Knowing You

Books by Tracie Peterson

*with Kimberley Woodhouse **with Karen Witemeyer, Regina Jennings, and Jen Turano

For a complete list of Tracie's books, visit traciepeterson.com.

Knowing You

TRACIE
PETERSON

BETHANYHOUSE

a division of Baker Publishing Group
Minneapolis, Minnesota

© 2023 by Peterson Ink, Inc.

Published by Bethany House Publishers
Minneapolis, Minnesota
www.bethanyhouse.com

Bethany House Publishers is a division of
Baker Publishing Group, Grand Rapids, Michigan

Printed in the United States of America

ISBN 978-0-7642-3744-7 (paperback)
ISBN 978-0-7642-3745-4 (cloth)
ISBN 978-0-7642-3746-1 (large print)
ISBN 978-1-4934-4364-2 (ebook)
Library of Congress Cataloging-in-Publication Control Number: 2023018332

Scripture quotations are from the King James Version of the Bible.

This is a work of historical reconstruction; the appearances of certain historical figures are therefore inevitable. All other characters, however, are products of the author's imagination, and any resemblance to actual persons, living or dead, is coincidental.

Baker Publishing Group publications use paper produced from sustainable forestry practices and post-consumer waste whenever possible.

23 24 25 26 27 28 29   7 6 5 4 3 2 1

Prologue

Seattle, Washington
May 1899

L eave her alone!"

Thirteen-year-old May Parker hurried to get to her feet. She dusted off the skirt of her dress and scurried to stand behind Leander Munro.

"Why are you standing up for her, Lee? She's Japanese."

"She's also my friend, and if you bother her again, I'll knock your teeth out. All of you."

May's three attackers stood their ground. "There's three of us, Lee, and just the two of you."

"Bradley Anderson, I don't care if there are six of you. I can hold my own and take you all on. You've seen me fight, and you know I can do it. Leave her alone, or I'll make sure you never bother her again."

"I don't understand why you'd stand up for her. She's not one of us."

May peeked around Lee. "I'm half white."

"Yeah, but you're also half Japanese," Bradley replied and spit on the ground. "You people were banned from Seattle, and I don't know why you're still here."

"You're talking about the Chinese Exclusion Act. It wasn't for the Japanese," Lee countered. "Learn your history, Bradley, before you go spouting it off and prove just how ignorant you really are."

"They're all the same. The yellow menace. My father works with other businessmen to rid the city of the Japanese, as well as the Chinese. They've put some five hundred Japanese out of Seattle's Southside. He's very proud of that."

"It's hardly a thing to be proud of," Lee replied.

"We don't need their kind here. This is a white man's world, and the only reason her parents were able to buy into this neighborhood is because her father is white," Bradley said, and his companions nodded. "But she isn't, and neither is her mother. They need to go back to where they come from."

"I was born in America!" May exclaimed. "Right here in Seattle. I am where I come from."

"Doesn't matter. You belong in Japan."

"Bradley, you'd do well to take your friends and go home. If I hear that you so much as look at May with a frown, I'll finish this once and for all."

May so admired Lee's strength and bravery. At fifteen, he was everything she thought a man should be. Just like her father.

Bradley seemed to consider Lee a moment, then shrugged. "Come on, fellas, let's go to my house. Cook is fixing us a grand lunch with cherry pie for dessert."

The other two went without protest, and May came out from behind Lee. She watched the boys move off down the street. Bradley lived only three doors down. His father was a wealthy investor who owned properties all over Seattle. Most of them commercial. Father said the man had more money than he knew what to do with, yet he still wouldn't fix up his buildings to be safer.

May's and Lee's families had plenty too. She knew they were blessed. Father had told her that over and over. His work in Asian imports had earned him good money, and he'd invested it wisely over the years. Lee's father owned one of the largest fish canneries on the West Coast, and he, too, had invested wisely and now had an entire fishing fleet that provided for his cannery. He was, as Lee had once said, *"Dependent on no one but God."*

"Are you all right?" Lee asked, looking at May as if for any sign of injury.

"I'm fine. He'd just started on me when you showed up." May dusted off her clothes once again.

"I don't know what you're going to do after I move away."

"That won't be for a long time." May looked up into his blue eyes and frowned when they narrowed. He was hiding something. "What is it?" she asked.

"Walk with me, May."

She nodded and kept in step with him as they headed back toward her house. She waited, wondering when he would answer her. Something was clearly not right.

"Lee, what's wrong?"

"I don't know how to say what I must tell you. We've been friends for such a long time, and I've never had this trouble before now."

"We have been friends for a long time, since I was very little." Some of May's first memories were of Lee, her next-door neighbor. They had been boon companions, often sneaking out to meet in the garden at night and gaze up at the stars for hours on end. Lee had talked of how he wished they could fly up into the skies and see the stars up close.

Sometimes they accidentally fell asleep and were discovered by the servants in the morning. Their mothers had been appalled when they found out.

May could see that he was very upset and put her hand on his. "Just tell me what you must, and we will talk it through."

"My parents bought another house, and we're moving away. I won't be around to protect you."

The pain in his expression matched the ache in her heart. May felt the air go out of her lungs. How could this be true? She twisted one of her black braids. "But why?"

"You know the answer to that as well as I do. They hate people who aren't white. There are now three families in the neighborhood who have either a mix of races or aren't white at all. My mother says it's ruined everything. She said it was hard enough living next to a woman who was Japanese. You know the things she's said about your folks."

May nodded. "But she's very unkind even to her white friends."

"Yes, Mother is a snob. She thinks that because she was born the daughter of wealthy New Yorkers she has a right to look down on everyone else. She was raised that way."

"So we must forgive her." May frowned, and her shoulders drooped. "I can't believe you're going to leave me. You've been my best friend. None of the other children will even speak to me. Or if they do, they call me all sorts of names and tell me to go back to Japan. What they don't know is that I would actually love to see it and meet my Japanese family there. My mother, however, will not even consider it. She hates Japan, although I don't really know why. She won't talk of it, and Father says we must respect her wishes. We both have difficult mothers."

"Perhaps, but yours is kind. She has always been nice to me."

"That's because you are nice to me. But now I'll have no one. I suppose I will stay in the house and paint and never come outside again."

Lee shook his head and touched her shoulder. "You must be brave. You mustn't let other children make you feel bad. You are a wonderful girl, May, and you belong to Jesus. Because you are His, you will always have the best of friends right here with you—in your heart. Jesus won't let you face the world alone."

Tears came to May's eyes. "But it won't be the same. I thought you and me . . . I thought we'd always be friends."

"We will be. I'll always be your friend, May. No matter how far away I move or how much time passes. I will be your friend until the day I die."

"I promise to be yours too." She wiped the tears away and forced a smile. "But it won't be the same."

"No." Lee's voice was edged with sorrow and resignation. "It won't ever be the same."

1

That's such lovely work, May." Mrs. Pearl Fisher stepped forward to better observe the photograph that May was touching up. People were often willing to pay for color to be added to their exposition photographs, and May was just the artist to handle the matter.

"I'm so glad we hired you to do this." Mrs. Fisher dabbed a cloth to her throat. The warmth of the day had left all of them perspiring.

May glanced up at the older woman. "Thank you."

Mrs. Fisher was such a nice woman to work for at Fisher Photography, temporarily set up at the Alaska-Yukon-Pacific Exposition. The expo had only a month to go until it would close down on October sixteenth, and Seattle would go back to the way things were before all the hoopla and planning of a world's fair took over the minds of its citizens.

The expo had been an amazing experience for May. Not only because she was able to put her interest in painting to use and be paid for it, but because of the incredible display on Japanese history in the Japan building. May had gone there every day during her break at lunch. She had sometimes taken her sketch pad along and drawn pictures of the various garments displayed. There was also a Japanese village on the Pay Streak Avenue walkway, and May had gone there on many occasions. It was fascinating to see the history of her mother's people presented at the fair.

"Otis and I have talked about having you come work for us at the new shop downtown. Would you be interested in continuing to touch up photographs?"

May smiled. "I would. It's such an enjoyable way to pass the time."

Mrs. Fisher rubbed her oversized abdomen. She was expecting her first baby in a matter of weeks. "We can speak more about it later," she said as two of the Camera Girls came into the shop.

Mary and Esther put the cameras they carried on the counter and waited to be given two more. This was the routine. The Camera Girls would go out and take pictures of tourists and their families with Kodak's new Brownie camera, then when the ten pictures of film were used, they would bring the cameras back with little notes about the pictures. Mrs. Fisher or Mrs. Hanson, the Camera Girls' supervisor, would oversee the development of the photographs and take the notes made by the girls to ensure the right picture was marked for the correct family. Some of the people paid ahead of time for their photos to be mailed, while many showed up in the shop later to see the photographs before buying them. When they saw what May could do, some paid extra money to have colored paint added to their souvenir pictures.

"Here you are, Mrs. Fisher," Mary said, putting several coins on the counter. "I marked who paid and wants the photos mailed. Their addresses are in the notes."

"Thank you, Mary." Mrs. Fisher moved to the far end of the counter and brought her another camera, already loaded with fresh, unused film.

Mary took the camera and headed for the door. "See you later."

Esther followed suit. "Most of my people wanted to see the photographs first. I only had one who wanted the postcard mailed."

"That's quite fine, Esther. Let me get you a camera." Mrs. Fisher went to retrieve another Brownie while Esther came to where May was working in the front window. A couple of people had stopped outside the little building to watch her work.

"You have fans," Esther said.

"People have been stopping by pretty regularly," May admitted. "I think they are surprised to see someone painting on the postcards. Then they realize what I'm doing and sometimes get very excited about it."

"Do you suppose we will ever have film that takes colored pictures?"

May shrugged and picked up a brush that barely had any bristles. "I suppose the right person will have to figure it all out, but I don't know why it couldn't be done."

"They've already created a process, but I don't think it's readily available," Mrs. Fisher said, returning with the camera. "Here you are, Esther."

"Thank you, Mrs. Fisher." Esther didn't quite look the woman in the eyes.

May had heard that Esther had been a bothersome girl in the first weeks of her working for the Fishers. There had been some trouble with Addie's brothers, and Esther had gotten herself involved with the oldest one. The entire matter was quite the sensation of the expo. Addie's brothers had held her hostage, knowing their sister had hidden gold she brought back from the Yukon. They nearly killed her, but in the end, it was they who died.

May felt sorry for Esther. None of the other girls seemed to want to get close to her, despite Addie encouraging everyone to forgive and befriend her. May had taken it upon herself to be extra nice to Esther. She knew what it was to be ignored or worse, bullied and picked on for being different.

"Are you having any luck selling the camera?" May asked.

"I've tried. We never know until Mrs. Fisher tells us later because we don't take the cameras out with us to sell on the grounds."

May nodded. She knew how the system worked. The girls handed out souvenir business cards with the Fisher Photography studio information on one side and the official Alaska-Yukon-Pacific Exposition logo on the other. Each girl would pencil her name at the top, and when someone bought a camera, it was credited to her as being the official salesperson. They each earned a commission on the cameras they sold, and this constituted the better part of their salary.

Thankfully, the cameras had been popular at the AYP, as the employees of the expo called it. The girls had done well with their commissions, and the Fishers had sold enough of the cameras that Kodak had made their shop an official provider. Mr. Fisher was even going to take the train back east, where Kodak was located, for some special training regarding the cameras once the expo was concluded.

"I'll see you later," Esther said, heading for the door.

May gave her a little wave, then gently touched her brush, what little there was of it, into the honey-brown color she'd created and dabbed it onto the photograph to highlight the woman's hair. She'd seen the couple earlier and thought the woman's hair quite pretty. She hoped to capture that in her work.

When the clock chimed five, May put away her paints and brushes as the Camera Girls filed back in one by one. There was a great deal of chattering about the day and all that had taken place.

"Tomorrow is Japan Day," Mary told May as she took off the camera from around her neck.

"I know. I'm very excited to see what all they do." May continued cleaning her station.

"I heard there would be a parade from the Japanese village to the Japan building," Mary added. "It's first thing in the morning."

May smiled. "I have the day off and intend to watch it all and listen to the speakers and hear the Japanese musicians. I am quite excited."

Mary nodded and returned May's smile. "I hope you enjoy yourself. If I were off, I would join you, but I'll probably be too busy photographing people. Maybe I can come find you at lunch."

"One of the restaurants is going to serve authentic Japanese food. I want to try it all," May said with a laugh.

Her mother never allowed Japanese food to be served in the house. On more than one occasion May had snuck downtown to the Japanese area of Seattle—Japantown. Bordered by Yesler Way and Dearborn on the north and south ends, and Fourth and Fourteenth Avenues on the east and west, Japantown offered May a glimpse into a world she had only dreamed about. It was here she had sampled a few classic dishes, but she'd never told her mother. She knew the older woman would have been very upset to know that May was even interested in such things.

But she was.

She longed to know about her Japanese ancestors and the culture of Japan. She had tried so many times to get her mother to open up and talk about it, but it almost always resulted in either tears or silence. Japan, her father had once told her, had been most hurtful to her mother, and she left many bad feelings there when she got on the boat for America.

When May had first heard of the expo and its plans for promoting Japan and other Pacific Islands, she knew she wanted to somehow be a part of it. Upon visiting, she'd seen the advertisement at Fisher Photography for Camera Girls. When she went in to speak to the owner about the job, somehow the conversation had turned to May being an artist. One thing led to another, and Mr. Fisher asked if she thought she could touch up the photographs with color. May was confident she could, and so she was hired. It turned out to be the perfect job for her, although she was also trained on the Brownie.

"Maybe I'll see you out there." Mary headed for the back room. "If not, I hope you enjoy your day."

May gave a wave, then gathered her things. She secured her straw boater atop her head and stuck a hatpin through to hold it in place. She wore the same uniform as the other Camera Girls because from time to time she would actually go out and take photographs if they were shorthanded. She didn't mind, however. The black skirt and high-necked white blouse were simple and comfortable. Besides, most of the time she wore a smock over her clothes when she painted and kept the straw hat hanging by the door.

"I'll be going now," she told Mrs. Fisher.

"Be careful."

"I will." May headed for the door with one backward glance at her station. Everything was in order.

She headed for the front gate and the trolley. She couldn't help thinking of tomorrow and how much fun it was going to be. She hadn't told her family yet of her intentions but supposed she would have to do so that evening. They would expect her to have the day off as she did most Saturdays. May had considered lying, but her Christian values wouldn't let her. She knew she would be restless and sick to her stomach unless she told the truth. So she would just start with the truth. If Mama got too distraught, she would think of something to say or do to calm her.

"Please don't get upset, Mama. I haven't asked you to talk about Japan in a long time. I've tried to be considerate, but you must understand. I'm twenty-three and long to know about my family. Your family and the land you were born in."

Father gave May a shrug and smile. "We must be patient. Those memories are difficult for your mother."

Her mother's brown-black eyes closed as she drew in a long, heavy breath. This was typical of Mama trying to calm herself. "I'm sorry, May. It's just . . . so much happened."

"Please try to understand my heart, Mama."

"May's right, Kame," Father declared. "She should go to the celebration of Japan Day. It will do her good."

"Japan was never good to me." Mama opened her eyes and looked at May. "But you can go if it pleases you. I will not forbid it."

"Thank you, Mama." May got up and put her arms around her mother. She kissed her lightly on the cheek, then hugged her. "I love you so much."

Her mother sighed and patted May's arm. "I love you too, my darling. I only want to save you pain."

May let go her hold and straightened. "But maybe if you allowed me to share the burden, it wouldn't cause you quite so much pain and sadness."

"This burden is one of great shame, May. I cannot desire that you share it," Mama said, looking up at her. She placed her napkin on the table as May reclaimed her seat. "I will go and rest now." She got up from the table and smiled at May and her father. "You are the only ones who matter to me. The past holds nothing but sorrow." With that, she left the room.

May couldn't help but feel saddened by her mother's retreat. She was running from the past as if it could hurt her all over again if she dared to speak of it.

"Why can't she just let go?" May whispered the question, not really expecting an answer.

"I don't know. I've tried to help her do exactly that for years," May's father replied.

"Why can't you tell me about it?" May looked to her father, whose emerald eyes matched her own. It was one of the only features she'd inherited from her father. Otherwise, she was the spitting image of her mother, but with more muted Asian features.

"May, it is your mother's story to tell. Even I don't know all of the details." He placed his napkin on the table. "What I do know is that your mother suffers greatly from her memories. She always has. I keep praying that God will release her from the power they hold over her."

"I pray that as well. I pray, too, that one day she will tell me about Japan and the family we must surely still have there."

"Just don't push her too hard, May. Have mercy on her." Father got to his feet and smiled. "And remember, I have told you plenty of stories about my family. At least you have that much."

"But that's only half," May replied. "And it makes me feel as if I'm only half a person. Will I never know the whole person?"

Her father smiled. "I think you are a beautiful young woman, and in time you will know what you need to know. Now, I will go sit with your mother and make sure her sorrow passes."

May watched him go and thought of the pain she'd caused. She hadn't meant to hurt her mother. *But I knew this would cause her pain. I'm a cruel daughter to do such a thing.* She glanced heavenward. "But what do I do, Lord? I am equal parts Japanese and American. I long to know who I am and who my people are and why the past is so hard for my mother to deal with."

She left the dining room and headed to her art studio. This was the only place of solace for her. Father had arranged it for her sixteenth birthday, giving her a first-floor room that had once been a small parlor for receiving guests. Mama had agreed that the larger parlor was more than enough for them. They didn't hold parties or entertain that much. May had been overjoyed at having her own studio. It had perhaps been the most thoughtful gift anyone had ever given her.

Closing the pocket doors behind her, May breathed in deeply. The scent of paint and turpentine, canvas and charcoal, lingered as a faint reminder of projects she had in progress. The ceiling was high—some fourteen feet with four large windows that started a couple of feet off the floor and ended a couple of feet from the crown molding. With the draperies pulled back, the light flooded the room during the day. At night, Father had arranged for her to have special lamps that put off a great deal of light. There were easels for her canvases. Tables and cabinets for her paints and brushes, and in the corner, a couple of chairs so that May could sit and contemplate or sketch. It was really all that she could want.

She pulled on her smock and walked around the room as she did up the buttons. She was anxious to get back to work on a landscape she'd sketched out down by the lake near the expo. Raising the covering from the canvas, May whispered a prayer for her mother.

The barely started painting was little more than brush-strokes of color and smudged shadows. Layer upon layer, May would work the paint to become something defined and understandable. She supposed her desire to know about the past was no different. There were the hints of life in Japan. The shadows of hidden sorrows . . . bursts of light revealing concealed secrets. The details needed careful crafting by one who knew the truth of each event. And that wasn't May.

She frowned. For now, she needed to put her desires aside. Tomorrow she would explore the generalized history of Japan. Maybe somewhere in the middle of it all, she would find her part of that mysterious country.

"Kame, you mustn't continue to carry this," Russell Parker told his wife. "My dear, you must allow God to heal you from the past."

"I want that more than I can say," she admitted. "I hate the pain it has caused."

"It has created a wall between you and May. She's entitled to know about her history—her family."

"They are no more."

"There are others. You are not without relatives. What about the letters that came to my company? You have relatives who desire to know where you are and how you are doing."

"For what purpose?" Her pale face was streaked with tears.

"Perhaps for the purpose of love and forgiveness. Perhaps a new start."

"I will continue to pray about it, Russ. I promise. Right now, however, my head is splitting, and I must rest. Forgive me." She turned her back so that he might unfasten the buttons on her silk gown.

"There is nothing to forgive." He finished with the buttons and placed a light kiss on her neck. "I love you, my dear. More now than even when I married you, and my love for you then was fierce." He turned her to face him. "You are my life, and I will do whatever I can to protect you from harm."

She wrapped her arms around his waist and rested her cheek against his chest. Nothing more needed to be said. Russell knew she would push back all the memories that threatened to surface. She would cover them over with happier thoughts and refuse to consider them anymore. In the morning, she would awake refreshed and happy. This was her way of survival and had been for the last thirty-two years. All he could do was continue to pray for her.

2

Leander Munro was never fond of his parents' Friday night suppers. There were always additional people invited, and the meals were served very late. Lee preferred to enjoy an early dinner at five thirty or six and then an equally early bedtime. His work in law enforcement came with early mornings, so the schedule suited him well. Not so, his folks.

As he sat at the ornate oak dinner table with his parents, the Reverend Cornwall and his wife, and Glynnis Faraday and her parents, Lee felt a familiar desire to bolt from his chair and make for the front door. Large dinner parties had never been his area of comfort, but smaller ones were even more disquieting.

For example, tonight he knew that his parents had invited the Faradays with the sole purpose of putting him and Glynnis together. It was their parents' plan to see Lee and Glynnis married, but that was never going to happen. This was a point on which he and Glynnis agreed. She had already lost her heart to a musician with the local symphony, and Lee had vowed to never marry. He saw no purpose in it. He wanted neither the obligation nor the legacy.

He glanced at Glynnis, who gave him a sympathetic half smile. Lee kept her secret regarding the violin player. Her parents would never approve, and Glynnis had told him that upon reaching her twenty-first birthday, she intended to take an inheritance left to her by her grandparents and elope. He had agreed to play suitor to her in the meanwhile so as to put both sets of parents at ease. Just another month and they could drop the façade altogether.

"We do hope there will be an engagement announcement soon," Lee's mother was telling the pastor.

All gazes turned to him, and Lee smiled. "I'm afraid my mother has never been known for the virtue of patience."

"It just seems you two have been courting for long enough."

"A couple needs time to know each other," Lee assured.

"Goodness, Leander, but you'll have time during the engagement to get to know each other."

Mrs. Faraday nodded. "Yes, they'll have plenty of time after the engagement is announced. We must have at least six months to a year in order to plan a proper wedding."

Lee had heard it all before and wasn't about to be told by the interfering matrons when he should propose. Especially since he didn't intend to propose.

"You and Glynnis have known each other a very long time," his father interjected. "Since you were sixteen, if I remember correctly. That makes it a full nine years. I would think that is long enough to know a person. I set my sights on your mother and knew almost immediately that she was the one I wanted to marry." He nodded toward his wife.

"Not so with us, I'm afraid," Reverend Cornwall said, smiling. "Samaria and I knew each other nearly twenty years before the idea of marriage came to us."

His wife gave a light laugh. "It's true. We were childhood

friends as well, but such a union was never a part of our thoughts until much later."

Lee's father picked up his wine goblet and paused. "Well, the point is that marriage has been a part of Lee and Glynnis's thoughts for a long time, and I think it's time they make a formal announcement."

Lee made no reply and instead focused on eating the last bit of his dinner roll. He knew that his parents were displeased. No doubt the Faradays were as well, but it didn't matter to him. He would endure for Glynnis's sake.

"How are things going at the cannery, Artimus?" Mr. Faraday asked Lee's father.

"As well as can be expected. I keep trying to rid myself of Asian workers, but there don't seem to be enough white men to cover the shifts."

"Thankfully that's not something I have to deal with in the world of finance. They aren't smart enough to hold positions in my firm."

Lee bit his tongue to keep from making a scene about the men's obvious racism. He'd dealt with it his entire life and felt nothing in common with such thoughts. He had known brilliant Chinese and Japanese men. Men who were no doubt more brilliant than Mr. Faraday.

"I weary of those people. I thought there were going to be laws to remove them from America," Mrs. Faraday said with a tone of exasperation. "Yet I see them everywhere."

"At least they aren't allowed in this part of town," Mother added. "There's some respite here."

"Yes, I suppose we should be grateful for that. I can't imagine having to live next door to the heathens."

"You know, many of the Asians are turning to Christianity," Reverend Cornwall threw out with a smile. "I have found their desire to know Jesus quite exciting. So many English-speaking Asians have shown interest, in fact, that I've started a Sunday afternoon service for them in Japantown."

"Goodness, can they really be saved?" Mother asked.

Lee couldn't keep silent. "Mrs. Parker and her daughter, May, were both Christians. Surely you remember that, Mother."

She looked at him oddly. "Yes, well, they said they were, but can they really be saved? I can't imagine they have the same kind of soul that we have."

Lee fisted his hands under the table to keep from pounding them on the top and rattling his mother's favorite German china.

"Mrs. Munro, have no doubt that people of every color have a soul that very much needs and desires a relationship with their heavenly Father." Reverend Cornwall's voice was firm but kind. "Remember the Bible tells us that God doesn't look on man's outward appearance. He sees neither skin color nor gender nor size nor shape. God looks at the heart."

Mother said nothing but instead rang the bell. White servants immediately appeared. She would never trust a person of color in her service. "We'll take our coffee and cake in the music room."

"None for me," Lee announced and got to his feet. "I have an early day tomorrow. Being the detective in charge at the expo, I have an obligation to be there before the gates open at eight."

"I'll be so glad when that terrible fair is dissolved and all the people go back to where they belong," Mrs. Faraday declared.

"Oh, so will I," Mother said. "It's ruined Seattle and increased our crime something terrible. Lee was just saying before dinner that the pickpockets are running rampant."

"I didn't exactly say that, Mother," Lee interjected, "but they are plentiful at the fair."

His mother sighed and shook her head. "Foreigners are always causing problems."

His father was already getting to his feet to assist Mother from her chair, and Mr. Faraday did likewise. Lee knew it was expected of him to help Glynnis, so he wasted little time.

"Thank you," Glynnis said. She really was quite lovely. Blond hair placed in perfection atop her head. Beautiful blue eyes with dark, sooty lashes. And a figure that needed no help from a corset, but of course got it all the same.

Lee smiled and leaned close to her ear. "One month."

She giggled. "Yes. David said we should get together sometime for lunch."

"I'd like that." He really didn't care one way or another, but it seemed the appropriate thing to say.

"That looks promising," Glynnis's father said, grinning. "They're sharing secrets."

Lee straightened and sobered. "Mother, Father. It was a lovely evening. Mr. and Mrs. Faraday, I wish you well with your new business venture." He turned to the pastor and his wife. "Reverend and Mrs. Cornwall, I look forward to seeing you at church Sunday." He took a slight step back, kissed Glynnis's hand, and gave a bow. "Until then, I bid you all good evening."

"Oh, Lee, do stay. At least for a little while," Mother encouraged.

"The fact is that Mrs. Cornwall and I need to be going as well. Lee, can we give you a ride to your apartment?"

"That would be quite nice. I'll get your driver to bring

your carriage around," Lee replied and hurried from the room before anyone could stop him. He knew the procedure should have been to ring for the butler to notify the stableman, but he didn't want to wait and risk someone talking the reverend into staying longer.

Lee didn't breathe a sigh of relief until he was seated in the carriage across from the Cornwalls and the driver had put the horses in motion.

"Thank you again for the ride home." A light drizzle of rain had started, and Lee had no desire to walk home.

"Of course, Lee. I always enjoy our time together. Although I must say, your mother's belief that Asian people lack souls is rather troubling." Reverend Cornwall shook his head. "I find racism quite distressing."

"As do I. My best friend as a child was the young lady I mentioned at dinner. May Parker is half Japanese with a white father. She was quite devoted to reading her Bible and praying. Of course, my mother would say that it was only the white side of her that craved such a thing. But I know for a fact that her mother, who was full Japanese, sought the Lord as well."

"People are funny with their reasonings, Lee. As missionaries get the Gospel message out to the world, more and more people of various shades and cultures are choosing to follow Jesus."

"The Holy Ghost is hardly limited by the color of a person's skin."

"Very true. So tell me, do you still talk to this friend, May Parker?"

Lee shook his head. "No. I think of her often. As I said, we were the best of friends. My parents, however, didn't want to live next door to a woman of Asian blood. Something happened to them before I was born that formed their minds against people of Asian descent. I don't know what it was, but it hardened their hearts, and we moved to an exclusively white neighborhood when I was fifteen. I haven't talked to May since then."

"But why?" Mrs. Cornwall asked. "If she was your best friend, I would have thought you would have kept up with the relationship."

"My parents forbade me to return to the old neighborhood or to have anything to do with her. My older brothers were quite firm on the matter as well. They told me there would be no end of trouble should I fail to adhere to my folks' desires. So I obeyed, even though I kept wondering how she was and what kind of young woman she'd grown up to be."

"You care a great deal about her even now. I can hear it in your voice."

Lee considered the reverend's words for a moment. How strange that he could see such a thing when Lee could hardly recognize it for himself.

"Yes, I care. I took it upon myself to be her protector when we were children. There were quite a few bullies in our neighborhood. Children who had taken up their parents' attitudes and hatred. I've always worried that they made her suffer all the more after I left."

"Now that you are a man on your own, have you not thought to look her up and see how she is?" the older man asked.

"I . . . well . . . to tell the truth . . ." Lee gazed out on the wet streets. "I think I'm afraid of the answer."

"I see. She might have been hurt in your absence."

"Or even killed," Lee admitted. "Her family could have

been forced from the country, although with a white father I don't think that is likely to have happened. Still, I worry about what she's been made to suffer."

"But the only way to know for sure would be to go see for yourself."

The carriage came to a stop in front of Lee's apartment building. "Yes, that's true." He waited as the driver opened the door. "Thank you for the ride and discussion. I apologize for my parents and their hatred. Unfortunately, they do not limit their feelings to the Asian community alone. They equally hate all people of color or difference. My brothers feel just as they do, but I could never quite understand it."

"Racism is a difficult matter to stomach and understand. Human beings, such as they are, are always comparing themselves to one another. Rather than loving each other as Christ commanded." The reverend smiled. "I do hope we'll have another chance to talk, Lee. I very much enjoy our conversations."

Lee nodded. "As do I. It's always nice to speak to someone who is like-minded. Good evening, Mrs. Cornwall. Reverend. And thanks again for the ride home."

Saturday morning dawned bright and clear. It couldn't have been a more perfect day, and May was enthusiastic about her plans. She had confessed her desires to her parents, so she could move forward with a clear conscience. And even though she knew her mother wasn't supportive of her fascination with the Japanese culture, she hadn't forbidden May to learn.

The trolley was packed with people, nearly eighty if her

count was correct. They seemed quite excited about the day too. Many hadn't yet been to the expo and were discussing it with their children or each other in animated style. When they disembarked from the trolley, May saw that the entry gates were overflowing with people. Thankfully, she had an employee pass to get her past the crowd.

Without needing to worry about work, she strolled the grounds slowly and made her way to the midway point between the Japanese village and Japan building. She figured this might be the perfect place to watch the parade and paused at Union Circle on Pacific Avenue to await the celebration.

The sides of the streets quickly filled with people, signaling it was nearly time for the parade. May could hardly contain her excitement, and before she could grow impatient, the parade came into view with Japanese geishas, fierce-looking warriors, and silk-kimono–clad women with their black hair done up in intricate fashion atop their heads. Their kimonos were so beautiful that May couldn't help reaching for her drawing pad. She wanted to at least get down a rough sketch of what she saw. Hopefully later she could talk one of the women into posing for her. That way she could mark the details of the kimono and maybe later create a painting of the costume. Of course, she'd have to hide it from her mother.

After the parade concluded in front of the beautifully designed Japan building, there were speeches and music to celebrate Japan's participation in the expo and its importance in the world. Having just defeated Russia only four years earlier in the Russo-Japanese War, Japan had taken great pride in standing out as a power to be reckoned with.

"Isn't that building unusual?" a woman beside May asked.

She started to respond, then realized the woman was speaking to the man on her right.

"The Japanese architecture is quite unusual," he replied. "I don't care for it myself."

May frowned and glanced at the Japan building. What was it about it he didn't care for? She thought it quite fascinating and had sketched the building on several occasions but never tired of it. Tucked into a grove of fir trees, the building had been designed by a Mr. Ikeda in traditional Japanese fashion with several floors separated out with curved tile roofs and painted red—a color of celebration. May had once seen an explanation of why certain colors were used in Japan once while inside the Japan building.

Red, or *aka*, was a color known to ward off evil spirits and was often used in festivals and other celebrations. It was also a color of authority and promoted peace and prosperity among all. Blue, known as *ao*, was the color of the common people. For a long time ao was used to describe both blue and green. The color reminded the people of the sky and sea, the latter being especially important to the Japanese since they were an island nation. Orange symbolized the sun, and gold represented wealth and power. There were marks of gold to highlight various places on the Japan building. There was also white, which was often associated with death.

All in all, May had very much enjoyed learning about these things and had even asked one of the Japanese guides, Mr. Akira, to pronounce the words for her so that she could memorize them. It made her feel just a little bit connected to her ancestors.

She turned to ask the spectator what he didn't like, but the couple had already moved on, and May decided she should probably leave well enough alone.

This was further affirmed when a Japanese man dressed in formal American attire took to the podium. He spoke of the day and of Japan's desire to partner with America in every way that would be beneficial to both countries. He shared various points of interest that the visitors would find inside the building and explained why they were important.

May knew all about the silks, porcelain, lacquerware, and kimonos that had been displayed. There were also presentations of food that were popular in Japan like peanuts and ginger, canned codfish, and various oils. Her favorite exhibit was a display of samurai armor. The man spoke of it, along with the histories that people could read regarding the samurai and shogun. She was determined to create a painting of the samurai piece. Or rather pieces. Japanese armor was made up of many pieces of iron, wood, and leather, and she was only now learning the various names of those parts.

Once the speeches were concluded, the people began again to move about. Many went inside the Japan building, where there would be further discussions of the exhibits. One of the restaurants was set up to serve Japanese food, just as May had told Mary. May was quite anxious to enjoy that as part of the day. Still, she wanted to savor every aspect of the celebration, so she took a seat across from the red building with its curved hip-and-gable roof to wait until the crowds thinned out. While she waited, she sketched the scene surrounding her.

"You're really good at that."

May glanced up and found Bertha, one of the Camera Girls, watching over her shoulder. "I love to draw and paint," May admitted. "I have done it since I was quite little. I guess it's just a natural talent."

"Did you take special classes?"

May frowned and looked back to her sketch pad. "I've had some training, but no one wants to train a Japanese girl for long."

"Why not? You're half white, doesn't that count?"

May gave a laugh that sounded harsher than she'd intended. "No, it doesn't. A glass of water spoiled with even the tiniest bit of poison is still undesirable . . . as I've been told many times."

"That's a terrible way to look at things—especially considering many of the people in America come from other countries. My family is German and Irish. I've always enjoyed talking to the foreigners who've come here. I think people from other places are quite interesting. I like hearing about their countries and beliefs. My grandparents used to tell me stories of their countries, and I loved what they had to say."

"I enjoy people of every place," May agreed, "but it doesn't always come back to me in kind. My teachers were unhappy to have me in a white school. My father, however, had money and influence, and they had to yield to his desires. But that didn't make them treat me kindly or with any consideration toward things I enjoyed."

"I'm sorry to hear that, May. I guess it makes me more mindful of my own behavior. I'll be sure to treat people better in the future."

"You are a good woman, Bertha. I wish everyone could have such a heart."

3

May still had her mind on the celebration of Japan when she came to work on Monday morning. She planned to go back to the building over her lunch hour and study some of the photographs and perhaps get one of the guides to talk to her about kanji, the Japanese art of writing. It fascinated her that those beautiful symbols represented words. She couldn't help but wonder if her mother knew kanji. Of course, she must know it. Mama was educated, so she must be able to read and write in Japanese fashion.

"Are we still going to plan on lunch together tomorrow?" Esther asked as May pulled on her smock.

"Yes, please." May smiled as she did up the buttons. "Unless, of course, you have something else to do."

"No, I just wanted to make sure you still wanted to . . . well, spend time with me."

May touched Esther's arm. "I've very much been looking forward to it."

Esther seemed to relax and gave a hint of a smile. "I am looking forward to it too."

"Good morning, ladies," Addie Hanson said, coming in

from the back room. "Isn't it beautiful outside? The taste of fall is in the air, and the temperatures are cooling fast. I was actually cold this morning. We had a fire going in the house, and I didn't want to leave."

"Yes, it was chilly," May agreed. "Especially when the breeze blows over the water." She glanced around. "Is Mrs. Fisher here today?"

"Not until later. She has an appointment with her doctor, so she and Mr. Fisher will be late. Too bad Eleanor isn't still with us, as there is plenty of film to develop."

Eleanor Bennett had married William Reed and moved off to Alaska, where she planned to take photographs of the vegetation. She had been one of May's favorite people and had a background in photography after working in her father's shop in Kansas.

"Eleanor could definitely be helpful," Esther agreed.

May hoped Eleanor would write to her soon and let her know all about her adventures, but for now she needed to get on with her job. "Mrs. Fisher was supposed to leave the photographs that she wanted me to touch up. She said there would also be a list that coordinated with them to suggest the colors for various items."

"Yes," Addie said, nodding. She reached for a stack of pictures. "These are the ones she had in mind, and here's the list." She handed it all to May. "She told me all about it last night."

"Oh good." May looked things over. "I can have these done by noon."

"How is Mrs. Fisher feeling?" Esther asked.

"Good. She is doing quite well, and the doctor has been encouraging." Addie began placing loaded cameras on the counter for the girls to take.

The bell over the door sounded as Mary and Bertha came in. "Oh, Addie, you should have seen the lake this morning. It was so beautiful—just like glass, and Mount Rainier was out in all of its glory."

"Mary couldn't stop talking about it all the way to work," Bertha declared. "I told her she was starting to sound like Eleanor in her enthusiasm for nature."

"We were mentioning Eleanor as well," Addie said. "Mr. and Mrs. Fisher won't be in until later, and I thought it would have been nice if Eleanor were still here. She could be working on developing pictures in Otis's absence. She really was quite talented."

"Has anyone heard from her yet?" Mary asked.

"Well, it's barely been a week since they left, what with having to remain behind to make certain all the legal issues were resolved with Mr. Masterson."

May recalled that the man had murdered an old woman in the apartment where Eleanor's sister-in-law lived. He had also been determined to kidnap Eleanor's sister-in-law, but thankfully that had been thwarted.

"She promised to send me a letter from Seward." May shrugged. "But I have no idea how long it takes to get to Seward, nor how long it takes to get a letter back."

"At least a week each way. Possibly more depending on whether the ship is stopping anywhere else," Addie said. "I wouldn't look for anything just yet. Now, come on ladies, we need to get this day started. Let's sell as many photographs and cameras as possible."

The girls went to work, and May settled into her window desk to work on the photographs. She buried herself in the postcards and set each aside in the window to dry when she finished. True to her word, by noon she was done.

She cleaned up her brushes and put away her paints and smock and was just leaving for her break as Mr. and Mrs. Fisher arrived.

"How are you doing?" Addie asked from the counter.

"The doctor is quite pleased. He believes the baby will be born very soon," Mrs. Fisher answered.

"He told her to stop being on her feet so much. She has water on the ankles," Mr. Fisher added.

"Yes, I suppose I'll have to start staying home, but that worries Otis because I'll be alone."

"Well, perhaps I could stay part of the time with you." Addie tapped her finger against her chin. "But who would be in charge of the girls?" Her eyes widened. "Mary and Bertha could trade off taking charge. They're both quite reliable and very capable of handling things."

"Oh, but that seems like a lot to expect in such a short time," Mrs. Fisher replied.

Mr. Fisher waggled his finger at Mrs. Fisher. "Addie is right. They can manage. Addie will show them what to do."

"Yes, I will. And maybe Otis can take his time coming to work in the morning and stay with you while I come here and check up on everything and make sure we keep plenty of inventory. Then we can change places. He can come to work, and I can come and be with you. It will all work itself out very easily."

May smiled to herself at the way the problem was being resolved. This was the way things always seemed to be accomplished since Addie had rejoined them full-time. "I'm going to head out now. The photographs will shortly be dry and ready for folks to pick up. Still, advise them not to touch the face of the picture until tomorrow."

"I'll let them know. Have a good lunch, May." Mrs. Fisher

gave her a wave. "I'm sure the people will be more than pleased."

With that May took up her satchel and headed out of the shop. The day truly was a harbinger of fall. There was just a sense of change that couldn't be ignored. It was intangible details like that May wished she could capture on canvas.

She made her way to the Japan building and hurried inside. There were only a few people in the entire building, which served her purpose quite well. Glancing around, she spied the man who'd helped her last time. He often led guided tours through the building, but at this time of day, he stood quite idle.

"Mr. Akira," May said, greeting him with a slight bow as he always did with her. "I wonder if you have time to speak to me about kanji and Japanese writing?"

The older man smiled. He was probably in his late fifties and seemed like a grandfatherly sort. "I would be happy to talk to you. Let's go to the room at the back, where there are some wonderful examples."

Leading the way, Mr. Akira didn't even bother to look over his shoulder to make sure she was following. He knew she would come. Her enthusiasm for all things Japanese was well-known to him.

"As you know, the kanji comes from the Chinese," he told her as they walked. "Japan did not have a written language for a long time. Then they borrowed kanji, and everything changed."

"The writing is so grand. I love the way it looks and wish I could read it."

"It is not hard to learn. You should start with kana, however. That is written letters like the American alphabet, though Japanese has only twenty-one letters. There is also katakana, which is like American printing and used for only certain things. Then there is hiragana—more like the cursive writings. Children learn hiragana first and then kanji."

He stopped in front of a silk tapestry painted with kanji symbols. English was written beneath each kanji to explain what the symbols represented. May had seen it on Saturday and found the beautiful display fascinating.

"It's truly a piece of art," she murmured.

"You are correct. There are those in Japantown who write for hours upon silk and sell to the Americans. Sometimes they paint flowers and other things on the silk as well. Bible verses have been very popular to sell."

May smiled. "I can well imagine." She took out her sketch pad and a pencil. "Is there a special way to make these symbols?"

"Oh yes, stroke order is very important," the man revealed. "It will not look right if you do not follow that." He motioned to the kanji for "person," 人. "You start here at the top and sweep down and to the left. Then start just a little bit below the top and sweep to the right."

It looked like an upside-down curved V. May practiced it on her sketchbook, but it wasn't quite right.

"If I may," the man said, holding his hand out for the sketchbook and pencil. May handed them over to him and watched as he drew five separate characters.

"So again, this is kanji for 'person' or 'people.' And this is 'mother.'"

She watched as he wrote 母. After he made the full symbol, he broke it down and showed her the stroke order. He did this for each kanji.

"This is 'father.'" He drew 父 beneath the symbol for 'mother.' It reminded May of a pair of curved crutches crisscrossed on each other. "The Japanese read down and from left to right. This is 'child.'"

子 was placed beneath the kanji for "father."

"And last of all . . ." He drew two symbols side by side. "'Japan.'"

May looked at the final kanji, 日本.

"The first is the kanji for 'sun.' The second one is 'origin.' So this means 'origin of sun.' Thus, we are the land of the rising sun. But when saying the word in Japanese, we say *Nippon.*" He smiled and drew out the stroke order for each kanji.

Handing her back the sketchbook and pencil, he bowed. "You take and practice. You will see how easy it is to learn."

"I have so little time. The expo will only last another month."

"You can learn much before that time is done. Besides, my wife and I live with our son's family in Japantown. You could come there to see us. My son has a small restaurant, Akira Roku. Akira Six, because there were six of us when it was started." He smiled as if the memory pleased him. "We are near Sixth and Jackson."

Did she dare go to Japantown on a regular basis to learn about her culture?

"Could you teach me to speak Japanese as well? At least a little?" May knew her mother must surely remember the language, but also knew she would never help May learn it.

"Of course. When there is time, I will teach you to write it and to speak it. May I?" He held out his hands for the sketchbook and pencil.

"'Person' is *hito*. 'Father' is *Oto-san* when you address him, but if you talk about him to me you would say *Chichi*." He wrote out each word. "'Mother' is *Oka-san*, but a lot of children call their mothers *mama*."

"That's what I have always done." May smiled and watched as he continued to write.

"And 'child' is *kodomo*." He finished and handed her the book and pencil once again. He gave her a broad smile. "I think you will learn very fast."

May put the sketchbook and pencil in her satchel, feeling as though she could take on the world.

"Thank you so much, Mr. Akira." She gave a little bow. He bowed in return.

"'Thank you very much' is *domo arigato gozaimasu*."

May tried the words on for size. "Domo arigato . . . gozai . . . masu."

He smiled. "See, you are doing very well."

Tobias Hillsboro was a tall, slender man with slate-blue eyes that seemed cold and lifeless. Mario Bianchi knew the man and his reputation, and the eyes made perfect sense. People often spoke of eyes being like passageways to a person's soul, but not so with Hillsboro. Bianchi wasn't even sure the man had a soul. He certainly had no conscience.

"I approached the Japanese officials, and they refused to sell me the samurai armor," Hillsboro said.

"What did you expect? It's a relevant piece of their history. They aren't a people who believe that everything has its price. It's all about honor and legacy for them. They honor their dead ancestors, for pity's sake."

"I don't care who they honor, I want that armor."

Hillsboro fixed him with a gaze that actually chilled Mario to the bone. He refused to show the effect, however, and shrugged. "You can't always get what you want."

The taller man crossed his arms and smiled. "You know me better than that, Mario. I always get what I want. There are museums all across Europe that bear the proof of that. How many of your forged paintings now hang where originals were once enjoyed?"

Mario smiled. "I suppose enough to have given you the idea that I can replicate the armor and replace it at the expo."

"Exactly. I want you to get your best men on it."

"I'll have to telegraph them to get here on the double. It will cost you plenty."

"I don't care. I want that armor, and I mean to have it before the end of the exposition. That gives you a month."

Mario swallowed the lump in his throat. This wasn't going to be easy, but with Hillsboro it never was. "I'll try to figure out the cost and get you a price as soon as possible."

"I don't care what it costs, Mario. Just make it happen."

Mario felt the shift of power. Hillsboro needed him. He couldn't begin to accomplish what he wanted unless Mario came through for him. It was empowering and caused Mario to stand a little taller.

"I'll make it happen, but you must be ready to pay the price."

Hillsboro's eyes narrowed. "Have I ever failed to come through with the money?"

Mario shook his head. "No, but they often say there is a first time for everything."

"I think you know me well enough to know that isn't a problem in our case. I have plenty of money, and you have plenty of talent. I will help you, and you will help me. It's that simple. Now, do we have an arrangement?"

"Of course." Mario turned to leave. "I'll be in touch."

He left Hillsboro without another word and took his hat

and gloves from the valet as he crossed the hotel room. The suite was grand and opulent, as was befitting a wealthy swindler like Hillsboro. Mario might have laughed at a lesser man, but not Hillsboro. The man was ruthless and cruel. He thought nothing of taking what he wanted and killing anyone who stood in his way.

But the man paid well, and Mario had managed an entire career in helping men like Hillsboro get what they desired. He was the best forger in the world. At least many had deemed him that, and Mario didn't argue with them on that point. He was exceptional, and Hillsboro was right. There were many famous paintings now in the possession of numerous individuals while his forgeries hung in prestigious art museums around the world. No one was the wiser because Mario Bianchi had done his finest work.

He'd never attempted to make a suit of armor, but how hard could it be? He would go to the expo immediately and study the piece in question. The problem would be in how to get a thorough study without raising suspicion.

Outside the hotel he had the doorman signal a cab. There wasn't any time to waste.

"Take me to the exposition," he told the driver. "I have business there."

That evening, May took a piece of sketch paper from her book and clipped it to her easel. Next she took up her paintbrush and black paint. She had practiced the various kanji over and over in her book using a pencil, and now she wanted to give it a try with brush and paint as she had seen the artists in Japantown do on various pieces of fabric.

Mindful of the stroke order, she carefully swept the brush across the paper. Something about the action resonated deep in her soul. Was it possible for her to connect so much with her Japanese ancestry that she could feel it course through her body? May wanted to be able to speak to her mother about it. She had so many questions and longed to know why they never spoke of her mother's life in Japan.

She studied the kanji she'd just drawn. It was the one for "mother"—almost as if it demanded to be placed upon the paper first.

"Oh, Mama, please help me to understand."

4

May took several photographs of the samurai armor before putting the camera away and pulling out her sketchbook. It had been more than a week since Japan Day, and she couldn't get this armor out of her thoughts. Mr. Akira had known very little about the armor, but thankfully someone had created a visual aid denoting the various pieces and what they were called.

Starting with the helmet, or *kubuto*, May drew the various pieces that formed the neck and throat guards. Hundreds of pieces of metal and leather, lacquered for added strength, made up the kubuto. They were riveted in place, and to these were added face guards and decorative pieces to display the family's crest and other design elements.

She worked carefully, making sure she drew each detail in a precise manner. May had already decided she was going to make a painting of this armor.

"Excuse me, please," a man standing behind her said.

May turned and found a man no taller than herself dressed in a well-worn suit. Beside him was a woman dressed in a simple kimono. They looked to be in their fifties—perhaps sixties.

"We are the Tamuras," he said, bowing.

May returned the bow. "My name is May Parker."

"You are making many sketches of the armor, yes?"

"Yes." She smiled. "I hope to make a painting of it at home."

"You paint? That is good for us to hear. You see, the armor belonged to my wife's family. After the Satsuma Rebellion, it was taken by the government. My wife wishes to know if you could make us a painting of the armor. She would like to have both front and back on the same canvas."

May had never considered doing her painting in that manner. She glanced at the armor and then back at the Japanese couple. "I suppose I could."

"We would pay you very well. Any price you asked, in fact."

May had never considered asking to be paid for her paintings. She had been so careful about even showing her work to anyone, yet this man was offering her whatever she wanted, and he didn't even know that she could really paint.

"But you don't know me. You haven't seen my work. How can you offer me any price?"

"I can see by your sketch that you make much attention to detail." He smiled. "I believe you would do good work."

"I see." May was surprised at his comment, but more so by what followed.

"I will pay you one hundred American dollars, but I will need the painting very soon. We will leave in a short time for Japan."

May wished she could boast the same thing. "One hundred dollars is a lot of money. I will do as you ask, but only because I had planned to paint this for myself. If you don't like the work I do, you won't owe me a cent."

The man nodded. "And you can make this very fast?"

"I can try," May replied. "The painting will be done in layers and has to dry. I still need to take more photographs of the armor and sketch out some of the more intricate parts. I can start painting it tonight. Of course, it won't be ready that quickly, but I'll be better able to tell you how much time I'll need to complete it."

"I will meet you here on Saturday and see where you are in the process."

"Very well. Let's say around two in the afternoon on Saturday."

The man bowed, as did his wife. May wasn't sure, but she thought she saw tears in the woman's eyes. They left as quickly as they'd come, and May turned back to the armor. She put away her sketch pad and drew out the camera again. She would need to get more pictures and have Mr. Fisher develop them before she left for home.

As she photographed the *dou*, May noticed a tiny detail on the chest piece. Just there by the right arm were symbols. They were barely noticeable. She motioned Mr. Akira over.

"What does this mean?"

He looked closer and smiled. "'Courage' or 'bravery.'"

May nodded. "I suppose it was to encourage the wearer. Did you see that couple who was here earlier?" Mr. Akira nodded, and May continued. "They asked me to make a painting of the armor. The man told me the woman's family had once owned it."

Mr. Akira's expression looked like a cross between sadness and anger. "The samurai were forced to give up their family armor. It caused great sorrow. That way of life was then forbidden. They were even made to give up their katanas— their swords. All in order to make Japan like the Western countries. It was a very sad time for the people. They suffer still."

May thought about that the rest of the day. She knew this was all somehow connected to the sorrow her mother bore. What little she'd been able to read about the Satsuma Rebellion fit the time period of her mother's life in Japan. No doubt it had been a huge influence on her.

Please, God, let her be willing to talk to me about it.

Although it took until the end of the day before Mr. Fisher could develop her photographs, May nevertheless made it home in time for supper. As she sat down with her mother and father, she went over and over in her thoughts how she might approach the subject of the samurai. She had once overheard her mother say something to Father about them. May had been quite young, but she remembered there was some sort of family connection. She knew her mother had grown up on Kyushu Island, and Mr. Akira said this was where the rebellion took place.

Throughout their meal, May bided her time. She spoke of the delicious roast and vegetables, as well as the lovely weather they'd enjoyed that day. Father talked about things going on downtown and newspaper articles about the success of the expo.

"It would seem the expo has made a great deal of money for its investors, many of whom are common citizens in Seattle. I'm sure that came as a pleasant surprise."

"I'll be glad when it's over with," Mama said. "The women at church who live near the expo tell me it's been a difficult time for them. The noise is deafening and doesn't end until midnight sometimes. I know people are gathering to have fun, and I don't hold that against them, but it has caused so many problems for those who live nearby."

"Well, the end is in sight."

Mama nodded. "Yes, but then there will come the tear-down. That will be difficult to bear as well."

Dessert that evening was a cheese custard with blackberries and whipped cream. May nibbled at it and waited for the proper moment to bring up what she knew would be a most unpleasant topic. Her opportunity soon presented itself.

"May, you seem rather caught up in your thoughts," her father commented.

"I wish to discuss something, but I don't want to make things uncomfortable for Mama."

She looked to her mother, who seemed to understand what May meant to discuss. Mama dabbed her napkin to her lips and to May's surprise gave her a smile.

"I have been praying and trying to understand what I should say and not say," Mama began. "I know that my sorrow and pain cannot be allowed to continue, but it is not without difficulty that I face this."

"It is not without difficulty that I ask you to," May countered. "I don't want to make you sad. There's just so much that I want to know. But right now, I want to tell you something, and then maybe you will understand why it's so important to seek answers from you."

"Go ahead," her father said. "I'm sure we both want to hear what you have to say."

"Yes. Please," her mother added.

May took a sip of her water, then placed the glass on the table. "I have been asked to paint a picture of the samurai armor that is on display in the Japan building. I was there sketching it and taking photographs because I desired to make my own painting. I was approached by a couple who said the armor was something that had been possessed by the woman's family, but that the government had taken it from them after the Satsuma Rebellion."

Mama looked down at her half-eaten custard. "It was the way of things."

"They offered me one hundred dollars, but I would have to paint it for them quickly, as they are heading back to Japan."

"That is a great deal of money," Mama said, looking to Father. "Isn't it?"

"It is." Father leaned back in his chair. "It seems more than is reasonable for an unknown artist."

May couldn't agree more. "I told them I would try, but that I could not think to force them to buy a work that they had never seen. They don't even know if I'm able to provide the quality they want, but I do wish to try."

"Are you seeking permission?" her father asked.

"In a way, but also asking to better understand. I feel I know so little about the samurai and their ways. What was the Satsuma Rebellion, and how did it affect our family?"

Mother leaned back in her chair. "I cannot tell you a great deal about the rebellion itself. I was just a girl of thirteen. Our family had long been a part of the samurai. There were many who had served, and when the samurai were disbanded and forbidden to carry their katana swords, it provoked many to war.

"The Imperial Navy came in the dead of night to our island, where there were two weapons factories and some ammunition depots. The government wanted to confiscate all weapons and ammunition and store them in another place. There were many of the former samurai on our island, and they did not approve of this. They had been the military to guard and protect Japan—to serve—as is the meaning of the word *samurai*. They rose up to fight, thinking they knew more about military actions than these new armies and navies of farmers and commoners. My father was one of those men—a samurai who thought it was his duty to keep Japan for the Japanese. The government wanted to Westernize the country. They saw great benefit in trading with the United States and other places, but my family did not see it as a good thing. They felt Japan was being betrayed and feared we would lose our culture and identity."

"So they fought." May barely spoke the words.

"Yes. And we were all so afraid for them—afraid for ourselves too. My mother and I left our home and gathered with other family members as the men went off to fight. It did not bode well for the samurai. Many were killed in battle, while many others died at their own hand. They committed *seppuku*."

May had heard of this ritualistic suicide. A warrior would use his own knife or sword and plunge it into his abdomen. Another would stand by and cut off his head with a single stroke after that. May thought it all very barbaric and had no idea her grandfather had died this way.

"My father committed seppuku as a means of dealing honorably with the loss," her mother said with a steady voice. "Upon learning this, my mother was unable to bear the grief and took poison. I was left alone, and our family dishonored. It was a shameful and terrible time. The government called them traitors and were harsh and cruel to those left behind. Those of my family who lived were bitter and angry because my father had urged them to fight. I was forced to live in that, and it forever changed me."

"I'm so sorry, Mama. I can see why you would rather forget."

Her mother shook her head. "It wasn't only the loss of the

war or the death of my parents." She paused as if to steady her nerves. "Our way of life changed. Everything changed practically overnight. The aunt I had to live with cursed the samurai way and hated my father—her brother—because his encouragement to fight had brought about the death of her husband and son. Left in her care, I was treated with great contempt. I came to hate Japan and all that it stood for. Sadly, I came to hate my family as well for their cruelty and betrayal."

"It was easier for them to blame your father, I'm sure, than to face up to their own responsibilities." May tried to let all that her mother had said sink in. She had never guessed that her mother—just a girl of thirteen—had faced such a situation. "I'm sorry, Mama, for what you had to endure."

"I arrived in Japan to take a position with the same export business that your grandfather had previously worked for," her father said, looking at May. "I met your mother and eventually fell in love with her."

"And I begged him to take me away from Japan," Mama added. "I wanted only to leave it all behind me and have nothing more to do with it."

"How hard that must have been. To set aside all that you knew and loved." May couldn't imagine how difficult such a task might be. It was little wonder that her mother became emotional just talking about it.

"When I married your father, my family wanted nothing more to do with me, and that was fine by me." Mama looked heavenward. "I felt completely betrayed by them, but your father taught me about Jesus and His love. It changed my heart forever and allowed me to let go of those things which hurt me so much. At least to a point. I forgave my family, but

I could not forget. I knew that I needed to do so, however, so I vowed to never speak of it again." She looked at May. "I'm sorry that I've been so unwilling to share with you the stories of my youth. I know that you long to know about Japan, and I promise I will try my best to share with you what I can. Just, please, be patient with me."

May got up and went to her mother. She bent and wrapped her arms around Mama's shoulders. "I am sorry that I have caused you pain in the telling, but I thank you so much for sharing this with me."

"You deserve to know."

Straightening, May smiled. "I am learning kanji and kana from a man at the fair. Maybe in time you could help me instead. He told me I could visit him at his son's restaurant in Japantown, but I would rather learn from you, Mama."

"Goodness, I haven't used either one in a very long time."

"Maybe you can both learn," Father said, smiling.

May could see a sort of relief in his expression. No doubt this had been a terrible burden for him to bear as well.

Later that night after May had finished the foundation of her canvas for the samurai armor, she kissed her parents good-night and made her way to her room. As she dressed for bed, she thought of the day and all that it had brought. She was so grateful that God had opened Mama's heart to share about her youth in Japan. Perhaps one day they would even go for a visit, and May would be able to meet her relatives. Oh, how she prayed it might be so.

She unbraided her hair and sat down to brush the silky strands. She glanced in the mirror and caught sight of her green eyes. They were striking—vivid just like her father's eyes. People had often commented on her eyes. It was obvious from their almond shape that she was of Asian descent, but the green was almost alarming. It was most unexpected and always caused people to ask questions.

Still, throughout her life, May had endured the comments and curses of those who hated anyone different from themselves. She had been severely bullied as a child. Being of mixed race was not widely approved nor accepted. Such thoughts always brought up memories of Lee Munro. How she'd missed him after he'd gone. It'd been ten years, and she still longed to know if he was all right. Happy. May wondered often about the kind of woman he might have married. She would be beautiful and smart. Lee valued intelligence and always encouraged May to read and learn as much as she could. Yes, Lee would have found himself a wife who could converse with him about the affairs of the day.

May finished with her hair and crawled into bed. She listened for sounds of her parents heading upstairs to bed but heard nothing. Perhaps they were taking extra time in prayer tonight. She smiled at the thought. Lee had always told her that Christians had no idea of the power they held in prayer. She had once mentioned that to her father, and he assured her that he and her mother were more than aware of that power. That God had blessed their life over and over through their prayers. And tonight's conversation about her grandparents was answered prayer for May.

"Thank you, God. I so value what I have learned and know that no matter what else comes my way, You are the One who has provided." She continued to pray and asked for blessings on her mother and father, as well as Lee. She always prayed for him. And she knew without a doubt that somewhere he was praying for her as well.

5

W hat is this summons from the Japanese officials all about?" Lee asked one of the police officers assigned to the expo.

"I was told there is a young woman who comes every day to sketch and take photographs of one of the displays. The samurai armor, I believe. They are concerned as to why she is spending so much time there and fear she might be planning to steal it."

Lee nodded and folded the note. "I'll go and see what I can learn." As one of the main men in charge of security now, Lee wanted to prove himself capable and hopefully earn another promotion. He'd only recently been assigned to the expo after a young woman had nearly died from an attack. There had been other situations that demanded his attention as well, and the expo officials were quite concerned that such attacks wouldn't bode well for the fair.

Pulling on his tan suit coat, Lee left the administration building and headed out, passing by the main entrance and down Pay Streak Avenue. Pay Streak was alive with entertainment and activities. It was here where the expo rides could be found. The Ferris wheel and Fairy Gorge Tickler rides had long lines as people waited to be thrilled with roller coaster–type twists and turns and basket rides high in the air. The Dixieland Band struck up a rousing song that featured trumpets. People all around the stage began to clap and stomp their feet. Lee smiled. He liked the music.

He cut across to Klondike Circle, then made his way to the main artery of the exposition—Arctic Circle, where the beautifully created water cascade drew crowds for photographs. From here, he made his way down to Rainier Circle and the Japan building. The sound of trumpets faded into a cacophony of voices and other fair delights.

An official was summoned, and while Lee waited, he admired a display of silk kimonos. He thought of May Parker. Not that she ever had a kimono. Her mother forbade anything Japanese in the house. May had once told him that her mother felt deeply wounded by Japan, but she had no idea why.

"I am Mr. Nakamura." The Japanese man gave a little bow. "How may I be of service?"

"I'm Detective Munro. You sent for me?"

"Ah yes, there is a young woman," Mr. Nakamura explained. "She comes every day and is sometimes here for quite a long time. She takes pictures of the samurai armor displayed in one of the south rooms. She makes drawings too. We have apprehensions that she may be up to no good."

"In what way? It's my understanding that there are quite a few people taking photographs of the displays." Lee really didn't see a cause for alarm.

"She is here so much that we are concerned. Would you at least speak to her?"

"Of course." Lee headed for the door. "Show me where I can find her."

The official nodded and gave Lee a bow, then led him to the room where the armor was displayed in the center. There were quite a few people milling about, but near the armor stood one lone woman with her back to them. She held a sketch pad and seemed to be drawing.

Lee lost little time crossing the room. "Excuse me, miss."

The woman turned and looked up. Lee momentarily lost himself in those green eyes he remembered so well. "May?" His normally stoic expression changed to one of delight. "As I live and breathe. Is it really you?"

"Lee?" she replied in a tone that suggested awe. She surprised him by taking hold of his arm. He put his hand over hers.

"I have so often thought of you."

She smiled. "And I you. I was just praying for you last night."

"And what prompted that?"

May gave a shrug. "I pray for you daily. I always have since you went away." She shook her head and gave his arm a squeeze. "I can't believe you're really here."

"Come talk to me. I'm here on official business. The Japanese officials are concerned about your interest in this armor. They are worried that you're up to no good."

"Truly?" She looked around the room as if to find her accusers. "I'm photographing and sketching so that I can make a painting. I've been asked to paint the armor for the price of one hundred dollars."

"That's a lot of money. Do you often get these kinds of requests?" He led May out of the building to a bench where they could sit.

"I've never had this kind of request before," she admitted. She pulled her satchel forward and put her pad and pencil away. "I still can't believe it's you. All these years later. You are very handsome. Exactly as I had imagined."

"And you are beautiful, just as I knew you'd be."

She laughed. "And you are working for the exposition?"

"Actually, I am a police detective here in Seattle but assigned to the exposition. There were so many fears about illegal activities that they felt they needed more attention to keep the fair attendees safe."

"And I am one of those making things unsafe?" She seemed amused by this.

"You know how people can be."

"Well, I can tell you everything about my being here. I work with Fisher Photography on Pay Streak Avenue. You probably know about the Camera Girls. They take photographs of people attending the expo, and then the people can buy them for ten cents and have a lasting souvenir of the fair." She raised her hands and motioned to her clothes. "This is the uniform. Black skirt, white blouse, and a straw boater hat with black ribbon."

"And you roam around taking photos?"

"Well, actually I don't do that as much. Only when they're shorthanded. Mostly I add paint to some of those photos for an extra price to colorize them."

"Sounds like something you'd enjoy." He studied her a moment and shook his head. "I can't believe we're together. I've often thought of coming to see you."

"Why didn't you?"

Her tone wasn't accusing but convicted him nevertheless. Lee shrugged. "I'm not sure. You know how my parents felt. They're worse now than ever. Their prejudice, in fact, led me to leave their house for an apartment of my own. Before that I wasn't in town. I lived in Boston for a time and moved around quite a bit from there. You see, I worked for an investigating detective agency—the Pinkertons."

"I've heard of them. I would imagine you have many exciting tales to tell."

"I've only been back in Seattle a little more than a year. I had hoped to find my parents changed, but that wasn't the case."

"I'm sorry they're still so lost in their hate. It's sad that they hold such contempt for people who are different. I had hoped that when you moved away perhaps your father and mother would lessen their hatred."

"No such luck. The neighborhood they chose is exclusively white and looks down its collective nose at anyone who isn't rich and of the same color. Even most of the household servants are white. There is such a mistrust of anyone different."

"I'm sorry, Lee. You have such a tender heart for everyone that I know it's hard for you to contend with that attitude."

"Yes." He drew a deep breath and let it go. It was as if the years fell away and he and May were children again. Or rather that the years of separation had never happened. "I'm glad you're still working with your art."

"Well, you should be credited in part. After you left, I was quite sad. No doubt you will recall you were my only friend."

"I never understood that. You have such a wonderful personality, and you were kind to everyone you met."

"Yes, but I'm half Japanese, and that seems almost worse than being full-blooded. My parents were often condemned for having a marriage of mixed races."

Lee nodded. "My parents often commented on the Bible saying that was a sin, but they could never show me Scriptures to support their beliefs besides Deuteronomy seven, where God tells the Jewish people they weren't to marry people from other countries because they served other gods. Even more vague, they would talk about how God made animals each their own kind, and somehow they believe this forms up the opinion that God didn't want people to marry people from other countries and races. I didn't see it that way myself. Why should your ancestry or skin color prevent you from falling in love with someone?"

"Exactly. I agree with you on that account, but so many do not." She looked away, and the expression on her face left Lee feeling a momentary emptiness that he knew she experienced every day.

"So how did being sad help with your artwork?"

She turned back to him and smiled. "I focused day and night on my art. After school, I would come home and hide myself away in my room and sketch and paint. Father arranged for me to have lessons from a real artist. He didn't seem to mind that I was part Japanese, but after only a year, he passed away, and we couldn't find another teacher. Father bought me some books that explained technique, so I used them to further teach myself. When I was sixteen, Father turned our small parlor into an art studio for me. He bought me everything I needed for my work. So in my loneliness and fear of people treating me badly, I have created a great many paintings and drawings. You should come home with me to see it all. I know my folks would love to see you again."

"I'd like that too."

May got to her feet. "Then come now. We'll catch the trolley. We still live in the same house."

"We needn't get the trolley. I have my horse and carriage at the expo livery. I'll meet you at the main entrance. How about that?"

May smiled, and it sent a wave of unexpected feelings through Lee. How he had missed her. It was like a part of himself had been missing and was now returned to make him complete. How could he not have realized how important she was to him? How could he have let all these years go by without seeing her again?

"I'll be there," she told him. "And you will let the officials here know that I am not seeking to damage their property or cause trouble?"

Lee chuckled. "Of course I will."

May had been completely taken off guard by Lee's appearance. She had often thought of meeting up with him again, but she hadn't expected the rush of feelings that his appearance provoked.

As she waited for him to come to the main entrance, she reflected on how handsome he'd grown. His dark brown hair and blue eyes had always enhanced his perfect face, but it was like he had grown into all of his features and now was only that much better for having aged.

She smiled knowing that her parents would be quite happy to see him again. Perhaps Mama would even talk him into staying for supper. May imagined sitting around the table discussing their childhood and all that had passed since. She was anxious to show him her art studio and the photographs she'd taken of the armor. It was strange that she had been reported as a possible troublemaker. Had they spoken to Mr. Akira, he could have told them what May was up to and why. She had just yesterday explained to him about the couple offering to pay her for a painting of the armor.

When Lee approached in his carriage, May noted the fine black gelding and quality carriage. Lee was used to the very best.

He set the brake and jumped down to help her up. "I still can't believe you're here," he said as she settled into the leather seat. He joined her and took up the lines. "I've missed you, May."

"And I have missed you. I pray for you all the time. I remember how you taught me the importance and power of prayer."

"I still believe that," he said, releasing the brake. He urged the horse forward and glanced over to May with a smile. "I pray for you too."

"You said you have your own apartment now?"

"Yes, near the police station where I work. They even have a carriage house and stable, so it's quite convenient for me. It is expensive—probably more than I should wisely spend—but I like having transportation at my fingertips. Sometimes on my days off I take long drives into the country."

"Oh, that sounds wonderful."

"Would you like to go along sometime?"

May felt overcome with joy at the thought of spending a day with Lee. "I would very much enjoy that. But I have to ask, do you not have a wife or at least a fiancée in your life?"

"No, there's no one." He glanced at her and smiled. "I honestly haven't found a single woman who suggests that role in my life. There is one young lady I am currently pretending to be interested in, but we're only friends."

"Pretending? Why would you do that to her? That doesn't sound like the Lee I knew."

He chuckled. "She's in on it too. She's in love with a lowly musician who plays in the Seattle Symphony. Her parents, however, are determined she marry a rich man like me."

"Are you rich, Lee?" she asked, unable to contain her amusement. A giggle escaped, and she began to laugh. "Oh, it's so good to see you again. It just makes my heart happy."

"Mine too," he admitted.

"My mother and father will be so happy to see you again.

I know they missed your company when you went away. You were like a son to Father. He always enjoyed the conversations you two had."

Lee nodded. "Your folks were better to me than my own were. I don't know why I didn't seek you out before now."

"Sometimes it's easier to let a thing go." May thought of her Japanese heritage. For years it had been easier to let it go than to beg her mother for answers, especially since those answers appeared to cause great pain.

"Here we are." Lee directed the horse up the drive and set the brake. He jumped down, then helped May off the carriage. "I brought a feed bag for Gaspar, so he'll be occupied for a short time." He reached under the carriage seat and retrieved the bag.

May watched him deal tenderly with the horse. Lee had always had a fondness for animals. She and Lee had found an injured dog once. They took it back to her house and bandaged its wounds. The animal recovered quickly and one day simply moved on.

Leading the way into the house, May wondered what Lee would think of seeing it all again. Not a lot had changed. They were all older, but she knew he would find her parents pretty much as he had left them.

"Mama! Father!" she called from the entry foyer. May glanced up the stairs and called again.

"Goodness, May. Why are you yelling?" her mother asked, coming from the back of the house.

"Look who's come to see you."

May's mother approached slowly and looked Lee over from top to bottom. "Leander Munro, is that really you?"

"In the flesh." He gave her a big grin. "How are you, Mrs. Parker?"

Mama laughed and clapped her hands. "It is you. How wonderful." She came forward and gave Lee a hug. "I thought we might never see you again."

"What's the commotion?" Father asked, descending the stairs. "I was just changing my clothes." He spied Lee and stopped a couple of steps from the bottom. "Lee, how good to see you again."

"He's working for the police now," May explained. "I was making sketches of the Japanese armor that I'm going to paint, and the officials thought I might be up to no good." She winked at Lee. "Lee came to arrest me."

"Hardly. I was merely there to question her as to her interest in the armor, Mr. Parker. I would never arrest my good friend."

"How wonderful to have you with us now," Father said. "You look quite fit. I'd say life is agreeing with you. How are your folks?"

"Well, sir."

"Lee recently moved out. He lives in his own apartment downtown."

"You will stay for supper, won't you?" May's mother asked. "Our cook has made fried chicken. As I recall, you liked that very much."

"I do. And I would be happy to join you for dinner."

"I'll see that another place is set," Mama said, disappearing down the hall.

"I was just going to show Lee my art studio, Father."

He finished coming down the stairs and put his hand on Lee's shoulder. "I'm glad you're staying for supper. I would love to hear about your life after leaving the neighborhood."

"I'll be glad to share it with you."

Father looked at his pocket watch. "I would guess we'll

eat in just a few minutes, but you two go ahead and check out the studio. I'm sure you'll hear the bell when it's time."

May led the way and pushed open the large pocket doors that separated her studio from the larger room where her family often liked to gather in the evenings. The bigger room had a large fireplace done up in black marble. There was already a blaze in the hearth as the evening had turned chilly and damp.

Inside May's studio, there was a smaller woodstove, but it was cold. May switched on the lights and stepped to one side. "Here it is. As you can see, I've tacked up several photos and sketches of the armor."

Lee moved forward to inspect. "May, this is wonderful. I'm so happy that you have a space in which to work. I know how important that was to you when you were young and can only imagine how dear it must be now." He stepped closer to study the photographs and stopped abruptly.

He pointed at one of the pictures. "When was this taken?"

May came forward and shook her head. "It was just two days ago—Sunday. It was in the afternoon."

"This man," he said, pointing to a man standing on the opposite side of the armor. "Do you know him?"

She leaned in closer. "No. I've seen him there a couple of times. I wondered if he might be an artist, the way he studied the armor."

"He's a forger. Mario Bianchi. I've dealt with him before. We thought for a time that he was dead."

Lee gave the photograph careful scrutiny. "When I was with the Pinkertons in Washington, DC, he was being sought for having stolen a painting from a local art gallery. As the years went by, he gained a reputation for forgeries and more thefts. I was put on the case and chased him all over the Eastern Seaboard, going to any major city that reported art thefts or missing pieces being returned. He's notorious, and it's been my heart's desire to catch him and see him pay for his crimes."

"You said you thought he was dead?"

"Yes, there was a massive fire, and Bianchi was known to be in the building at the time. We found the body of a man who matched Bianchi's stature and hoped it was him. But it turned out it wasn't. It wasn't long at all before Bianchi was up to his old tricks. I wanted more than anything to catch him, but I left the Pinkertons before we had our man. Seattle offered me a tremendous opportunity to be in charge of my own department. That, along with the fact that it was home and I was tired of avoiding it just because of prejudicial people, encouraged me to return. I've always rued not getting Bianchi, though."

May could hear the determination in Lee's voice. "I don't know anything about him, but if I see him again, I could certainly try to get him to talk to me. Maybe I could ask him why he shares my interest in the armor."

"No, stay away from him, May. He's dangerous. If you see him again, just send someone to get me. I have an office in the administration building. I'll come if you get word to me."

She nodded. Lee's entire countenance had changed. His blue eyes seemed somehow darker—his expression quite serious. This Mario Bianchi was definitely a thorn in Lee's side. She had never seen such a look on Lee's face except when he'd dealt with her bullies.

"I'll get word to you," she promised. Just then the bell for dinner rang. "That would be our cue for supper." She had hoped to wash up and change her clothes, but now it was too late. "Come. I know you know the way, but I want an excuse to touch you and make sure you're really here." She looped her arm through his.

Just having him near made her feel so happy.

6

"Miss Parker is no threat to your samurai armor display," Lee told the Japanese official. "She has been hired to make a painting of the armor for a Mr. and Mrs. Tamura. Apparently, the armor has some connection with the woman's family, and she wanted to have it painted."

"That is good news," Mr. Nakamura declared. "I have since talked to one of the men who guide the visitors. He told me Miss Parker was harmless and that he has been teaching her kanji and some Japanese."

Lee wasn't surprised even though May hadn't spoken of the matter. "There is, however, another matter I wish to discuss. I looked over the photographs Miss Parker took of the armor, and in one of the pictures, I spied a man who is notorious for art thefts and forgeries. His name is Mario Bianchi. He is wanted by the law in several countries."

Mr. Nakamura's expression remained stoic. "I am not familiar with this man."

"Few are. He always manages to stay in the background, but from time to time, he steps out and is quite dangerous. He usually carries weapons with him and isn't afraid to use them if he feels cornered. Do you know any reason why he would single out the armor being displayed?"

The man shook his head and grew thoughtful. "It is a fine example of samurai armor but not famously owned. The government thought it worthy of the exposition. That is all I know."

A short man who had stood behind the official in silence stepped forward and whispered something to the official.

Mr. Nakamura nodded. "Yes, I remember now. There was a man named Tobias Hillsboro. He offered to buy the armor. He wanted it for his collection. We refused, and he offered a larger sum. We made it clear the piece was not for sale."

Lee took out his notebook and jotted down the name. "Tobias Hillsboro. Do you have any information about where he lives or is staying?"

Again, the shorter man touched the older man's arm. At the official's nod, he spoke up. "We wrote down his information. He was hopeful the government might be persuaded to change their mind and sell him the piece."

"We told him it was a treasure of our country and no amount of money would be valued over our ancestors and their legacies. He did not understand." Mr. Nakamura frowned. "Perhaps you should speak with him."

"I will."

Mr. Nakamura nodded and spoke in Japanese to his aide. The man hurried away, while the official looked again to Lee. "He will write down the information and bring it to you. I must go now. I am late for a meeting. I thank you for what you are doing to help me in this matter."

"That's why we're here."

Lee waited for the aide to return. It was about ten minutes later that he finally approached Lee with a piece of paper.

70

"This is all of the information we have."

Lee took the paper and read it. Hillsboro was staying at the Sorrento Hotel but lived in New York City. He looked up at the man. "Thank you."

He immediately retrieved his horse and carriage and made his way downtown to the Sorrento Hotel. The grand Italian Renaissance creation was highly praised as the finest hotel Seattle had to offer. Built to accommodate the exposition visitors, the hotel boasted over one hundred fifty rooms, styled and fashioned in such grandeur as to please even the wealthiest of guests.

After handing over his horse and carriage, Lee made his way inside and headed to the front desk. He was directed to Mr. Hillsboro's suite with assurance from the manager that the man had not left his room all morning.

Lee knocked on the door and waited. It wasn't long before a stately old man appeared. "Yes, may I help you?"

"I'm here to see Mr. Hillsboro. My name is Detective Munro. I'm with the Seattle Police Department."

"Very good, sir. Please wait here."

The man crossed the small foyer and made his way into the large open sitting room, where Lee spied a man standing at the window. He glanced toward Lee as the old man spoke to him in a hushed tone. Finally, he nodded, and the man came to retrieve Lee.

"Mr. Hillsboro will see you now."

Lee crossed the room in a few long strides and extended his hand to Hillsboro. "Mr. Hillsboro, I'm glad to meet you. My name is Detective Munro."

"And to what do I owe this unexpected visit?" He shook Lee's hand, then crossed his arms over his chest.

The man was around Lee's six-foot height and about the

same build. His sandy blond hair held tiny hints of silver at the temple, and his gray-blue eyes seemed cold and indifferent, but Lee could tell the man missed no detail.

"I work for the Seattle Police Department and have been assigned to the Alaska-Yukon-Pacific Exposition."

"And what has that to do with me?" Mr. Hillsboro turned his gaze back toward the window.

Lee glanced in the same direction. From this sixth-floor room, there was an exceptional view of the Puget Sound. He thought of May and how she might enjoy painting the vista.

"I understand you desired to purchase the displayed samurai armor at the Japan building."

Hillsboro didn't so much as blink. "I am a collector of fine arts and antiquities. The armor intrigued me, and I made the Japanese government an offer. Why should that be a matter for you?"

"There was some concern about the safety of the armor. Can you tell me why that piece in particular was of interest to you?"

Hillsboro turned and faced Lee. "As a collector, I value a great many pieces. I like what I like, Detective Munro. I saw the armor and found it quite pleasing. As is my habit, I approached the officials in charge and offered to purchase it. End of story."

"I see. And do you know a man named Mario Bianchi?"

Hillsboro's eyes narrowed. "Should I?"

"As a collector of fine arts and antiquities, I would have thought you would have heard of him. He's a forger of such things."

"I'm a wealthy man, Detective. I got that way through hard work and attention to detail. I would never accept a forged piece." He gazed toward the ceiling.

Lee could see the man was growing bored with the conversation. He also knew there was nothing wrong in what the man had done. However, he had a feeling the man was not being completely honest, a detective's sort of sixth sense.

"I'm sorry to have bothered you, Mr. Hillsboro. If you should have any encounters with Mr. Bianchi, I would appreciate it if you would get word to me." Lee pulled out a business card and extended it. Hillsboro merely looked at it.

Lee wasn't easily shaken, and Hillsboro's demeaner was one he'd dealt with many times before. "You can reach me for the time being at the administration building at the exposition. You can also leave word for me at the address given. That's where the station is located. There's also a telephone number."

"I'm sure that I'll have no need of it, but feel free to leave the card with my valet."

May inspected her area one final time, making sure everything was put away. She was anxious to get home and continue her work on the samurai armor painting.

"I can't tell you how popular your painted touches have been on the photographs," Addie Hanson declared, coming from the back room with a stack of pictures. "May, you do such beautiful work. Given your talent, I think Mr. Fisher would like to have you working for him full time in the new shop."

"I enjoy what I do," May admitted. "However, I have a commission to paint a portrait of the samurai armor and am quite excited by that as well."

"I've seen that armor. It's quite detailed. I'm told there

are hundreds of lacquered pieces that make up the headpiece alone."

"It's true. I've studied it over and over. The armor is finely detailed and made in such a handsome manner. A warrior would surely have looked fierce in it."

"My thoughts exactly."

The front bell rang, and Lee came into the shop. May smiled. "Addie Hanson, this is Lee Munro. He's a police detective who works here at the expo."

"Miss Hanson."

"Mrs. Hanson, actually. It's nice to meet you, Mr. Munro," Addie said, nodding. "I could have used someone like you back in June and July when my brothers tried to kill me."

"So you're the one." He grinned. "It was your case that forced them to bring me on as added help with the safety of the expo. In fact, a great many officers were added to the security force here."

"I'm glad. It might have saved us all a lot of trouble."

"Lee and I grew up together," May offered. "He's an old friend."

Addie laid the stack of photographs on the counter. "Then do I presume correctly that you're here to see May?"

"You do. I was checking to see if she was ready to leave for the day."

"I am. I want to get home to my painting." May took up her satchel and put it over her shoulder. "Addie, I may need to take a few days off. Remember I mentioned that I was hired to make a painting for the Tamuras? Well, I was supposed to meet them on Saturday and let them know when I thought the painting would be ready, but Mr. Tamura caught up with me this morning. He said they need the painting by the twenty-fifth."

"Things have slowed down considerably since school started once again. Not as many people traveling now either. I think we can spare you for a couple of days, although as I said, your painted touches are becoming more and more requested. I think you could have a permanent job with the Fishers."

"If Mr. Fisher asks me, I might take him up on it." May smiled and headed for the door. Lee opened it for her and stepped aside. "I'll check in with you in a couple of days."

"After you, milady."

May said very little on the ride home. She was already planning out her strategy for the samurai armor painting. The concept of lean over fat came to mind for the purpose of finishing the piece faster. Most artists preferred fat over lean. A higher content of oil, or fat in this case, would give richer, glossier colors and keep the paint more flexible and decrease cracking. But the drying time would be longer.

She needed to turn over the painting right away, so lean painting would make more sense. She would dilute the oil paint with turpentine. This would give less sheen and faster drying. As she thought of the old piece of armor, it seemed appropriate and perhaps would even benefit the details she hoped to include.

"You're very quiet."

May looked up to find Lee watching her. She smiled knowing he would understand. "I was already painting in my mind. I'm not sure why I agreed to do this. The rush is going to be difficult. I can only do so much to speed the process. I probably should have just suggested having it professionally photographed."

"I think your efforts, no matter how rushed, will be greatly appreciated. Obviously, the armor means a great deal to them."

"I think it does. The woman was actually tearful when they approached me. If it's a part of her family's history, then I can understand. I'm going to have to find a way to ensure as much quality as possible in the little time that I have."

"If anyone can do it, it's you."

"You have an awful lot of confidence in a woman you haven't even known for ten years."

He shrugged. "You've always been steadfast in your thoughts, May. Your faith in God is strong, and you know your abilities. You neither brag because of nor pretend to be without skills and talents. I've always liked that about you. Despite not knowing much about your lineage, you've always been well grounded. That impressed me from the earliest days."

She was rather surprised by his comments. She'd never really considered herself well-grounded simply because there were all those missing pieces from the past. What was one to ground themselves on if they weren't allowed to know where they had come from? Of course, she had Father's family, but she longed so much for an understanding of her mother's ancestry. At least Mama had been willing to speak briefly on the past. Perhaps in time, additional information would be forthcoming.

"Why isn't there a man in your life, May?"

She laughed. "Who says there isn't?"

Lee slowed the horse. "If there was someone, you would have been talking about him without ceasing. I know how you are when you are truly enraptured by something. Remember the red dress you wanted when you were twelve?"

"It wasn't red. It was burgundy, and how is it that you remember such a thing?"

"Because you were completely impassioned about having it. You talked about it all the time. If I were talented in drawing, I could sketch that thing just from the memory of your description alone."

She shook her head, marveling that he had such a mind for detail. "There isn't anyone in my life. I'm not white enough for most Americans and not Japanese enough for those from Japan. I don't fit into either world."

"Of course you do. You just haven't met the right man yet. But when you do, watch out. You will talk about him all the time, and I will learn every detail of who he is and where he's from. And if not from you, then I shall research him myself to make sure he's good enough for you."

"And what of you, Lee? You said you were pretending to be interested in that young woman who is in love with the musician. Is she the only woman in your life? Is there no one you fancy?"

"I've been too busy with my work," Lee replied. He directed the horse down May's street and shook his head. "I don't know of anyone in my social circle that I could fancy. Most are of the same attitude and opinions as my parents, and I disagree with so much that they favor."

"That's really too bad. You're handsome and kind and would make a wonderful husband."

He looked at her oddly for just a moment, then returned his gaze to the street. His silence gave her concern that she'd embarrassed him, but she'd only spoken the truth. He was handsome—dashingly so. And his love of God had always directed him to respond to people with kindness and gentleness. He was all that any woman would want in a husband.

"By the way," she said, hoping to ease any discomfort, "I did get that dress, and it was perfect."

❧

"He knows your name and that you're in town," Hillsboro told Mario Bianchi.

Bianchi shrugged and pursed his lips as he rolled his gaze heavenward. "It is unimportant."

"I hardly think so. Why else would he come here asking after you? He is worried about the armor and doesn't seem like the kind of man to let a thing go once it has a hold on him."

"Leander Munro is of no concern. By the time he figures out what's going on, I'll be gone." Bianchi lowered his gaze to Hillsboro. "We'll both be gone, and the armor will be yours."

"I wish I had your confidence."

"I tell you what," Bianchi said as an idea suddenly dawned. "I'll arrange for some thefts around the exposition grounds. Things of value that I can sell later. I can have a man or several men search the exhibits and steal whatever seems of greatest importance. Munro will find himself so caught up in finding the thieves that he'll forget all about the armor. I've also hired a Japanese couple to have a young lady make a detailed painting of the armor. The Tamuras are down on their luck and can be trusted to keep their mouths shut. Once I have the painting, it will be easy enough to create a believable copy. I already have men forming the lacquered pieces, silk bindings, and creating the basic formation."

"I suppose a distraction couldn't hurt."

Bianchi leaned back and gave a satisfied smile. "And don't worry about Detective Munro. He'll be so busy giving each case his utmost attention that he won't have time to worry about a thing that hasn't even happened yet."

The week of September twentieth started as normally as the other weeks had, but by the twenty-fourth Lee was inundated with reports of theft in various locations at the expo. He looked over the details of each report, then made his way to each place. One by one he heard the stories. A rare book had been taken from one exhibit. Several priceless pieces of jewelry from another. Two different buildings were missing money that had been kept in their offices. Last but not least, the Alaska building was missing several pieces of carved ivory valued at several hundred dollars.

When he finished with the last report, it was nearly eleven o'clock. He was out of sorts and hungry. He wondered if May would have time for an early lunch with him. He made his way through the exposition grounds, noting the crowd had thinned out considerably. He knew that by evening the number of attendees would swell again, and since it was a Friday, there would be even more than the usual evening increase.

He paused in front of the photography shop and watched May work. It was rather brilliant of Fisher to position her in the window. where people could easily see for themselves the quality job she did and how it enhanced the photographs in a most artistic way.

He had seen May at work when she'd been younger. She was always quite intense when focused on her canvas. He had seen her contemplate an object for lengthy periods of time, studying it, memorizing each curve and subtle shading. She looked at the world with different eyes, he had once told her.

May paused to clean a brush and glanced up. She smiled at Lee in a way that suggested she was absolutely delighted to see him. She always looked at him that way. He couldn't help but feel an odd sensation course through him. He had always enjoyed her company and conversation. She was one of those people who made others feel better just by being around them. How he had missed her all these years.

He returned the smile and headed for the door. The bell rang overhead, and one of the Camera Girls behind the counter greeted him.

"Good morning, can I help you with something?"

He shook his head. "I'm here to see if May might join me in an early lunch."

May was putting her brush aside. "I'd love to. I am famished. I left late this morning and didn't stop to have breakfast." She stood and unfastened the buttons of her smock.

"I thought I'd like to try the St. Louis Café over by the main entrance."

May turned to the woman behind the counter. "Mary, have you tried the St. Louis Café?"

"Bertha and I have eaten there several times. I think you'll enjoy it," the girl replied.

"Then we'll give it a go." May joined Lee. "I'm ready."

He opened the door for May and followed her outside. It seemed that the crowd had grown some just in the short time he'd been inside.

"What have you been doing this morning?" May asked.

"There have been a number of thefts reported, and I had to check them out."

"Is it that Mr. Bianchi you told me about? Do you suspect he's the one responsible?"

"Well, it's not his regular style. His method is to replace the pieces he steals with forgeries. He goes to an art gallery or museum and studies a piece for several weeks or even months. Then he makes a forged copy and finds a way to exchange it for the original. These were out-and-out thefts where the person took the piece and ran."

"I'm sorry to hear that. Do you have any leads?"

"Not a one."

"It's rather strange that they should all come at once when nothing much has been going on prior to this. Perhaps your Mr. Bianchi needed to create a diversion."

Lee looked at her for a moment, then nodded. "It does seem strange. There has been the odd theft here or there, but nothing like this." Perhaps this was the kind of distraction Bianchi would use. Get Lee busy elsewhere.

"I'm supposed to meet the Tamuras tomorrow. They insisted I bring the painting as they are leaving soon for Japan. I told them it would still be wet in places because I have to finish adding a few touches. I've really had to rush to get this done, and it hasn't been easy. Thankfully, I've had my photographs and sketches to aid me."

"I'm sure it will be perfect." He couldn't quite stop thinking about Bianchi and found it hard to concentrate on what she was saying.

They'd reached the main gate area, and the St. Louis Café looked to already be full of people. Lee was about to suggest they go elsewhere when he glanced up to see the trolley coming down the slope. Something wasn't quite right. It was going much too fast. They'd never be able to stop at this rate.

In no more time than it took to blink, the streetcar hit the curve near the main entrance of the exposition and pulled away from the track. The body of the car separated from the wheels in what seemed like slow motion. Lee could see that it was headed straight for them and grabbed May's arm.

"Run!" He pulled her with him, but her legs seemed frozen in place. He lifted her to his side and carried her. He cast a quick backward glance. The trolley was nearly upon them. He angled them to the east, feeling certain the momentum of the trolley would continue past them.

Screams from the people rushing to get out of the way were nothing compared to the cacophony created by the thirty-six-ton streetcar grinding against the pavement and the impact of it on the buildings. Lee shielded May the best he could, praying they wouldn't be injured. She clung to him, wrapping her arms around him and pressing her face against his chest. He knew she was terrified, but there was nothing more he could do. When the trolley finally came to rest on its side, it was as if the world went silent.

Lee pulled back from where he had pressed May against a wall. "Are you hurt?"

She shook her head, peeking out around him. "No, but look at what that trolley did." Lee turned to see the destruction. The small cigar shop was demolished, and the café had a huge gaping hole in its side wall.

People gathered around the trolley, and Lee knew he needed to go to work. "I have to do my job, May. I'm sorry."

He left her standing there and hurried to where the trolley had come to rest.

"Back away," he commanded. "I'm with the police."

May watched Lee go to work clearing away those who could offer no assistance and organizing those who could help. At first there was absolute stillness after the accident. It was as if the entire world had fallen into a state of shock. Even the expo rides and thrill seekers seemed to be silenced. Then little by little the sounds returned, with moaning coming from the trolley and inside the damaged buildings.

People started to emerge from the streetcar. Most had some type of injury. Lee dispatched a man to get the medical staff from the expo's emergency hospital. A couple of women stepped forward, announcing they were nurses. Lee put them in charge of assessing the wounded.

May glanced at the damaged café and saw that people were trying to exit. She hurried to the front doors and found two men already working to help people out. As customers nearest the doors filed out unharmed, May slipped inside the building to see if she could help those less fortunate. She wasn't sure what she could do, but it made her feel better than standing idle.

She maneuvered to the area where the most damage had occurred. Tables were overturned, and people could be seen beneath the debris. The wall had been shattered, and splintered wood was everywhere. Had the structure been built for permanency perhaps it might not have sustained such damage, but as it was, those who'd been in the path of the trolley were definitely in trouble.

"May."

She frowned. Who had whispered her name? May glanced around to see who had summoned her.

"May, help me."

She saw a familiar figure pinned beneath the wreckage. "Esther!" May knelt down and began moving what she could away from Esther's slender body. Already she could see blood from a scalp wound.

"Oh, Esther, don't move. I'll do what I can to get you out of here."

"Don't leave me, May. It hurts so bad."

"I won't," May promised. She moved a large piece of wood from where it rested atop Esther's hips and legs. The removal revealed that a metal pole, whose origins May had no idea of, had fallen across Esther's shoulder and abdomen.

"I can hardly breathe. I'm scared," Esther half whispered, half moaned. "I don't want to die."

"You aren't going to die, Esther. Stop talking like that." But May could see the woman's ashen color and noted that blood now trickled from her nose.

Esther reached to take hold of May's hand. "I don't know what to do."

"Just pray. Keep still and pray." May tried to move the pole, but it was quite heavy. She did her best to heave it upward, but the movement just seemed to further Esther's pain.

She glanced around to see if someone could help her, but the others were already busy moving injured folks from the restaurant. Taking her own advice, May prayed like never before, asking God to send help.

"May, I don't want to go to hell."

Esther's comment momentarily stunned May. She stopped trying to move the pole and knelt beside her friend. "You don't have to go to hell, Esther. God is quite willing for you to be saved."

"I've done terrible things. I'm a bad person, and God can't forgive me. I've tried to pray, but I don't think He hears me."

"Of course He hears you. Oh, Esther." May smoothed back the girl's bloody hair. Esther coughed, and more blood came from her nose and mouth. Reaching into her pocket, May produced a handkerchief and wiped the blood away as best she could.

"It's going to be all right, Esther. The Bible says that the Lord isn't willing for any to perish, but that all should come to repentance. He will save you if you ask Him to."

"I don't know what to do," Esther said, her words turning to sobs. "I've tried to be good."

"None of us are good enough to save ourselves, Esther." May found a spot on the handkerchief that wasn't soaked with blood and dabbed at the tears running down Esther's cheeks. "You're obviously sorry for the way you've acted."

Esther nodded. "I'm so sorry."

"And do you believe that Jesus is the Son of God who came to die in our place for all of our sins?"

The injured woman nodded again. "I do, and I want to believe He died for my sins too."

May smiled. "He did, Esther. He did. Just believe in Him and confess your desire to be forgiven and saved from sin. Jesus is more than willing. He loves you so much that He died for you. Are you willing to turn away from sin?"

"Yes, I want to be a better person. I want to please God." She sounded weaker by the minute.

Esther closed her eyes, and for a moment May was uncertain if she had fainted or died. She reached for Esther's shoulder.

"May, are you all right?"

May turned and saw Lee not three feet away.

"I need help, Lee. Hurry. Esther is pinned down by the pole, and I can't budge it."

Lee tapped a fellow near him. "Come with me."

The man complied, and the two of them lifted the metal off Esther's body. She moaned from the action but May saw that as good. At least she wasn't dead. Esther opened her eyes.

"I prayed, May. God heard me."

May smiled. "Of course, He did." She patted Esther's arm.

"If I die . . . tell my folks what happened here. I want them to know that . . . that . . ." Her breathing sounded more labored. "Tell them. Promise."

"I will, Esther, but you aren't going to die. You must live. You're my friend, and I don't want to lose you."

"Let me lift her up and get her outside. There are doctors and nurses waiting," Lee said, reaching to pull Esther into his arms.

May stood and backed out of the way. The man who had helped Lee move the pole now tried to help free Esther's skirt from a table leg. Together they managed to get her up and into Lee's arms. May followed Lee from the café.

"Make way," he called. "I have an injured woman."

The crowd shifted enough for them to pass through. May felt strangely at peace. Esther had accepted Jesus as her Savior. No matter what happened now, she was safe.

Just as Lee had said, there was an area off to one side beyond the accident where men and women appeared to be caring for the injured. Lee carried Esther to one of the tables that had been set up for patients. He gently placed her atop the table and stood back. Esther had passed out, and May could see that the movement had caused more bleeding.

A man stepped forward to examine her. "Do you know her?" he asked Lee.

"No, but my friend does." He motioned to May. "What's her name?"

"Esther Danbury. She works at Fisher Photography as a

Camera Girl." The man wrote on a notecard, then handed it to a woman, who jotted the information down in a notebook. When she was finished, she took a pin and secured the card to Esther's collar as a means of identification.

"I lifted a heavy metal pole off her," Lee offered.

"And she was buried under a lot of other debris," May said, taking hold of Lee's arm. Despite the peace she had about Esther's condition, the events of the day were starting to overwhelm her.

"I suspect internal bleeding. We need to get her to Seattle General Hospital."

May saw two men carrying a stretcher with a covered body. Apparently at least one person had already died from their injuries. This was the kind of accident where there might well be many deaths.

"There are ambulances on the way, Doctor," a woman told him. "They've telephoned for as much help as we can get."

"This patient has priority when they arrive."

"I'll see to it," she promised.

The doctor turned to Lee and May. "There's very little I can do here. She needs a good surgeon. You can wait with her if you like. It would probably be of comfort to her should she regain consciousness."

May nodded. "I'll stay with her."

"If you know her family . . . it might be wise to get word to them," the man told May.

Lee put his arm around her. "I'm going to go help the others, but I won't be far."

She met his gaze and saw the concern he held for her. "I'll be fine, Lee. Go do what you must."

He hesitated, then leaned forward and kissed her forehead. The gesture surprised May, but she bowed her head so that he couldn't see her reaction. She knew without him, she would probably have fallen apart.

Wailing sounds and outright screams could be heard as people were helped from the trolley and buildings. May had no idea how serious the injuries of others were but knew that Esther was badly hurt. She wished she could let the others at the photography shop know and looked around to see if she might spot one of the Camera Girls in the growing crowd of onlookers.

She noticed a man had set up a tripod and was preparing to take a photograph of the mangled trolley, but she saw nothing of the familiar straw boaters with their black ribbons. She had nearly given up when she spotted a familiar face. She didn't know the man all that well but knew he could help her in getting word to her friends.

"Mr. Hanson!" She waved and called again. "Mr. Hanson!"

Addie Hanson's husband crossed to where May stood. "Are you hurt, Miss Parker?" He looked her up and down.

"No, I wasn't in the accident. But Esther Danbury was badly injured, and they are sending her to the General Hospital. We need to get word to her family. Oh, and I'm going to go with Esther to the hospital if they'll allow me to."

He nodded. "I'll let Addie know. Do you know if any of the other girls were hurt?"

"I don't know. I stopped helping when I found Esther." May felt her eyes well with tears. "I don't know if she's going to make it, but she accepted Jesus as her Savior before she lost consciousness. It seemed to give her great comfort."

Isaac Hanson reached out and patted May's arm. "Don't be afraid. God will see us through this. Rest in Him, May."

"I will." She squared her shoulders, feeling bolstered with those few words and drew a deep breath. "I will trust in Him."

8

At Seattle General Hospital, Esther was quickly taken into a room for examination. May sat in the waiting area, wondering if she'd ever see her friend again. Poor Esther. She had gone through so much emotionally, and now she was struggling for her very life.

It was hard to imagine facing death. May had never really contemplated dying. Since having received Jesus as her Savior, death no longer held fear for her. Oh, there was the question of how it might come, but May usually pushed that aside in favor of thinking more about what heaven might be like.

She could still see the fear in Esther's eyes. May had figured the girl was already a Christian. It was something May just took for granted that a person would be. She forgot that some people didn't even believe that God existed. It was just so hard to imagine that people could actually think that way. How could you look at the beauty of creation—at all the complexities of life—and not believe in a Creator? How could you endure the tragedies of living without a strong faith in God?

"May?"

She looked up and saw Addie Hanson. "Addie." May moved

over on the bench so that Addie could join her. "They've taken Esther to surgery. She has internal injuries."

"Oh, poor girl." Addie sat down beside May and took hold of her hand. "Mr. Munro said that you were very nearly a victim as well."

"Yes, if not for his quick thinking, I believe I would have stood there gawking at the trolley bearing down on us. I doubt I would have even had the sense to run and get away from it."

"I'm so glad you weren't hurt." Addie squeezed her hand and continued holding on. "There were so many injured. I know Isaac said at least one man was dead."

"I hope there won't be others, but it would take a miracle." May gave a heavy sigh.

Addie nodded and gazed off down the hallway. "Where is the surgery?"

"I don't know. The doctor promised to return here to let me know about Esther's condition after he tended to her. They've only been gone about an hour. I have no idea how long it will take."

"No, of course you don't. We will just sit here and pray and support each other while we wait. My husband will be here later. He wanted to stay at the expo and see if he could offer any help."

"Lee felt that way too. He cares so much about people."

"As an officer of the law, I'm sure he feels it's his obligation to help."

"He would feel that way regardless," May countered. "Since we were young, he was always the one who helped others when they were injured or when someone set out to picking on them. He saved me more than once from horrible children who hated people of Asian blood."

"How awful. I'm sorry you had to endure that."

May shrugged. "The world is full of people who find it easier to be afraid and hate than to learn and perhaps share friendship."

"It's true. I've seen that for myself," Addie admitted. "It's so easy to hate. That's why I was determined to put hate aside even after my brothers were so cruel. It wasn't easy, but few good things are."

"I'm sorry you were treated so badly." May had heard only enough to know that Addie's life had been in jeopardy at the hands of her brothers.

"Greed makes people do as many horrible things as hatred does. When I was in the Yukon, I saw that every day. People killed for that little glint of gold. My brothers were greedy and driven to have more than they did. They ended up in prison for trying to take what they wanted. Here at the expo, they picked pockets and stole things and never gave it a second thought. They told me as much. They felt somehow entitled to have what belonged to other people, and they were conniving enough to take it."

May shook her head. "Strange notions for a person to have. I grew up around one terrible boy who often shared the thoughts of his parents regarding how people of color shouldn't have money or possessions—that they didn't deserve the same things that white people deserved. I could never understand such thinking."

"Nor do I." Addie shifted her weight and leaned back against the wall. "I don't suppose I ever shall."

May gazed down the hallway at the closed double doors. Occasionally a nurse or white-clad orderly passed through, but otherwise the place was silent. It was hard to wait and wonder about Esther's condition.

For a long time, May and Addie said nothing. People came and went. Some of the injured arrived from the expo but didn't seem in too bad of shape. There was one man whose leg had been mangled. He'd been riding the trolley and May heard the stretcher bearers explaining his situation to a doctor as they were directed to the same room where they'd first taken Esther. Another was a woman who had lost a bunch of her teeth. Her face was cut, and swelling was already distorting her appearance. Thankfully, very few of the injuries seemed life-threatening.

After what seemed like forever, the doctor reappeared and came to where May and Addie waited. Both got to their feet in hopes of good news.

"Your friend came through surgery and is doing well. We were able to stop the bleeding inside of her, but she'll be recuperating for some time."

"May I see her?" May asked.

"No, she's not awake. We're keeping her sedated for at least twenty-four hours. You could come back tomorrow evening, perhaps, but it would be better to wait until Sunday."

"We could come after church," Addie suggested. She turned to the doctor. "I'm Mrs. Hanson, Esther's supervisor at the expo. I'll let her parents know about her situation. They don't have a phone, or I would have called. Do you wish for me to tell them anything else?"

The doctor shook his head. "Just tell them their daughter was badly injured but is now stable. I have no way of knowing whether an infection will develop or if any other complications will set in. Only time will tell."

"I understand. I will stress that to her family."

"If you'll excuse me, I need to check on a new patient."

"Thank you, Doctor. I appreciate that you came to talk

to us." May waited to let out a long breath until he had headed back down the hall. "I'm so glad she made it through the surgery. I was quite concerned about her. She looked so bad."

Addie put her arm around May's shoulders. "We will just continue to pray for healing. God has this. No matter what, given Esther's decision to ask Jesus into her heart, she's going to be just fine."

"I know, but I'd kind of like her to be around for a while longer. I made it my goal to be her friend. It doesn't seem like she has many, and given the way she acted, I do understand the apprehension of others to take her on. I'm glad, however, that I don't have that past with her, and I can reach out and offer friendship. I believe that's what God has called me to do."

Addie smiled. "I'm sure He has."

"Addie!" Isaac Hanson smiled when he spotted her. He came to her and placed a kiss upon her cheek. "How is she?"

"We just heard that Esther is out of surgery," Addie replied. "We won't be allowed to see her until Sunday, however."

"Perhaps as soon as tomorrow evening," May added. She hated the thought of waiting until after church on Sunday.

"Is she going to be all right?"

"The doctor doesn't know exactly. He said she came through the surgery well, but that infection could set in. Sounds like it might be a few days before we know."

Isaac nodded. "Are you ready to go home?"

"No, we need to make our way to Esther's home. Her folks don't yet know about her situation. I need to tell them what's happened."

"Of course. I'll drive you. Do you have the address?"

"Yes, I wrote it down before I left the shop." She turned to May. "Would you like a ride home?"

Just then, May spotted Lee standing at the entrance. She gave a wave until he saw her, then turned back to Addie. "I'm sure Lee can see me home."

He joined them, a grave look on his face. "Did she make it?"

"She did. She came through surgery and is now resting," May said. "The Hansons are going to her home to let her parents know what has happened."

"How many are dead?" Addie asked.

"Only one, miraculously enough. Frank Hull from Tacoma." Lee shook his head. "I don't know how that is even possible, given the way that trolley was torn up. It split in half when it hit that telephone pole. There were some eighty passengers inside, but most of the injuries were superficial. There were a few broken bones and more serious injuries, but for the most part everyone came out of this without too much damage. Of course, the cigar shop and St. Louis Café were completely destroyed."

"Will they worry about rebuilding them?" Addie asked.

"They were already clearing the debris away and planning what to do. I think they'll probably set up tents. After all, there are only a couple of weeks left."

May calculated the time. "Three to be exact."

"Hardly worth worrying about," Isaac said. He looked to Addie. "We should probably get going before the traffic gets too heavy."

Addie nodded and reached over to hug May. "Will you be at work tomorrow?"

"No, I have to finish up my painting and meet with the Tamuras. I doubt the canvas will even be dry, but they insisted. They can't wait any longer."

"Then I'll see you Sunday here at the hospital after church," Addie said. "Good day, Mr. Munro." Addie extended her hand.

"Please, call me Lee." He shook her hand and then did the same with Isaac.

"Call me Isaac. You too, May." Isaac smiled and took hold of Addie's arm. "Good day."

May waited until they were out of sight before moving back to the bench. She sank down and closed her eyes. "I'm exhausted."

"Hungry too, I'd imagine. Come on, let's go get something to eat."

She shook her head. "I'm a mess. I have blood on my blouse and skirt, along with dirt and a snag or two. I should just go home."

"Well, at least let me drive you there."

"That would be good. Thank you." She got to her feet. The events of the day were starting to get to her again. She could still see the trolley careening toward them.

"I haven't really thanked you for saving my life," she said as they made their way outside. "I could barely move. Had you not taken hold of me and dragged me along, I'm sure I'd be dead."

"Life is very unpredictable, to be sure. I have a feeling I'll be seeing that trolley heading at us in my dreams."

"Me too."

Lee helped her into the buggy, then followed her up. He took off the brake and snapped the lines lightly over the horse's backside. "Walk on, Gaspar."

The horse moved forward, and May leaned back and closed her eyes. There was still so much to do, and even painting lean, she knew the canvas wouldn't be dry when she met the Tamuras early tomorrow afternoon.

She didn't know when she'd dozed off, but when Lee touched her cheek, May sat straight up to realize they'd reached her house.

"I'm so sorry. I didn't mean to fall asleep. This day has just taken all of my strength."

"Promise me you'll eat something before you get to work," Lee said, helping her down. "You skipped breakfast, and then we didn't have lunch. By my calculations, you haven't had anything for going on twenty-four hours."

"Ever the man of details." She smiled. "I promise. I'll go see the cook first thing. Then I'll have to explain all that's happened to my folks. I'm sure they'll want to forbid me to return lest another trolley comes careening my way."

"I'm sure by now the Seattle Electric Company, which runs the trolleys, is checking all of their brakes."

"Brakes?"

"Yes, the motorman in charge said the brakes failed. They picked up speed coming down the hill, and the trolley was unable to manage the curve. The poor man said he yelled out to the passengers to brace themselves—that he couldn't help them. Then he told them to pray."

"I see. Well, you never know what small detail is going to have a major impact on your life."

"That's true." Lee took hold of her arm and walked her up to the house.

May opened the door, then turned back to face him. "I'm so glad you're all right. I was very proud to watch you in action. You are an amazing man, Lee Munro."

She saw his face redden just a bit as he looked toward the ground and cleared his throat.

"I was just doing my job."

"No, it was more than that, and we both know it. You're

a good man—a godly man who cares for others and puts them first before his own safety. I'm proud to call you friend, Lee."

He met her gaze. "And I'm proud and deeply blessed to call you the same."

May learned from the cook that her parents were having dinner out that evening. It was a relief to know she wouldn't have to make excuses for why she couldn't sit down to the table and share an hour or more at dinner. She made arrangements for a sandwich and piece of pie, then rushed upstairs and shed her damaged clothes.

Willa, their lady's maid, came in to assist and was terribly shocked to learn about the trolley. May explained what had happened and allowed Willa to help her wash up. Once that was done, May donned an old but serviceable brown skirt and navy blouse. She was hardly fit to receive and hoped that no one would stop by that evening, but just in case, she found the housekeeper, Mrs. Moore, and explained.

"I won't be available for visitors this evening," she told the older woman. "I'll be painting and must be left to finish my work."

"Very good, miss."

May made her way to the kitchen, where the cook already had the food waiting on a tray. The stocky woman smiled and adjusted her cap as May crossed the room.

"I put a glass of milk on there as well. Thought you might get thirsty."

"Thank you. I do appreciate it, and to prove as much, you may take the rest of the night off." May smiled, knowing the woman halfway expected the announcement but would be pleased, nevertheless.

"Oh, thank you, miss. I'm gonna go visit my sister. I told her I'd come at my first chance. She just had a baby."

"How wonderful. I will pray for them both to be healthy."

"Thank you, miss."

May nodded. "Now, I'm going to get to work on my painting."

She took the tray of goodies and headed to her art studio. She wasn't at all comfortable with giving clients a wet painting, so she hoped she could get as much done in the next hour as possible. She saw the painting completed in her mind and knew there wasn't that much left, but it bothered her. One hundred dollars was a lot of money.

The light was already on in the studio, and a fire had been lit in the stove. Mrs. Moore had no doubt seen to that. The woman was always two or three steps ahead of everyone. May put the tray on the table nearest the door and picked up the roast beef sandwich. She took a bite as she crossed the room to close the drapes. Next, she turned on her special lamps and went to the wall where she had tacked up her photographs and sketches of the armor.

Munching on the sandwich, she plotted her strategy. There was no way she could include all of the detail no matter how hard she tried. At least she was faithful to the colors. The red-and-black lacquered armor stood out in bold contrast to the ecru-colored background that she'd settled on. The gold trim on the helmet horns and crest stood out, as well as the decorative pieces on the dou. She had painted the armor facing forward and then to the back. They stood side by side, and while she didn't find it particularly appealing, it was exactly what the Tamuras had asked for.

Her gaze fell on the photograph with Mario Bianchi in the background. Lee had told her to keep an eye out for him, but she really hadn't had much of a chance. Although she had popped in a few times to double-check something regarding the armor, May hadn't had time to stay long in the Japan building. If Bianchi was there, she hadn't seen him.

She went back to the tray and picked up the glass of milk. It was creamy and cold and really hit the spot. She started to put the sandwich aside, then remembered her promise to Lee and resumed eating. Once the sandwich was gone, she finished off the milk, then wiped her hands. The pie could wait until later.

"All right, my fierce Japanese warrior," she said, approaching the canvas, "let's see you completed."

9

The painting isn't completely dry," May told the Tamuras. "You'll have to be very careful, or it will smear in places. As you can see, I've done what I can to keep it safe. Let me show you."

She put the framed canvas on a nearby table. It was covered, leaving them unable to study her work. She reached up to pull a pin from the corner at the top of the canvas. "I've covered the painting with a piece of corrugated cardboard and secured it with pushpins." She removed the pins from the other three corners and pulled the cardboard away. "You can see that the four corners of the canvas have pieces of cork attached. They've been cut thick enough to keep the cardboard from touching the wet paint. This will help you to protect it, but if you press up against the cardboard, it is close enough that it can still damage the painting."

"It is not a problem," Mr. Tamura told her. "I will guard it with my life." He leaned in to study the painting. "It is beautiful. You are most talented." He gave her one hundred dollars in various bills.

May resecured the cardboard and handed him the canvas.

"If you hold it at the corners," she said, showing him precisely where to handle the piece, "you should be safe."

He nodded and took the painting. "You have made us very happy."

Smiling, May quickly put the money in her purse. "I'm glad I could help."

"I wonder if we could have your sketches and the photographs you took?" Mr. Tamura surprised her by asking.

She considered this for a moment. She had intended to use those to make another painting for herself. But it would be easy enough to take more photographs and even make new sketches.

"I suppose so."

"I can meet you back here just before closing," the man added.

"Today?" May hadn't planned to return to the expo. She wanted to take a chance and try to visit Esther. But the doctor had been rather clear about the matter. She sighed. "I suppose I can meet you here just before five."

The man smiled and gave her a bow. "I thank you. I will return."

He spoke in Japanese to his wife, and the two turned almost in unison and headed for the door.

May watched them go and then remembered the money in her purse. It made her nervous to be carrying that much money since there were so many pickpockets around the expo. She had already decided she was going to use the money to help Esther. Her family was so dependent upon her wages, and now Esther wouldn't be able to work for some time. May had explained this to her mother and father, and they thought it admirable that their daughter should be so giving. But for May, it was more an act of obedience.

Something in her spirit told her to help Esther, and that was what she was going to do.

Clutching her purse close, May headed out of the Japan building and ran into Lee coming up the stairs.

"I'm glad you're here," she said, smiling.

"Well, I'm glad to be here. I hoped I'd catch you before you left."

"I just turned over the painting to the Tamuras." She stepped closer to Lee and lowered her voice. "It makes me nervous to have so much money on hand."

"I agree. It's not safe. Where are you headed?"

"Home. Mr. Tamura asked if he might have the sketches and photographs I made, and I agreed to meet him back here just before five."

"Why does he want the sketches and photographs when he has the painting?" Lee frowned, looking quite disturbed by this new prospect.

"The armor was in their family. I don't think it odd that they would want as much information and as many pictures of it as they could get." May shifted her purse, trying not to appear too nervous. "I agreed to bring them. You could accompany me, if you like. Even ask him why he wants them."

"I think I should. It seems strange to me that he should ask for such things." Lee still looked worried. "I'll drive you home, and you can leave the money. We can collect the sketches and photographs and be back here in time to meet Mr. Tamura. Then I can ask him why he wants those things. It might be nothing more than you say—just a man who wants to document the armor that once belonged to his wife's family. I tend to start questioning everything when Bianchi is involved."

"I would appreciate your company. I know I'd feel safer

regarding the money." She paused a moment. "Do you really think Mr. Bianchi is involved?"

"It's possible. For a long time, I chased after that man when I was with the Pinkertons. It was such a frustration to me when I thought he'd died. I wanted very much to catch him and force him to give us a list of all the paintings he had forged. So many people suffered because of him, and knowing I have another chance to catch him, and perhaps get him to share that information, drives me ever forward."

"Why would he tell you the truth? It would just mean more trouble for him."

Lee seemed to consider her question a moment. "Those in charge might be willing to lessen his prison term in return for finding the original paintings and the men who paid to have them stolen. They're just as guilty as Bianchi."

"And having Bianchi serve less time would be acceptable to you?"

"If the real treasures can be restored and returned to the museums, then yes. I detest Bianchi and what he's done, but I also want those pieces of art to be back in their proper places."

"And you're sure he's involved with the armor?"

"He may not be planning to do anything related to the armor, but he's up to something. The armor is worth a fortune, and there's a collector out there who already tried to buy it. It would be a real challenge for Bianchi, but also a real accomplishment. I can't help thinking he's intricately embroiled."

"If he is, I'm sure you'll be able to catch him this time."

Lee led her down the steps. "I'd rather you not give Mr. Tamura the photograph with Mario Bianchi. I'd like to keep that one myself."

"That's fine. I plan to only give him a few of the sketches and pictures. I'll keep the ones that I think will be difficult to recapture. I still plan to make a painting of that armor for myself."

"Why the fascination?"

"Because I, too, am intricately embroiled. It's a part of my heritage . . . in a way. My grandfather was a samurai. I only just learned this. Mama rarely speaks of her family, but after praying about it, she has decided to share more of her memories."

They walked to the livery, where Lee reclaimed his horse and carriage. The liveryman hitched Gaspar to the buggy in quick order, and they were soon on their way to May's house.

She liked these rides with Lee. It gave them time to talk and catch up on the years that they were apart. Today, however, May felt reflective about her life and the things she had dreamed of as a young girl. Facing the possibility of her own death yesterday had caused her to take a hard look at what she still wanted to accomplish.

"You're awfully quiet." Lee's expression softened. "Are you all right?"

She gave a brief nod. "I keep thinking about how I could have died yesterday."

"I know. It haunts me as well."

"I realized that I've accomplished so little of what I have dreamed of doing. Most women my age are already married with children of their own. I wanted that too, but few men want to marry a half-caste they don't consider an American."

"Don't call yourself that. You're complete and beautiful and perfect. You are as much an American as I am."

She smiled to herself. Lee had always encouraged her this way. It was the thing she remembered most about him from when they were younger. She had thought life difficult then, but adulthood had proved even harder, and Lee had been painfully absent.

"Most folks just don't look at it that way. A young man in high school pursued me for a time, and I thought him quite interesting. One of the teachers noticed our spending time together and mentioned it to his parents. The next thing I knew, he wouldn't even speak to me anymore. One of his friends told me what had happened. It was because I was half Japanese."

"Then he was a fool and nowhere near good enough for you."

She shrugged. "That's what my father said, but it's easy enough to make that comment when you aren't the one being slighted."

"I'm sorry, May. I didn't know how difficult it was for you, but I feared it would be brutal."

"If I hadn't had my art and faith, I think I might have wallowed in self-pity. God wouldn't allow me to do that, however."

"I'm glad you didn't. Tell me, what is it you hope to accomplish?"

"I'm not entirely sure. I know I want to fall in love and marry. I'd like to have children and continue with my art."

"Would you like to be a famous artist?"

May thought about this as they stopped at an intersection to allow a trolley to pass. "I don't know what I hope to accomplish with it. I just know I'd like to get better and better at it. Maybe take some additional lessons."

"Is that all that's on your list of things to accomplish before you die?" He put the horse back into motion and his attention back on the road.

"I'd like to go to Japan."

"Japan? Of course. I remember you talked about that when you were young."

"Yes. My mother has never allowed me to know much about her side of the family, and I want very much to learn about that part of my heritage. I need to know it for myself, and fear I never will. I want to touch and see and taste and feel all that I can of Japan. It's a part of me, and I don't even know enough about it to recognize it."

"I can understand that."

"I'm not sure I do." She looked down the tree-lined street and sighed. "I feel like a part of me is missing, and yet when I bring it up, it causes Mama sadness and pain. I try to remain silent on it, but sometimes I just can't help myself. I need to know."

They fell quiet for several miles, and May couldn't help but wonder if she'd ever feel whole. All of her life, people had been more than happy to point out that she was half this or half that. They made it clear that she wasn't complete, even if Lee said otherwise.

Did he have goals that were yet to be accomplished? Would he mind her asking? She had never known him to mind when they were younger.

"What do you still want to accomplish?"

Lee said nothing for a moment. He seemed lost in thought, and May wondered if he'd even heard her.

"I want some of the same things you do. I didn't think I did—at least I told myself I didn't want a wife and family. But in truth, I do. I just don't want them to be like most of the people I know, my folks included. Their hearts are so hardened against people who are different from themselves. It's not just a matter of skin color either. It's their social status.

Their financial means. The church they attend. My family and most of their friends are complete snobs. If you aren't like they are, then you aren't worthy of their acquaintance. I despise that attitude. I think it was one of the reasons I wanted to get involved with the police. There were so many people in law enforcement who have the same attitude, and I wanted to change that."

"Have you?"

"I've managed to convert a few guys here and there." He frowned. "But sadly, no, not really."

"I don't understand why people would rather divide themselves than join together with common causes."

"I don't either, May. Being a detective changed my life. It helped me see another side of life that my parents and their friends completely ignored. There are people out there who are suffering so much because of people like them. I hate it, but my mother and father have no compassion for the less fortunate despite their proclamations of Christianity. They sit in their lovely home and eat their rich foods, enjoying every convenience life has to offer and never thinking about those who are struggling just to exist."

"I know a lot of people like that, but thankfully my parents aren't. When I told them that I intended to use the money I made on the samurai painting to help Esther and her family, they were very supportive. In fact, they said if more help was needed, they wanted to share in what I was doing."

"Mine would have reprimanded me," Lee said, shaking his head. "They can't see their own fears and, worse yet, their lack of feeling for humanity."

They finally reached May's home and made their way inside without another word. Mrs. Moore met them in the hall, and May asked her to let Mama know she was there but only for a few minutes. The older woman left immediately to relay the information as May and Lee headed for her studio.

May took the money from her purse and put it in her desk drawer. "I'm glad to have that taken care of." She put the purse aside. "I'll hand the photographs and sketches to you as I take them down, if that's all right."

"Of course. Glad to help." Lee set his hat aside, then followed May to the far wall.

She started taking down the pieces that she'd decided to give the Tamuras. "I hope they enjoy having these. I can't imagine that they would be all that important to them. Some of these are nothing more than details of various pieces of the armor—not even the whole armor itself."

"It does seem odd."

She paused at the photograph that included Mario Bianchi. "Would you like to take this now?"

"It would be helpful. I'd like to show it to the police officers working at the expo. If they see Bianchi, I'd like them to arrest him. He's wanted for so many art thefts that I don't think we'd have any trouble getting him convicted."

She took down the picture and handed it to Lee. "I've not seen him around, but then I've not been much at the Japan building since I was using all my free time to complete the painting. I'll have to go back there now, of course. I think I'd like to create my own painting on a large canvas. Maybe something as big as four feet by two feet. Maybe bigger."

"I think that would be amazing. I'd even enjoy something like that myself."

"Since my family were a part of the samurai, it would make me feel somehow connected."

"Do you think your mother might tell you more about your family in Japan?"

"I wish she would, but I don't want to push her. I know it causes her pain."

"But it shouldn't," her mother said, surprising May from the doorway.

May left Lee holding the pictures and went to hug her mother. "I'm sorry, I didn't expect that you would hear me."

"It's all right, May." Her mother smiled as May pulled away. "I am resolved to tell you about my family—your family."

"I would love to know everything," May said, giving her mother a quick peck on the cheek. "Still, I have no desire to hurt you."

She studied her mother, noting how her face was still smooth and free of wrinkles. Her black hair bore no hint of gray. Kame Parker was a beautiful woman. One would never look at her and see the hardships of her past. She hid them deep inside.

"What are you doing with those sketches and pictures?" Mama asked.

"The Tamuras asked if they could have them. I didn't really want to give them away because I hope to make a painting for myself of the samurai armor. But at the time I had no reason to refuse and told them I'd bring them back before five o'clock when the Japan building closes."

"I see. And Lee brought you here?"

"Yes." May looked to him. "And he's taking me back to the expo."

"While you collect your things, I will tell you a story about my girlhood," Mama declared and made her way over to the stuffed chair by the window and took a seat.

"After the Satsuma Rebellion, many of our men were dead, and the government punished the rest of us for the rebellion.

Not long after we were at peace again, the export business sent your father to work in Japan and take my father's place.

"I thought he was one of the kindest and most generous people I'd ever met. He wanted to know about Japan, and I shared what I could, although I told him I felt we had been betrayed by our people and the government."

"Because of the way they treated the samurai and their families?" May asked, coming to sit beside her mother on a small stool.

"Yes. Even my own relatives were siding with the government, and all I could think of was how my father and mother were dead because of the government. Although now that I'm older, I realize they were dead by their own hand. Still, you must understand about Japanese honor. The Bushido code was followed by the samurai, and I was taught from my earliest years about the important virtues of this code."

"I've heard of it, but admit I know nothing about it," Lee said.

"It has good ways, even ways that seem Christian, despite it not being from the Bible," May's mother continued. "Bushido is a moral code by which the samurai lived. My father told me these were the very things that made him a man. There are eight virtues: justice, courage, compassion, respect, integrity, honor, loyalty, and self-control. For me, these were at the heart of what it meant to be Japanese.

"But as I watched my countrymen kill each other, I found none of those virtues prevailed. There was no justice, compassion, or respect for my father and relatives. There was no loyalty to be sure, and the integrity of my people seemed completely at odds. The government had no honor that I could see. The samurai had served loyally for hundreds of years and then were cast aside as if they were of no use.

They weren't even allowed to wear their swords as they had always done. My father was deeply sorrowed at all that he saw happening. He told me before he marched off to war that the eight virtues of the Bushido Code were important, and he wanted me to always remember them and practice them as a way of remembering him."

"They are indeed Christian virtues as well," Lee agreed. "They are very similar to the fruit of the Spirit in Galatians chapter five: love, joy, peace, long-suffering, gentleness, goodness, faith, meekness, and temperance."

Mama's expression was one of sadness. May reached out and took hold of her hand. As much as May wanted to know the truth of her family, she didn't want her mother to suffer.

"Tell me about when you met Father," May said, hoping to take away her mother's pain.

The older woman nodded. "I was just thirteen when my parents died. In the months that followed, the export company sent your father to Japan to take up where my father left off. Your father could speak Japanese because he had grown up with a Japanese gardener who taught him the language. Your father also fell in love with Japanese art and stories, so working in Japan was everything he could have wanted. He was young and handsome. I found him quite interesting to talk to because he could tell me all about America, and that was where I longed to go."

"Why America?" May asked.

"I had heard from others that it was a land of plenty with freedom for all. It sounded like such a wonderful place, and it truly is, despite society's shortcomings." She smiled. "I fell in love with your father almost from the start, but it took a while for him. When I was seventeen, he asked me to marry him, and I said yes, but only on one condition: He must take me away from Japan, and we would never speak of it again. My family was appalled that I would marry a white man and leave the land of my birth. They condemned me and told me if I did it, they would have nothing to do with me. I told them I didn't care because I intended to move to America and forget everything about Japan.

"Your father agreed to my terms, even though I know now that it cost him a great deal because he loved Japan and the people there. But I was full of anger and bitterness. That is why we have never talked about it—never allowed anything Japanese in the house. I wanted to forget it all—to be as disloyal to Japan as I felt it had been to me and my parents."

"I'm so sorry, Mama." May glanced to where Lee still stood holding the pictures and sketches. His expression was one of compassion, and she knew that Lee cared as much as she did about the pain her mother had endured.

"Over the years," her mother began again, "I have realized that keeping my anger and bitterness alive has done nothing but cause problems. That is why your father encouraged me to pray about my life in Japan, and as I prayed, I felt my fears release, along with the rage. I can look back and begin to remember good things, whereas before I never allowed myself that."

"I'm glad that God is helping you to feel better about these things." May squeezed her mother's hand. "I knew some about you meeting Father, but I didn't realize Father knew Japanese before he went to Japan. I always assumed you had taught him."

Her mother smiled. "No, he was quite accomplished and could even read a little Japanese. He is very smart, your father."

May knew this was true. Her father had always amazed

her with his vast knowledge. "Thank you so much, Mama. I cherish your stories, but Lee and I have to get back to the expo." She got to her feet. "I'll be back later."

"After she has dinner with me," Lee interjected.

May gave him a questioning look, and he laughed. "If she would be so kind as to agree to have dinner with me."

"Of course. You only had to ask." She felt her heart skip a beat at the thought of spending the evening with Lee. She was coming to see that her feelings for him were changing from mere friendship to something more. Maybe it was just that the near-death experience had caused her heart to shift in a direction that focused more on the future and those things that she had wanted since she was a child. Maybe it was nothing more than being grateful for another day of life. Whatever it was, it was centered around Lee and his place in her heart.

Lee studied the Tamuras as May handed over her sketches and photographs. They were nothing special, just an old Japanese couple. They didn't appear to be uncomfortable or the least bit suspicious. After the exchange, Lee watched them go, still battling the uneasiness he'd had since May told him about their request for the painting.

He walked to where the armor stood behind glass and pondered the piece until May came alongside him.

"It is beautiful."

He looked at her and gave a curt nod. "I just can't shake the uneasiness I have about it. There is something going on with this. I can feel it, and Bianchi being involved makes me certain that something criminal is afoot."

"But what? It's hardly possible for your Mr. Bianchi to remake the armor as he would a painting. These pieces are hundreds of years old. There would be no way to age the leather and lacquer and give it the same appearance."

"You don't know Bianchi. The man is a genius and knows things that would surprise you to no end. He has made paints and canvases seem the proper age, so why not samurai armor? Besides, I talked to the man in charge of this exhibit. The armor only dates back to the early 1800s—not even a hundred years old."

"Still, it would be very difficult to fool the experts who handle it."

"I suppose you're right."

"Maybe Mr. Bianchi was simply in the wrong place at the wrong time. Maybe he wasn't at all interested in the armor but was looking around to see if there was something else of value he could forge or steal."

What she said made sense, and Lee tried to put it all aside and instead focus on their plans for dinner. He smiled and offered her his arm. "Are you hungry?"

May smiled, and it lit up her green eyes in a way he'd always enjoyed. "I am hungry. Where did you have in mind to go?"

"How about Japantown?"

May sobered and took on an expression of gratitude. "I'd like that very much."

"I'm afraid I'm not very good at handling chopsticks," Lee said, laughing as he gave up the battle and put the sticks aside. Mr. Akira had already given them forks to use in place of the bamboo pieces. Lee picked up his fork. "This I can manage." He dug into the rice concoction and took a large bite.

May laughed at his antics. She must have found the instructions Mr. Akira had given to be quite simple, because she had mastered the chopsticks in no time at all. He wondered if, like everything else she'd attempted that was Japanese, it made May feel closer to her mother's family and Japan.

"This is very good," Lee said, pointing to his plate. "What was it Mr. Akira called it?"

"*Kuri-gohan.*" May took a sip of her hot tea, then continued. "Chestnut rice."

They had tried several dishes that evening, and the chestnut rice was a fine way to end the meal. Lee had always liked chestnuts, but he was used to having them roasted rather than boiled.

"I like it," May said, setting her chopsticks down. "I'm afraid, however, I'm quite full."

Just then, Mr. Akira came to the table. He held a small plate. "You must have some *taiyaki* to end your meal. *Anko*, a sweetened red bean paste, is used." He placed the plate between them.

"It's shaped like a fish," May said, sounding delighted at the prospect of dessert. Lee had witnessed her childlike pleasure all evening. She was truly enjoying her experience more than his company. Still, it didn't offend him. He knew how much she wanted to know her culture.

"The fish is a red snapper. It is a sign of good luck," Mr. Akira explained.

"Oh, Mr. Akira, this has been such a wonderful meal. Please tell your son how much we have enjoyed it."

The older man smiled. "I will tell him. It was our pleasure to have you and Mr. Munro to be our guests."

May was already pushing aside her bowl of kuri-gohan. "I can hardly wait to tell Mama about all the food we've tried tonight. Mr. Akira was so kind to make sure we had an extensive sampling."

"He really has been most attentive. I think he looks upon you as his own special project."

May met Lee's gaze and smiled. "Thank you for tonight. I've never had a better time, and I know that it's because of you."

Lee warmed as his gaze met her emerald eyes. She had such a way of making him feel complete. No other woman had ever stirred him in that way. He thought of Glynnis and tried to cover up his sudden discomfort by reaching for his chopsticks.

"I'm going to try once more to get this right," he told May, but in his heart he was trying to figure out how he could possibly make anything right.

10

I'm so glad you came," Esther said, her voice rough. "I
hate being here."

May glanced around at the pale green walls. The private room seemed nice enough with its simple furnishings.
"Are they treating you badly?"

Esther closed her eyes and shook her head. "No. Everything is fine, and everyone is kind. I just hate being sick. I
always have."

"But you aren't sick. You're injured, and you'll soon be
back on your feet. In a few weeks, you'll be as good as new."
At least that's what May hoped and prayed for.

"But in a few weeks the fair will be over, and I won't have
a job. I wanted to have another job lined up before that.
Now I have nothing, and I don't know how I'm going to
help my family."

"Don't you worry about that." May reached over and
patted Esther's hand. "I just earned a lot of money. I made a
painting of the samurai armor displayed at the Japan building. It was for a Japanese couple, and they offered me a
ridiculous sum of money. I prayed about it and talked to my

parents, and they agreed I could use the money any way I felt led. And I feel led to help you and your family."

Esther's eyes widened. "Help us? But why? You hardly know us. Besides, I couldn't take charity. My folks would be ashamed of that."

"We're friends, and you're in need. It's not anything to be ashamed of. You have so much that demands your attention, but now that you're injured, you need to focus on healing. That's where the church body should come in. It is our place to help take care of you."

"But we don't go to church."

"The church body is the collection of Christians," May explained. "Christians are supposed to take care of one another, and when we see someone in need, reach out and help. I'm just doing what I believe God has called me to do."

"No one has ever done that for me or my family. For as long as I've had memory, my father has been sick with one problem or another. Still, he was a very hard worker and earned enough to keep us in a good fashion. Then he got sicker still. The doctor says he has tuberculosis, and my mother says he won't live much longer."

"Can't the doctors help at all?" May questioned.

"I guess not. Of course, he refuses to go to the doctor most of the time now because of the cost. Mother says he would do better in a drier climate and wants to move to California, but of course that costs money."

"Well, try not to worry about your father or your job. Let yourself heal and pray about it. Now that you've got Jesus in control of your life, you can trust in Him. I find it gets me through all the bad and uncertain times.

"I'm sorry Addie couldn't be here," May said, changing the subject. "She was needed at the shop since Mrs. Fisher couldn't be there. You know it's nearly time for her to give birth."

Esther tried to shift a bit but grimaced at the pain. "I hope . . . Mrs. Fisher has an easy time."

"Can I help you move a bit? What do you need?" May was on her feet, leaning over Esther, in a heartbeat.

"I don't need anything. I've never been a good patient. I get so tired of just lying about, even though the medicine they give me makes me groggy." She smiled. "Tell me more about your Japanese dinner with Mr. Munro."

"I think I should probably let you rest. I promised the nurse I wouldn't stay long." May leaned closer, rather conspiratorially. "She didn't want to let me visit you at all. She was worried that I should let you sleep and told me not to visit you again for several days."

"But sleep is all I do."

May straightened. "That's what you need for now. Your body is healing. Rest. I promise there will be time to talk later." She turned for her things. "Oh, I nearly forgot." May reached into her satchel and pulled out a Bible. "I want to loan you this until I can arrange to get you one of your own."

"Your Bible?"

"Yes. I find great comfort in reading from it. I always have. I want to encourage you to start here." May opened the Bible to where a crocheted bookmark kept the place. "The book of John. There are other books with John's name. They are First John, Second John, and Third John. But this is just plain old John. My pastor once recommended it for anyone who really wanted to get to know the person and deity of Jesus. So I'm sharing that with you. I think you'll find it as wonderful as I did. However, if you feel confused or have questions, write them down, and we'll talk. If I can't help, we'll get the pastor to come visit you."

Esther took the Bible and touched the pages as if in awe. "I don't know what to say. Aren't you afraid I'll lose it or some harm will come to it?"

May smiled and shook her head. "Come what may, it's all in God's hands. I will deal with whatever must be dealt with if and when it comes to us. Now, I need to get back to work. I have a stack of pictures to touch up."

"Thank you again for coming to see me."

"Of course. You're my friend. You'd do the same for me."

Thursday was a surprisingly warm day for the thirtieth of September. May was working on her seventh postcard when Addie Hanson came into the room. She had been working on the books and now seemed ready to greet the public.

"Thanks for watching the counter, Mary."

Mary gave a stretch. "It wasn't a problem. Frankly, I'll be sorry when all of this is gone."

"Yes, there's not that much time left before the expo closes for good." Addie started lining up a display of Brownie cameras.

"It will be strange once the exposition is gone," Mary commented, adjusting her hat as she glanced at her reflection in a mirror they'd placed by the front door. "We'll all be out of work and in need of figuring out what we should do next."

"It will be different to be sure. However, at the rate Seattle is growing, I don't think you'll want for work," Addie said. "You're quite good working in sales. You might want to find something else along those lines."

"I'm rather jealous that Bertha already has a job lined up with the Fishers."

"Who knows, maybe Mr. Fisher will need more than one salesclerk. You should speak to him. What with Mrs. Fisher ready to give birth any day now, she'll be busy with the baby."

"I'll talk to him." Mary opened the front door, and a breeze flooded the room. "It's definitely autumn. Even smells like it."

May had to agree there was a damp, earthy smell that always accompanied fall. She concentrated on the photograph in her hand and wondered how soon it would turn cold.

Mary had no sooner departed than the bell over the door rang, and Mr. and Mrs. Fisher entered the shop. Mrs. Fisher looked exhausted.

"Pearl, what are you doing here?" Addie questioned, hurrying forward with a chair.

The older woman took a seat and put her hand to her swollen midsection. "I didn't want to be alone at the apartment. I'm not having any contractions, but I feel strange." She shifted uncomfortably. "I didn't want to bother the doctor."

"You're due to have a baby any day. I don't think coming out to the exposition is a good idea. Why don't you let me go home with you? I'll take care of you until Mr. Fisher can join you."

"I suppose it would make more sense to be at home. I know I'm causing everyone to worry, but I don't know what else to do. This is my first baby." At forty-five, Pearl was just as naïve regarding the birthing to come as a much younger woman might have been.

"I'd feel better if she was at home," Otis Fisher said. "I tried to talk her into staying there, but you know how she can be."

Addie laughed and untied her apron. "I will gather my things. You're in luck, Pearl. Isaac is here—just over at the administration building. Are you up to a short walk? He can take us in our carriage to your apartment."

Pearl got to her feet and nodded. "I think that would be good. My back is starting to ache something fierce." Then her countenance changed, and her eyes grew wide. She pressed her hand to her mouth.

"What is it, Pearl?" Addie asked, coming to her side. "Are you all right?"

"My water just broke."

"It's time for the baby!" Addie all but squealed in delight. "Oh, this is exciting. Otis, we must get Pearl home quickly. You too. Call the doctor and tell him that the baby is coming."

"But I've had no pain. Just the aching back."

"Apparently that's pain enough." Addie put her arm around Pearl's shoulders.

Pearl let out a moan and nearly doubled over. "I can feel the baby moving lower. Oh, help!"

Addie looked at May, who shrugged. She knew nothing about the birth of babies nor the care of expectant mothers.

Otis looked frantic. Just then, Isaac came into the shop. He grinned at his wife, then took a step back at the expression on her face. "What's wrong?" he asked.

"Pearl's going to have the baby, and it would seem things are happening very fast. Her water just broke. I was going to suggest we drive her to their apartment, but I don't think there's time. We need to get her over to the emergency hospital here at the expo."

Isaac wasted no time. He scooped Pearl into his arms. "Let's go!"

"And then they were gone," May told Lee later as she and Bertha waited in the closed shop. "We locked the doors at five but didn't feel like we should go. We haven't heard yet what happened. I had hoped Addie would stop by and let us know."

Lee had been surprised by all the news when he'd come to see if May needed a ride home. He hadn't even really expected to find her there, since it was nearly six thirty. "Maybe they had to move her to another hospital. They have a nice facility here, but it's not as good as a more permanent hospital."

"I do hope Mrs. Fisher will be all right."

The sound of a key in the lock drew their attention. All eyes were on the door as it opened. An exhausted-looking Addie stepped in. "She's had the baby. It's a boy."

"Is she . . . are they doing well?" May asked, moving a little closer to Lee.

"She is. The baby too. They named him Joseph after Otis's father. She'll stay at the hospital for the night. The exposition officials graciously offered to deliver the Fishers home as soon as the doctor says it is safe. I just wanted to stop by and let you know and see that we got the shop locked up safe and sound." Addie glanced around. "Looks like you ladies have everything under control."

"We were rather concerned," Bertha said, unpinning her straw hat. "I was going to come to the hospital if we didn't hear something soon."

"Well, everything is quite fine. The doctor said that Pearl's back pain was in fact labor pains. She didn't realize they could be located in the back more than the front. I suppose we've all learned something today," Addie said with a chuckle. "Come on. Let's go home."

Lee smiled at May. "See there, everything is fine."

"I'm so glad. It was a great worry. Pearl is older than most new mothers."

"Will I still see you tomorrow, Addie?" Bertha asked, heading for the door.

"Yes, of course, Bertha, but I'd like you to open the shop and handle things until I can get here."

"Don't forget, you promised to go with me to see Esther tomorrow," May reminded.

Addie glanced around the room one more time. "Yes, and once we know Pearl is home, we can stop by and see if she needs anything, and then I'll come directly here and relieve you, Bertha."

May smiled. "I traded my day off with Mary, so I have the whole day to do as I please. I think that would be fun to see Pearl and her little one. I've never experienced a new baby. Do you suppose she might let me hold him?"

Lee heard the awe in May's voice and imagined her as a mother with a babe of her own. She would be a wonderful mother. Her compassion and gentle spirit would make her perfect for the job.

"I have to admit I'm hoping for as much myself," Addie said with a grin. "Now, we'd best hurry. Isaac is waiting for me."

Lee helped May into her cloak, then opened the door for the ladies.

May suppressed a yawn, and once he had joined her outside, she took hold of his arm.

Lee very much liked her nearness. "You're exhausted, aren't you?"

"I am. It's been a very full and exciting day."

Across the fairgrounds, Lee heard a band strike up. "Will you miss the expo when it's gone?"

May seemed to think about it for a moment. "I'll miss my Japanese connections. I've learned so much. I slip off almost every day to talk to Mr. Akira about kanji and the language. I want very much to master it all."

"As determined as I've always known you to be, I'm certain you'll find a way to accomplish it." He smiled at her. "Perhaps your mother will be strong enough to continue your lessons."

May glanced up at him. "That is my prayer. I would love to learn it all from her. The language and writing, as well as the history of our family that only she can tell."

Lee and May headed for the livery. The days were getting darker earlier, and already twilight had settled in. He'd sent word ahead, so the horse was already harnessed and ready. Lee helped May into the carriage, then joined her on the seat. She surprised him by moving a little closer to lean against him.

"What a day," she murmured. She was asleep before they were even a block away.

Lee continued thinking about May long after he'd dropped her off at home. Mrs. Parker had invited him to stay for supper, but he had business at home. Father had sent a message to the administration building earlier in the day to tell Lee that he'd be stopping by his place that evening. Given the extra time he'd spent at the expo, he had worried about making his father wait. There was certainly no time for a leisurely supper with May's family. Even if that was what he'd rather be doing.

He saw to Gaspar and the carriage, then made his way to

the second floor of his apartment building. A quick glance at the hall clock revealed he still had time to eat something before his father arrived. He couldn't imagine what the man wanted. Well, that wasn't exactly true. He could imagine a few things, and that was what had him on edge.

Cold roast and potatoes awaited him in the icebox, but that seemed like a lot of trouble tonight. Instead, Lee made toast and slathered it with butter and jam. He had just finished eating when a knock sounded on his door.

He opened it to find his father, hat in hand. "Good evening, sir."

"Lee. Good to see you're well."

"Won't you come in?" It was all so very formal. Not at all the casual manner in which he'd been greeted at May's. They were in so many ways more of a family to him lately than his own.

Father stepped into the apartment and glanced around the room. "Do you really enjoy living like this?"

Ah, the first salvo of the battle that was their relationship. Lee motioned to a chair. "Wouldn't you like to sit before you start in on the insults?"

His father eyed him for a moment, then took a seat. "I see no reason to pretend. You could have a much better life. That's the reason I'm here. George Faraday is quite concerned about Glynnis. He and I spoke yesterday, and he wants to know what your intentions are."

"I've made no mystery of my intentions."

"Neither have you made a declaration for her hand. She's nearly twenty-one, and George is concerned that she will remain a spinster."

"Glynnis is a wealthy heiress and a beautiful woman. She'll never want for suitors."

"But her father and I are determined that you two should marry. You've known each other for a long time now, even if you did go away for several years."

Lee moved to sit opposite his father. "I know what you are determined to see happen. Why can't you leave our romance to us and let time work out the details? If it's meant to be, it will come around."

"We are weary of waiting. I'm here tonight to help resolve your feelings on the matter. I am prepared to give you a healthy portion of your inheritance early—if you marry the girl."

"I see. And how soon do I have to marry her to meet your demands?" Lee tried to keep the anger from his voice. He was doing this solely for Glynnis. She needed just a few more days. It was less than a week until she could run off with her beau.

"We'd like to see the engagement announced immediately. Your mother is able to take care of that. She'll see it written up properly in the paper."

"I see. And then?"

"Then I am prepared to help you secure a house . . . a home of your own. It will be our wedding present to you. Mr. and Mrs. Faraday will gift you the furnishings."

"How very generous."

"It is. Both families, however, feel it is critical that you maintain a certain appearance in society. Mr. Faraday is quite willing to take you on and put you in charge of any number of his businesses and investments. He will train you, and it will be much more socially appropriate."

"Than what? Being a police detective?"

"Yes." His father wasn't in the least bit ashamed of his statement. "George has vast holdings all over the world. Why, if you and Glynnis wanted, you could even live abroad for a time. Think of how pleasant that might be."

Lee shook his head. "I rather enjoy living in America."

"Then live here. It doesn't matter. What matters is that they can announce their daughter is engaged to you."

"I see." Lee didn't want to do anything to threaten Glynnis's happiness. "I suppose if it is that important, I will speak to Glynnis on the matter." Surely they could hold things off a few more days.

His father's expression changed to one of disbelief and then to a rather hesitant smile. "You will?"

"That's what you want, isn't it?"

"Well . . . yes, but I haven't known you to be overly concerned with what I want in years."

Lee shrugged. "I think speaking to Glynnis will be in everyone's best interest. I'll try to arrange something tomorrow."

Father jumped to his feet. "You don't know how happy this has made me. I'll get to work immediately on locating you a property."

"There's no hurry. Let me arrange the matter of the engagement, then we can figure out the rest."

His father nodded. "You've made us all very happy. Your mother will start working right away on the engagement announcement."

"I'd prefer, of course, that she wait until we can make it official."

"I'll do what I can, but you know your mother. She will be so elated. I would imagine she'll discuss it with Mrs. Faraday, and the two will conspire to see it in the paper as soon as possible, so please arrange things with Glynnis. You know those two women are almost impossible to stop when they have something they feel needs to be done."

"Yes, but—"

"Give me a call tomorrow."

Lee stood but said nothing. He didn't want to lie, and he certainly didn't want to add fuel to his father's excited mood. Soon enough they'd all find out about Glynnis's plans. Poor girl. She was an only child, so it wasn't likely that her family would disinherit her, but they were certain to be quite unhappy at having a son-in-law who played in an orchestra instead of in stocks.

He saw his father out, glad to have him leave. Lee leaned heavily on the closed door and sighed. He'd have to send word to Glynnis tomorrow and see how she wanted to play this. Whatever she wanted, Lee would allow for it. She was a good woman, and he valued their friendship. Even more, he valued the thought of true love.

11

The next day, May and Addie made a quick visit to see Esther, then headed to the expo grounds. Addie had promised to check on the shop and then planned to go be with Mrs. Fisher while Otis came in. She explained that Mrs. Fisher wasn't up to anyone else visiting, so May made other arrangements. She had traded days off with one of the other girls and intended to go to the Japan building to start resketching the samurai armor.

The day was overcast and threatening rain, a complete contrast to the day before, but it didn't dampen May's mood. She'd had a wonderful summer. The exposition had turned out to be a tremendous place to spend her days, and she'd been able to reconnect with Lee.

Thoughts of him were seldom far from her mind, and May knew she was starting to feel things for him that she never thought possible. She supposed it was because she felt safe with Lee. It was rather fun to give pretense to there being something more to their relationship than mere friendship.

May couldn't help herself. She imagined letting herself fall in love with Lee. He was just the kind of man she wanted as a husband. He was fair and kind to all and generous with his time. He was faithful to God and often spoke in a praiseworthy manner. In fact, the other night when they'd had supper together, May had listened to him tell her about his youth after leaving their old neighborhood and how God had been there for him through all the lonely hours without friends. Of course, being from a wealthy family, Lee hadn't waited too long for friends, but nevertheless, he had stressed how those weren't the kind of friends he desired. Most were only there to get whatever they could for themselves. It was funny how so many wealthy people were self-seeking that way, he had told May. But while May had grown up with plenty, no one was seeking to court her for what they could get. The bulk of her white neighbors had nothing to do with her or her family. When she'd been younger, there were times when May thought she might die of loneliness.

Lee was one in a million, that was for certain. May had always felt that way about him, even when they were children. No one had ever cared for her the way he did. He had always been there to talk to and trust in. Just like now.

She glanced up to find it had started to sprinkle. Thankfully, she had brought her umbrella. She opened it just in case the rain fell in earnest. She had no sooner raised it when she heard someone calling her name.

She turned and found Lee hurrying toward her. "May, I'm so glad we ran into each other. There's something I want to tell you about."

She moved the umbrella to cover them both. "I'm on my way to the Japan building. I want to start my sketches again and take a few pictures as well. I'm quite excited to get started again on painting that samurai armor."

"The time will fly by, I'm sure." He took the umbrella

and held it for them. "Before we know it, the exposition will be over."

That thought made her sad. Where else would be appropriate to meet up with Lee? She frowned. "What is it you wanted to tell me?"

They began walking, and for a moment, May wondered if Lee had heard her.

"Remember I told you about my friend whom I am pretending to court?"

"I do remember. Why do you bring it up?"

"My parents may rush the situation and announce our engagement in the paper. I just didn't want you to be hurt by that . . . thinking I should have told you first because of our . . . friendship."

"Oh, Lee, you are possibly the kindest man I've ever known. Please don't worry about me."

His stern expression left her little doubt that he was worried about something.

May touched his arm. "What's wrong?"

"Nothing really. I don't want to lie to my parents, but I've allowed them to believe we will soon be engaged. Glynnis just needs a few more days, then she'll be able to marry, as she'll be twenty-one. I don't really worry for her because she's the Faradays' only child. After they get over the initial shock, they'll accept what she's done and find a way to live with it."

"Then what has you troubled?"

"I'm not exactly sure." He shook his head. "I've never pleased my parents the way my brothers did. I didn't follow in my father's footsteps and chose a profession that was far from what they thought appropriate. This is going to be devastating to them. They're counting on the marriage to solidify some business arrangement that our fathers have in mind. I hate hurting them, but I want even less to be married to a woman I could never love as a wife."

"I'm sure your folks will also be able to deal with it in time. You must be true to yourself—to your heart. You can hardly marry a woman you don't love."

He looked at her for a long moment. "I know that's true. Glynnis and I have talked about this on many an evening when our parents thought us to be deep in conversation about our future together. I've never been able to get them to see the truth of the matter."

They reached the Japan building, and a collection of men speaking near the front garden drew Lee's attention.

"Those are some of my plainclothes officers. I need to speak with them. Go ahead inside and I'll join you shortly."

He handed the umbrella back to her. May watched him engage the men in conversation. She still wasn't sure why he had felt the need to tell her again about Glynnis Faraday. She was glad to know they were only friends but sorry that Lee had gotten caught up in such a predicament.

May climbed the steps to the Japan building and folded the wet umbrella. She left it by the door, hoping no one would take it. She drew off her satchel and smoothed her coat. She had chosen to wear a walking suit with a long, embroidered navy jacket and matching skirt. The same lavish embroidery that graced the jacket also lined the hem of the skirt. The outfit had been made for her mother, but by the time she received the suit, she had changed her mind about the style. May loved the simple lines and had begged to keep it for herself. With a little alteration, the outfit was made over for her, and Mama even bought her the hat she now wore, a wide-brimmed creation in velvet and silk banding.

Making her way to where the samurai armor was displayed, May saw Mr. Akira and stopped to say hello.

"How are you, Miss Parker?" he asked.

"I am well. I'm still thinking about that wonderful dinner at your son's restaurant. I enjoyed how you explained all the samples and told us little bits of your family history."

"It was my pleasure." He gave her a smile. "I thought you and your young man made a striking couple."

"Oh, we're not a couple. Lee is a good friend from my childhood. There's nothing more between us."

Mr. Akira waggled a finger at her. "I do not think that is true. He looks at you with a tenderness reserved for those in love, and you also look at him that way. I think there is more to this than just friendship. Although, that is a very good place to start."

May had no desire to encourage further conversation on her relationship with Lee. "I have practiced the kanji you gave me, and I can now write out forty different symbols. If you have time, I'd like to learn a few more after I make some more sketches of the armor."

He smiled and bowed. "Of course."

She smiled and bowed as well. "I'm so grateful to have your help. I'm hoping my mother will lend me a hand with it once the exposition closes."

Just then, she spied Mario Bianchi entering the room with the samurai armor.

"If you'll excuse me, I have someone I need to see."

She walked to the armor room, trying to be as casual as possible. She smiled at a Japanese couple strolling out of the room and fumbled in her bag for her sketchbook and charcoal pencil.

Mario Bianchi stood on the other side of the armor and

snapped a photograph. He held one of the Brownie cameras that the Fishers were selling. She wondered if he'd purchased it at the shop.

May tried not to pay obvious attention to Bianchi. Lee was just outside of the building. He had made her promise to send someone for him if Bianchi appeared again. She glanced around, hoping Mr. Akira was nearby, but he wasn't. Several people entered the room and were drawn to the armor. As they drew closer to the case, May slipped behind them and headed for the exit.

She hurried outside and down the steps and found Lee and the men still talking. She went to Lee's side and tugged on his coat. He didn't even acknowledge her as he drove home a point he was making.

"Without additional help in the market area, they will continue to struggle with the thefts. It's not a simple matter, and I'll do what I can to get Captain Brewers to understand how difficult the situation is. If something isn't done, the thefts will continue to even higher levels."

May tugged again on his coat. Lee reached over and placed a hand on her arm. "Please let your men know what to expect in the days to come. It's critical that we put an end to this as soon as possible. We don't want word getting around that such behavior will be accepted—that we'll merely look the other way."

She couldn't get his attention. What if Bianchi left the building? They were all just standing here, and he might slip by. She looked around and noticed a gardener had left a stool nearby. If she could whisper in Lee's ear . . .

A quick glance back at the steps to the building showed no sign of Bianchi, so May pulled away from Lee and went to grab the stool. She brought it to his side, then, holding on to his arm, she stepped up on the stool and brought her face even with his. She started to speak but knew it wouldn't be enough to get his attention. He needed something shocking. She smiled and reached out to take his face in her hands. Without warning, she pressed her lips against his.

She had only meant to give him the briefest of kisses, but Lee wrapped her in his arms and pulled her right off the stool. His friends roared with laughter and egged him on.

May momentarily forgot all about Bianchi. There in Lee's arms, kissing his warm mouth, she felt as if something long missing in her life suddenly fit into place. Lee seemed in no hurry to end the kiss, but it dawned on May that she'd done this with a purpose other than romance. She pushed against him, and he pulled away just enough to look at her.

"Bianchi is in the Japan building," she whispered.

He looked at her with a silly grin on his face, but then the words registered, and he all but dropped her and ran for the stairs. The plainclothes officers looked at her for explanation.

"A man he's been trying to catch is in that building."

The men raced after their fearless leader while May stood in stunned silence.

She had just kissed Lee Munro.

Lee searched through each of the exhibit rooms and saw nothing of Bianchi. He asked a guard if he'd seen him and gave the man a detailed description. The guard had seen him earlier but couldn't say how long Bianchi had been there or when he'd gone.

"Any sign of your man?" one of the officers questioned as they caught up to him in the armor room.

"No." Lee punched his fist into his hand. "He was right here. He couldn't have gotten far. Go in pairs and search the offices and backrooms." The man nodded and collected the other men.

Lee checked the exhibit rooms one more time, then conceded Bianchi had most likely fled the building. No doubt he knew every exit and had a plan for escape before ever coming into the building.

Lee gave a heavy sigh and made his way to the exit door. It was then that he thought of what had happened between him and May. She had obviously come to tell him about Bianchi, but he was too caught up talking about another matter. He chided himself for not having dropped everything to hear her out. Those few minutes might have allowed him to catch his nemesis.

But then there was that kiss.

She had *kissed* him. Kissed him with such passion that Lee couldn't help but return it.

He made his way outside and saw her standing at the bottom of the stairs. She looked just as confused as he felt. She glanced around, then caught sight of him. She lowered her gaze to the ground. Was she embarrassed by what had happened? Better yet, why had it happened?

"May, are you all right? Did you see Bianchi come out of the building?" He came down the stairs to join her. "Did he come past you?"

She looked up again and shook her head very slowly. Her green eyes seemed to search his face as if questioning him, but then she quickly looked back at the ground.

"I didn't see him at all. He had left by the time we got there."

"I couldn't get you to stop talking."

"I'm sorry. I should have listened to you." He chuckled.

"Although I've never had someone seek my attention in quite that way."

"I saw the stool and thought . . . well, I thought I could speak into your ear. I . . . I didn't want to interfere in something important. But then . . ." She shrugged.

"But then you decided to kiss me instead?" He laughed again. "That definitely got my attention."

"I know, and I'm sorry for embarrassing you in front of your friends."

"I wasn't embarrassed. Not in the least bit."

She dared to look at him. "Oh, Lee, I'm so sorry. I'm the one who's embarrassed. I don't know what came over me. I've never acted that way with anyone before."

"I'm glad to hear that, but you don't need to be sorry."

May seemed completely contrite. "I saw Bianchi taking a picture of the armor and knew there was no one I could send to get you, so I hurried to do the deed myself. I'm afraid I don't make a very good policeman."

Lee's friends soon joined them, and nothing more could be said about the kiss or how Lee's heart was still beating so fast it made him breathless.

"There's no sign of him. We searched everywhere. He must have escaped out the back."

"Well, keep an eye open. He's around here somewhere." He looked back at May. "What was he wearing?"

"A reddish-brown coat and gray trousers. White shirt with a gray tie and gray felt hat. Oh, and he was wearing black shoes and had a Brownie camera."

The artist in her had apparently noticed every detail.

"Got that, men? Now spread out and see if you can find him." He looked at May once again. "I've got to go, but I'll be happy to drive you home this evening. Will you be here, sketching?"

She opened her mouth as if to answer, then closed it and nodded instead. Lee headed off down Pacific Avenue toward Rainier Circle with the memory of their kiss permanently etched in his memory.

Mario Bianchi was no man's fool. He hadn't known for sure that Miss Parker was tied to Leander Munro, but as he slipped from his hiding place, he saw them interacting like a couple of shy lovers at the bottom of the building's steps.

He hid in the shrubberies and watched. He had gotten very good at reading lips, and when the group of men showed up and Lee addressed them, Bianchi surmised that these were additional officers dressed in civilian clothing. He caught the description the woman gave of his clothes and hurried to alter his appearance as he moved away from the site. He pulled off the tie and coat and tossed them and his hat into the bushes, before crossing the railroad tracks and heading toward the model farm exhibit. As he walked, he rolled up his sleeves as if he were one of the farm workers and reached down for a handful of dirt to smear on his white shirt and arms. Hopefully he'd look enough the part of field hand that nobody would give him a second thought.

He entered the largest barn and found an old denim jacket. He pulled it on as he continued to walk through the building and tucked the Brownie camera under his arm with the strap that held it still around his neck.

Lee Munro was a problem for Mario wherever they encountered each other, but Mario wasn't going to be defeated by the man. Munro was predictable. He was trained, as was every officer of the law, in a particular manner of doing things. That made it easier to anticipate his actions.

Mario pushed aside any concern. He'd made it all these years with Munro chasing after him. Now he had the Tamuras' painting, along with Miss Parker's sketches and photographs, as well as his own photographs. He didn't need to bother further with the armor until they were ready to switch it out.

"You there," a man called out.

Mario turned to face one of the men he'd seen with Lee. He smiled. "How can I help you?"

"Have you seen a man wearing a reddish-brown coat, gray hat and tie, and gray trousers? He's on the run from the law."

"I haven't seen anyone like that." Bianchi shrugged. "This place isn't going to be one he'd likely hide in. Too much going on." He nodded toward a large group of people entering the building with one of the guides. The man spoke of the model farm and all that they were seeking to accomplish.

The officer nodded. "Well, if you see him, try to let the police know. There are officers all over the expo, just tell one of them."

Mario gave a two-fingered salute and nodded as the man went running back out of the building. It was all just too easy.

12

By the time Lee picked May up to head home, she had come to regret her earlier actions. All day, even as she sketched the samurai armor, May continued to dwell on the kiss and Lee's reaction. He seemed jovial enough and even accepting. His comments hadn't been at all condemning, but she felt terribly guilty. She'd never had a kiss from a man, much less initiated a kiss. What had she been thinking?

Lee seemed rather sullen when he helped her into the buggy. His mood was considerably more subdued, and May couldn't help but wonder if, upon reflection, he was unhappy with what she had done. They were, after all, just friends. Maybe he worried that his friends would think otherwise and word would get back to his parents before Glynnis could elope. They had teased him a bit, and perhaps that had been unpleasant for Lee.

He headed the horse down East Fortieth Steet, taking the same route as the trolley would. While he focused on the road, May began to pray.

Oh, Lord, I didn't mean to ruin our friendship. Please don't let my silliness cause harm to it. Keeping Lee as a friend is so important to me.

May twisted her gloved hands together and wrestled with her conscience until finally she couldn't take it anymore.

"I'm sorry if my earlier actions upset you. I couldn't get your attention any other way—at least that's what I told myself at the time. I really wasn't thinking clearly."

He glanced at her, then returned his attention back to the horse. "What are you talking about?"

"You seem upset with me, and I can't blame you. I know that I shouldn't have been so bold as to kiss you, especially in front of your men." She sighed and shook her head, wishing she could take back her actions despite having enjoyed them very much. "It was wrong of me, and I am so sorry to have upset you."

Lee pulled the horse and buggy to the curb. When they'd stopped, he looked at her for a long moment. "You didn't upset me. I thought I made that clear."

"But you are upset."

"I'm upset because we didn't find Bianchi."

May could understand that but found it difficult to accept that this was the only thing bothering him. "I know you needed to catch him, but I can't help but feel like I wronged you."

He laughed. "You didn't wrong me."

"It's just that I could think of no other way."

"The fact is, May, I'd like very much to do it again."

"What?" She looked at him, completely perplexed.

"Kiss you. Only this time I'd like to initiate the moment."

She felt her cheeks warm. "I, uh, I wouldn't mind that at all. I mean, that is to say . . . you have my permission."

He leaned over and gently placed his lips upon hers. May temporarily forgot where they were. The kiss lasted only a moment, but when Lee pulled away, she was reluctant to open her eyes. She wanted the dream to go on and on.

146

Instead of saying anything, Lee put Gaspar back in motion. His actions had changed everything between them, and yet he wasn't at all sure what to say about it. Before May had come back into his life, Lee hadn't seen too much hope in courtship. Most of the women he knew played by the social rules their parents had written. They looked down on anyone who wasn't white. And not just any white. They needed to be Anglo-Saxon and Protestant in their religious beliefs. Sometimes exceptions were made for the French, Dutch, and Germans, but only if they had plenty of money. Lee had once pointed out that even their family had relatives who were Scottish, French, and, shockingly enough, Spanish. His parents had waved it off since that had taken place generations prior, and besides, those relatives had come from the best of families.

Lee knew he'd never be happy in a marriage where such prejudices were promoted. He wanted his children to grow up respecting people of all cultures. He wanted a wife who recognized that all were precious in God's sight. But many in his social circles didn't believe people of color even had souls. With attitudes like that, Lee had put aside thoughts of falling in love.

But then May kissed him.

Why had he never thought of May as a potential wife? Was it because he knew his father and mother would forbid it—eject him from the family once and for all for his desire to marry a woman of mixed race?

He frowned. If he followed his heart, it would cost him his family. His brothers would never speak to him again, and his mother and father would die of shame. Well, that was probably an overreaction, but they would suffer for it.

But he would suffer for it if he didn't pursue his feelings for May.

He was still contemplating all of this in silence when they reached May's house. What must she think of him? He'd kissed her and said nothing. He set the brake and turned to her.

"I don't know what to say, except that I very much liked sharing a kiss with you."

May nodded. "I liked it too."

"I have a great deal to think about, but I want you to know that I'm not sorry you kissed me. I'm not sorry that I kissed you. I find myself perplexed, however."

"Can you explain?" The look on May's face suggested she was worried.

"Well, the thought that comes to me first is—"

"Lee Munro, good to see you again." May's father approached the buggy. "Kame asked me to hurry out and invite you to stay for supper."

Lee met the older man's gaze, unable to shake his guilty feelings for having taken advantage of May with his kiss. After all, there were no other intentions but to enjoy the moment. At least . . . none that he had made openly known.

"I, well, I would, but I have to tend to some business." Lee still needed to go into the station and speak to his captain about all that had happened that day.

"Maybe another time, then. I'll talk to Kame, and we'll make plans for a night next week. Would that work?"

"Of course, Mr. Parker. I'd be honored."

"Then count on it. I'll let May know the date. Is there any time that would be bad for you?"

"No, I believe next week is open."

He started to climb down to help May, but her father waved him off. "I've got her."

Lee watched as May's father assisted her from the buggy.

She turned and met his gaze. She seemed uncertain of herself and looked away.

He felt momentarily awkward. "Uh, we'll talk tomorrow. I'll stop by the shop." He looked back to May's father. "Mr. Parker, please thank your wife for her invitation. I look forward to next week."

Mr. Parker smiled. "I'll let her know. I feel certain she'll be delighted."

Lee watched father and daughter head up the walkway to the house. A part of him wanted to forget his responsibilities and run after May. He wanted to declare his feelings for her, but in all honesty, he wasn't even sure what those feelings were or how to proceed with them. He released the brake and snapped the reins.

"Walk on, Gaspar. We've got work to do." And it wasn't all related to police business.

May prepared her framed canvas. Once it was secured on the easel, she picked up her palette and considered her paints. She had already decided she was going to create a person in the armor. A fierce samurai warrior in full battle gear. It seemed only right. The piece she'd made for the Tamuras seemed empty when she really thought about it. The fact that the warrior was missing made the painting seem incomplete.

"You were very quiet at dinner," her mother said from the doorway. "Is something wrong?"

May put the palette down, then wiped her hands on a towel. "I don't know. I wouldn't say that things are wrong. Just . . . different."

Her mother came into the room and joined May in front of the canvas. "Different in what way?"

May looked at her mother a moment. Her black hair was fashioned in a sleek bun at the nape of her neck. Her dark eyes surveyed May's face as if seeking to find some hidden truth. Mama was such a beautiful woman, but May knew she despised her Japanese appearance. In turn it had made May hesitant about her own. But rather than speak on the matter, May went in another direction.

"Mama, how did you know you were in love with Father? That it was really love?"

Her mother smiled. "Are you having feelings for someone?"

"I kissed Lee earlier today, and on the way home he kissed me. We both enjoyed it, but I have to admit I feel confused and a bit overwhelmed."

Mama's right brow arched ever so slightly. "I've always liked Lee. He is a kindhearted man."

"I didn't mean to kiss him. I needed to get his attention, and instead of just yelling or making a scene . . . of another kind, I kissed him. It was unlike anything I'd ever experienced. He stirs my thoughts like no one else has ever done."

Mama took her by the hand and led her to where they could sit. She motioned May to do just that and pulled up a wooden stool to sit at her daughter's knee.

"I felt that way about your father. From the first time we met, I knew he was someone special. I was just a young girl, but I'd endured so much that it had aged me—matured me beyond my years. And to be honest, your father isn't that much older than me. He lied about his age to get the job because he wanted so much to travel and see the world.

"There were so many fearful things happening around me. The soldiers had taken away many of the men in my family, even the men who hadn't fought in the rebellion but were known to support it. My family suffered greatly. My aunts and cousins were left without the help of their husbands, brothers, and fathers. Without the men to help, there was very little money to buy the things we needed for everyday life. We had our gardens and such, and we were able to fish, but it seemed there was never enough food. And of course, we were worried about what had happened to the others. So when your father came into my life, it was alluring in more ways than that of romance. I missed my father so much, and though he was young, your father offered counsel and wisdom in a way that my father had done."

"I'm so sorry, Mama. You were only a child, and you suffered so much. I wish I'd known. Perhaps I could have offered comfort. I certainly wouldn't have pestered you about Japan."

"You only wanted to know about our family. I don't blame you for your questions. However, I didn't want you to dwell on the sadness and pain. It was a terrible time, and before your father came into my life, I wished that I might die."

"Oh, Mama, no!"

Her mother gave a sad smile and patted May's hand. "I won't lie to you now that I've agreed to tell my story. It was a bleak and hopeless time for me. Then your father came into my life. He told me about Jesus and God's love for us—how God sent His only Son to die for our sins. He told me that any wrong or responsibility I bore was already redeemed at the cross. But of course, I told him my family didn't believe in the Christian God. He said that didn't change the fact that it was the truth.

"I loved him for saying so. I loved him for the way he made me feel the tiniest glimmer of hope. I said as much to him one day when I was just fifteen. He told me it wasn't him that gave that glimmer. It was Jesus through him. I didn't understand, but your father was more than willing to help me see the truth."

May thought of her father giving tender counsel. "I can just hear him. He loves to talk about Jesus and God's love for His children."

"You asked how I knew I was in love with your father . . . well, he made me feel safe and cared for. I knew that when I was with him, I could be myself and speak honestly. He didn't ask me to pretend and didn't expect me to be someone I wasn't. He accepted me for being me."

"That's how it is for me with Lee."

"From our first meeting, your father was there for me in ways I never expected, and he always knew exactly what I needed to hear. I believe God was directing his every word."

"Of course He was."

May looked up to find her father listening from the doorway. He came into the room and knelt beside his wife. "Hopefully He directs all of my words." He gazed lovingly into his wife's eyes.

May's mother smiled. "It was more than just his words about God. His kindness and loving spirit greatly attracted me, but so did his sense of humor and joy of life."

"I've cared for your mother since I first met her. She was so angry and lost—so alone. I decided to be a friend to her, and after she grew up, I realized that I held a deep love for her. Over the years, that love has continued to mature and grow deeper, and I thank God every day for giving her to me."

"As do I," Mama declared. "I feel certain I would be dead if you hadn't taken me under your wing."

May loved hearing their declarations of love, but it only served to confuse her more about her own feelings. "How do you know when that love is the right one? The one who will love you for the rest of your life?"

"Pray about it, May. God is good to show us when we

ask," her father replied. "The book of James tells us to ask for wisdom and says God will give it. I've found Him faithful to always do exactly that. Just when I've needed it the most, God's wisdom has been available for me."

Later, as May finished her work for the evening, she considered all that her mother and father had shared. She felt confident that they were right about putting her trust in God for the answers. It was funny that she had never really given any thought to a specific man being a match for her love. She had come to dread even pondering such matters because, as she recently told Lee, she was neither white enough nor Japanese enough. One side or the other always found her wanting.

Lee had never made her feel that way, but she hadn't truly considered him as a potential mate. Lee was a friend—one of the only ones she had ever had. Oh, there were girls here and there throughout her life who had been friends, but the relationships never lasted past the parents learning of May's heritage. It was truly amazing how easily people turned away, even from a child, and all because they were different.

May sighed and made her way upstairs. Lee had always been a source of kindness and encouragement. Even in the ten-year absence, May had found strength in the way he had once championed her. If that didn't speak of love—what did?

That evening, Lee sat in front of his fireplace reading until much later than he'd intended. The book was an old and comforting friend—his Bible. The day had stirred up feelings in him that he had never expected. The kisses he had shared with May left little doubt in his mind that she was more than just a girl from his past. He wanted her in his future as well.

After leaving the police station, Lee had gone in search of Glynnis to discuss the pretense of engagement. They both agreed they needed to somehow hold off any formal announcement for just a few more days, and then, hopefully, Glynnis and her beau would be married and on their way to Chicago. With that decided, Lee couldn't help telling Glynnis what had happened with May and how it made him feel. Glynnis had told him without a doubt he was in love and congratulated him on finally realizing it.

"Sometimes God puts a person right in front of us, but until it's time for us to notice them, they are simply a friend or acquaintance," she had told him. "Now May is more, and it's easy for me to see that she has awakened something very special in your heart."

He supposed she was right, but what should he do about it? As he'd already considered, his parents and brothers would never accept May into the family. They would instead tell Lee to go and never return, and while he hated their prejudice, they were the only family he had. Could he cast them off as easily as they might him?

Gazing into the fire, Lee knew there wasn't going to be an easy way through any of this. He felt confident that if he suggested to May he was in love with her, she would confirm her feelings for him. But where would that leave them? What could he do beyond loving a woman he could never marry without losing the only other people who had ever loved him?

He let out a heavy sigh. He contemplated the Scriptures he'd just read. "But seek ye first the kingdom of God, and his righteousness; and all these things shall be added unto you," Matthew six, verse thirty-three said. How could loving

May be a matter of seeking God first? Didn't Lee already seek God first? He certainly thought he did.

He gazed upward at the ceiling. "Lord, am I failing to seek You in some way? Am I not doing Your will? Show me what I'm missing. Show me what to do about my feelings for May."

For a long time he just sat there waiting, as if God Himself might come through the door with answers. Instead, Lee heard the patter of rain against the window and the chiming of the clock on his mantel. It was midnight, and morning would soon be upon him. Wearily, he got to his feet and headed to his bedroom. He had no answers for tomorrow.

Only then did he think about the verse that followed in Matthew six: "Take therefore no thought for the morrow: for the morrow shall take thought for the things of itself. Sufficient unto the day is the evil thereof."

He couldn't help but shrug. "I give it to you, Father. I have no understanding of where You want to lead me in this, but I trust You. Help me to trust You more."

Mario Bianchi looked at the progress his men had made that day. The armor was coming along quite nicely. Thanks to the photographs and sketches May Parker had given the Tamuras, along with the beautiful painting—which Mario himself intended to keep after everything was said and done—the armor would soon be complete. It had taken hiring more artisans than he'd anticipated. Most were happy to help, although he hated working with other people. They could bear witness against him, and that was a liability he didn't like having around.

Of course, the best way to rid himself of that problem was to eliminate the witnesses. He supposed he could do that if necessary, but they were good at what they did, and he might need them again. No, he'd find a way to keep them quiet. Threats. Rewards. Whatever it took.

He picked up a detailed sketch of the gauntlets. Miss Parker had put quite a lot of detail into her drawing. She really was an exceptional artist. Bianchi smiled. Perhaps one day she would be much sought after, and he would have her painting of the armor for his own. That would be one original he'd not need to steal.

Thinking of his home in Ontario, Mario couldn't help but chuckle. His house was full of beautiful, expensive pieces of art. Originals that he had stolen and replaced with copies. There were so many pieces of art hanging in museums around the world that were his exceptional copies. He was gifted at painting. Everyone had always said as much. What he lacked was originality. It wasn't his forte to dream up the subject or scene. He was a copy master, somehow interpreting the artist's style as if it were an intimate part of who he was.

If only he could rid himself of Lee Munro, all would be perfect. Unfortunately, Lee and his men were on the lookout for him, and Bianchi would have to be twice as careful to remain out of sight or, at best, disguised when going to the expo. And unfortunately, he still needed time with the armor. The photos and painting were only so much help. Miss Parker's sketches were quite good—impressive actually. They had helped even more than the photographs because she was so precise with the details. And it was the details that always gave him the edge.

He put the sketches aside and yawned. It was nearly two in the morning, and he needed sleep. Tomorrow he would work on some of the artistic detailing for the armor, and he would need a steady hand.

13

"You look so much better," May told Esther. Someone had combed and braided Esther's long hair into two plaits and put her in a fresh white shift.

"It's only been one week and two days since your accident," Addie reminded, "and the change is remarkable."

"I feel so much better," Esther admitted. "Although I find the stitches pull and tug when I move."

Addie nodded. "They will do that."

Someone had moved Esther to a ward with four other women, most of whom were sleeping after a variety of surgeries. There was one empty bed yet in the room of iron-framed beds and metal cupboards. The walls were painted the same soft pale green May had seen elsewhere. There was very little privacy to be had.

Addie stepped closer to the bed. "You do seem much healed. I have to say I'm impressed with the level of care they've given you. They were quite attentive to me as well, but I figured it was due to my husband's threats or insistence." She smiled. "Isaac can be quite influential when he wants to be."

"They've taken such good care of me," Esther admitted.

"And the doctor said my recovery is going better than he could have hoped. He said it was something of a miracle given my injuries."

"Yes, well, there have been a lot of people praying for you," May offered.

"I can definitely believe that," Esther replied. "I feel like I'm never alone, but in a good way. It's like I'm surrounded by . . . well, I don't know . . . maybe angels. Anyway, I feel quite improved, and everyone here has been so nice."

"What do you do with yourself all day?" May asked.

"They wake us early to tend to our wounds and take down information like our temperature and heart rate. I know, because I asked." She laughed. "One of the nurses' helpers washed my hair and braided it for me. I must say, I felt so much better just with that simple task."

"It is amazing how much little things can improve our situation," Addie replied.

"We have our meals, and the doctor comes to see us and judge our healing. Mostly I spend my time reading the Bible—thanks to May's loan. But tell me how things are going at the shop."

"We had a very busy day," May admitted. "Saturday always has more children, so there were lots of photos to be taken. And as soon as work was done, Addie and I hurried to come here and see you."

"That was so kind. I don't feel quite so lonely with you coming to visit. Mama and Papa haven't been able to make the trip just yet. My father hasn't felt well enough. Mama hoped they might come today." She frowned. "But they didn't."

Just then, May noticed a man and woman standing in the doorway to the ward. When they spotted Esther, they came forward at a fast clip.

"Oh, Esther," the woman said. "We're here at last. How are you feeling? We went to the room where they had you first, but you were gone. I feared the worst."

"Mama. Papa." She tried to straighten and sit, but although she was healing fast, Esther was still too weak. She settled back against her pillow. "I'm doing very well."

Her mother put her hand on Esther's forehead. "You don't have a fever. That's good. So often after surgeries, and even simple injuries, a person takes a fever."

"Mama, Papa, these are my friends and coworkers Mrs. Hanson and May Parker." Esther motioned to her parents and looked to May and Addie. "These are my parents, Mr. and Mrs. Danbury."

May noted that while the couple looked rather downtrodden, their clothes had once been of a quality and nature that would suggest a much better life.

"I'm pleased to meet you, Mr. and Mrs. Danbury," May said, offering a smile. "Esther is my dear friend."

"You're the Japanese girl Esther told us about. The artist."

May nodded, not quite expecting the comment about her heritage. It wasn't all that unusual for people to note her ancestry, but she hadn't anticipated it as an identifier in that moment.

"I'm Addie Hanson. I'm Esther's supervisor at Fisher Photography."

The couple exchanged a glance. May knew from things Mary had told her that there was once bad blood between Addie and Esther. However, Addie didn't reference this at all.

"Esther is most fortunate that she's so healthy," Addie said. "The doctor said she is healing fast."

"He did, Mama. He said I was healing faster than any of the patients he'd known."

"She's correct in that," a nurse said, coming in with a tray of medicines. "However, the limit on visitors is two per patient, and I'm afraid I must ask two of you to go."

"We were just getting ready to leave," Addie said.

May gave a nod. "She's right. We're going to go see Mrs. Fisher and the new baby."

"Mrs. Fisher is the woman whose husband owns the photography shop," Esther explained to her parents.

"Speaking of which," Esther's mother spoke up, "how soon can Esther return to work?"

The nurse set her tray aside. "I believe the doctor said she'd be here a few more days and then have to recuperate at home for several weeks."

"Weeks?" her mother said. She looked at her husband.

May noticed the way the man's gaze dropped to the floor, and his face seemed to grow more ashen. Esther had told her how sick he'd been. Some form of consumption—tuberculosis? He wasn't getting any better, and the results had cost him his job.

"I'm afraid your daughter had internal injuries. The doctor can help you to better understand," the nurse replied. She handed Esther a glass of water and two pills.

Esther took the pills with a few sips of water and handed the glass back to the nurse, who started to move on to the next patient.

"I don't know how we'll ever pay for all of this," Esther's mother declared.

The nurse stopped and turned back around. "There's no worry on that account, missus. The Seattle Electric Company has guaranteed all debts. They will be paying the full cost of Miss Danbury's stay. They are the owners of the trolleys, after all." With that she went on to the next bed.

Mrs. Danbury's expression brightened. "Well, at least that is something. I've not known companies to willingly accept responsibility for such things. Seems most have to be taken to court."

"Perhaps they realize that no one else could be responsible since it was the bad brakes on the trolley that caused the accident," Addie suggested.

Mrs. Danbury nodded and reached out to touch her husband's arm. "Did you hear that? The electric company has assumed responsibility for the medical debts."

"That's good," the older man answered.

May noticed the man seemed quite a bit older than the woman. Perhaps it was just his disease that made him appear so hunched over and pale. Though his hair had grayed, and his hands were wrinkled as if with age.

"I had no idea of that being the case," Esther said. "Of course, it doesn't help with my wages."

"Oh, that reminds me." Addie opened her purse and pulled out twenty dollars. She placed it on the nightstand. "Here's the pay and commission for the week before the accident." She looked to Esther's parents. "She's definitely been one of our best workers."

Her mother met Addie's gaze, then looked to Esther. "I thought you said there was no more pay coming."

"No doubt the injury caused her to forget," Addie interjected. "Esther, we'll be going for now, but May and I will come back and visit you if time permits. Please know that we'll be praying for you."

Esther gave Addie a look that suggested gratitude. Her words followed up that expression. "Thank you so much for everything. You've both been so good to me."

"Glad we could help," Addie said.

May came to Esther's side and took hold of her hand. "I'm blessed to see you doing so well. Please be obedient to what the doctors say and let us know if there is anything we can do."

"Yes," Addie said from the foot of the bed. "Just have someone telephone the expo and tell them to get word to Fisher Photography. Otherwise, we will stay in contact and check up on you."

May joined Addie and gave Esther a little wave. "It was wonderful to meet you, Mr. and Mrs. Danbury."

Esther's parents nodded and turned their attention back to Esther and the money. "What an answer to prayer that this money should come just now. With the first of the month, there was rent to be paid, and I didn't know how we'd ever make it."

May could hear them discussing what needed to be done even as they exited the room. She looked to Addie.

"I know she wasn't owed any money."

"No, but Isaac and I felt certain God would have us help them."

"I feel the same way. I told my parents I want to help Esther with the money I was paid for the painting. They agreed it was a wonderful way to share God's blessings and love."

Addie glanced back down the hall. "Things that Esther said make me believe her folks wouldn't allow her to take charity—that they wouldn't take it themselves. I'm not sure how we'll continue to bless them, but we'll figure out a way."

May considered how bad things might be in Esther's home. "They seem like good people who are just down on their luck."

"I agree. Esther's father is not well enough to work, and I know that has hurt the family greatly. Her mother is trying to do cleaning jobs and such but isn't making much at it. I suppose I might see about having her do some work around our house. We have a housekeeper, but perhaps I could speak to her about the situation."

"I wish they'd just take the money offered. I'd simply give it over to them if I thought they would accept it."

"I know. So would I." Addie exited the hospital and headed for the Fifth Avenue trolley stop.

The day was chilly and damp. May pulled her coat a little closer and did up the buttons. "Perhaps we can think up some way to get them to take the money. Maybe I could just send it in the mail with no return address. Or better still, mail it to Esther in the hospital. They surely wouldn't turn money aside if it was explained that God had laid it upon my heart to share it."

"Maybe not, but who can say? All we can do is try. I do like the idea of an anonymous gift." Addie smiled. "I'm sure God can prepare their hearts to receive His blessing. After all, we're doing this as an act of love for Him. To bring Him glory and not ourselves."

May smiled. "Yes, that's exactly what I was thinking. Surely God will bless it and change their hearts to accept it."

"I know he's posted a man to watch me," Hillsboro told Mario Bianchi over a late dinner. "I have always been able to tell when someone is on my trail. What I don't understand is why. No crime has been committed. There's no reason to watch me or anyone else."

"He's that way," Bianchi admitted. "He chased me from city to city for several years."

Hillsboro leaned back and steepled his fingers. "This Munro may be a difficult man to manage. Can he be paid off to look the other way?"

Bianchi laughed. "Never. He's devoted to law and order. Completely dedicated."

"It's been my experience that even dedicated men can be enticed."

"Not Munro. Believe me when I say this, he will challenge us every step. But"—Mario held up his hand as Hillsboro looked about to speak—"I've dealt with him before, and I feel confident of managing him once again."

"Well, I don't like having people watching me. I've had to go out of my way to get out of the hotel unseen. And now we're eating in a poor man's excuse for a quality restaurant. I don't appreciate it at all."

"Be patient, please. I assure you the end result will be worth your trouble." Bianchi smiled. "And if Leander Munro proves to be too difficult to deal with . . . I'll simply kill him."

"I find it hard to believe that Hillsboro hasn't left the hotel in three days," Lee said as one of his men checked in to give his report.

"I've watched the room. Maids and the valet have come and gone, but Hillsboro remains inside the room. He orders room service three times a day and has no visitors."

"So you've seen nothing of Mario Bianchi?" Of course they hadn't. Bianchi wouldn't be foolish enough to visit Hillsboro at the hotel. That's why Lee was certain Hillsboro was leaving the hotel to meet Bianchi.

"Nothing, sir." The man stood completely at attention, his eyes straight ahead.

"Very well. Who's on guard now?" Lee asked.

"Sheridan, sir. He took over at the end of my shift. I came straightaway to report just as you ordered."

Lee nodded. "Very well. Go home and get some rest or go to church. Whatever it is you do on Sundays. I'll speak with you again tomorrow." The man turned and headed out of Lee's office without another word.

Easing back into his leather chair, Lee tried to surmise what Hillsboro was doing to leave the hotel. Was it possible he was disguising himself? He could somehow have changed places with his valet. Perhaps he wasn't even in that room any longer. Yes, that was a possibility. He might well have changed rooms with no one the wiser. Probably paid the hotel staff a great deal of money to keep quiet about where he'd gone.

Lee frowned. If that was the case, then he was wasting time and effort in keeping men posted to watch his activities. Maybe if he took the officer off of watching the room and simply posted men around the hotel, Hillsboro might relax and make a mistake. After all, they had been able to follow him a few times prior to the last few days. Of course, each time the driver had managed to lose the officer in the heavy Seattle traffic.

He pounded the top of his desk with a single-fisted blow. "There has to be a way to figure this out. God, please help me."

He noted the time. If he was going to make it to church with his mother and father, he would need to get a move on. The expo wouldn't open until the afternoon, so at least he wouldn't have to fight that incoming traffic. This would be the last time he'd attend church with his family. He had already spoken to his pastor and planned to start attending with May and her family. On Tuesday Glynnis would be married and gone, and after that, there would be no reason to pretend anymore that he loved anyone other than May.

"He has to be one of the handsomest babies I've ever met," Addie told Pearl Fisher.

Of course, May knew the woman needed no encouragement on that point. She already adored her newborn son.

Pearl watched as Addie held the baby. "I just find it hard to believe he's really here. I feared I would never have a child."

"He seems like such a good baby," Addie said, handing him to May.

May took the baby in her arms and cuddled him close. He watched her the entire time with beautiful dark blue eyes that reminded her of Lee's. "He is beautiful," she agreed. She looked up at Pearl and Addie. "Do you know something? I've never held a baby until now."

Addie laughed. "Well, you seem quite natural at it."

"I agree," Pearl replied. "And little Joe seems very happy to be in your arms."

May looked at the baby again and smiled. "He's just so very precious. God is so amazing. He has created this beautiful baby out of pure love."

"He has indeed," Addie said. "Oh, Pearl, this is such a happy time. I'm so delighted that you are healthy and the baby is well. I would imagine Otis is quite beside himself."

"He didn't want to go to work today, but I told him you

were stopping by after church and reminded him he only needed to be there from one until five. Just four short hours. That seemed to soften the blow."

Addie nodded. "I will stay as long as you need me. May, however, has to go to work. There's a large stack of photographs for her to paint."

May handed the baby back to Addie, who in turn placed him in his mother's arms. May thought she would like to paint that picture. Mother propped up in bed, babe in her arms. A perfect and lovely moment.

"Thank you for letting me come and visit with Addie," May said before gathering her satchel and hat.

"Thank you for coming. I'm so glad you've become a part of our little family," Pearl replied. "I'll be praying for you."

"And I for you, Mrs. Fisher. I'll be praying for you and your son. Oh, and Mr. Fisher of course."

Addie escorted her to the door. "If you finish with painting the photographs, feel free to head home. Mary will help Otis close things down."

"All right."

The grandfather clock began to chime as May pulled on her coat and headed downstairs. The Fishers' new shop was strategically located in the heart of the city, where people were always passing by. She'd have to hurry to catch the trolley if she was going to get to work on time.

May ran the last block to the stop and barely managed to climb aboard before the conveyance headed out. She found a seat near the back and plopped down—grateful that she wouldn't be late.

She couldn't help but think about the baby and Lee. She wondered if there might be any hope for marriage. She knew it wouldn't be easy under any circumstances. She wasn't even sure Lee would see it as worth the price it would cost them both.

May gave a sigh and stared at her hands rather than meet the gazes of those around her. She was Japanese—might as well be full-blooded. How could it ever work out for her and Lee to have a future?

"We just met yesterday, so what could possibly be so important as to drag me out and risk being seen? I suppose you want more money," Tobias Hillsboro said, lowering his rain-soaked umbrella. He had only agreed to meet Mario Bianchi because the man had sent a message insisting. What else could it be but a plea for more money?

"Money isn't everything," Bianchi replied. He looked Hillsboro in the eye. "You wanted to know if I would have the armor ready to exchange by the fourteenth of October. The answer is no."

Hillsboro resented that the demanding little man had dragged him away from the warmth and comfort of his new hotel to meet under the awning of a run-down Chinese laundry. All to tell him something he could have sent a note about. He also resented the fact that Bianchi seemed completely at ease despite the damp cold.

"What is your solution?" Hillsboro finally asked.

"There is none. I'm simply telling you that it won't be done by the fourteenth. I will have it done on the fifteenth."

"The fifteenth?" Hillsboro wanted to throw something at the weasel. "And you couldn't have just sent word to let me know that, instead of a missive demanding I meet you here?"

"I wanted to explain," Bianchi said with a placating smile.

"You see, my friend, I had to send away for a special lacquer that I could only get in San Francisco. It will arrive on the train the day after tomorrow. We will of course continue our work to the best of our ability, but that lacquer has to be applied in layers, and the drying process is not an easy one. If I apply the lacquer too soon, it will crack, and the rush will be evident. Hence, we will need an extra day."

"As long as it's done and exchanged before the fair ends. I want it in that case being exhibited to the public. Then if there is any concern—any reason that the armor appears to be a copy rather than the original—it will come out immediately."

"I still don't understand your reasoning. If you allowed me to exchange it when the original is already packed and ready for loading, it would be much simpler. It would also buy you time to get away with your prize. The armor would ship back to Japan, and only then would it be unpacked and someone might notice that it's not the actual piece that they sent to display."

Hillsboro shrugged and gave Bianchi a hint of a smile. He didn't expect the man to understand. "It's the thrill of the thing. It's being able to pull it off under the nose of everyone. It's knowing that the officials will look at that piece and not even realize they're being duped.

"I intend to stand there and make another plea to purchase it. That will only add to the intrigue when they realize it's not the original. They'll remember that I begged them to sell it to me. Perhaps your police detective will even be there. I will watch them all as they hold their heads high, knowing they did their job and kept the armor from foreign hands. But all the while I will have the real piece packed and awaiting shipment."

It was almost more than Hillsboro could stand to have to wait until the sixteenth to experience the moment. "I will walk away in feigned disappointment and defeat and make my way to the train station, where I will leave for New York with the samurai armor among my possessions. It will be one of my sweetest victories."

Bianchi shrugged. "Seems it would be easier to simply take it at the docks, but however you want to play it. After you pay me, I don't care."

The rain had stopped, and it seemed the right time to leave. Hillsboro looked at Bianchi and shook his head. "It's a good thing you didn't ask for more money."

"Why is that?" the smaller man asked.

"Because I might have grown annoyed and killed you."

That had a sobering effect on Bianchi that gave Hillsboro great satisfaction.

"Now get back to work and leave me be. I already had to move heaven and earth to get away from the watchful eye of your detective friend. I don't need any more secret notes and rendezvous."

14

May had spent the morning working on her Japanese warrior. As he took shape, May imagined he was her grandfather. How she wished she had photographs of her grandparents. Mama said there were none—that such things had never been important to her father and mother. Plus she reminded May that photography was very new in Japan when her parents were still alive.

Still, why could they not have realized that it would be important to their descendants yet to come? Of course, the war had brought shame upon the family, so it was possible that if such photographs had existed, they would have been destroyed.

When she reached a point when the painting would have to dry before she could continue, May cleaned her brushes and put them aside. She tidied her studio, then took up a charcoal pencil and her sketchbook.

All morning she'd thought of Lee and how much she cared for him. It was funny how that simple kiss had opened a locked door in her heart. She could scarcely think of anything but how much she wanted to be with Lee—to see and talk to him about everything—anything.

Before May realized it, she was sketching Lee's face from memory. She worked to capture the serious expression he wore when working. He seemed almost fierce. Like her Japanese warrior.

She used her finger to smudge in his thick brown hair. He wore it a bit long around the ears and collar, so she accommodated that as well. His face was easy for her but not so much the stern expression. There was a determination Lee would get in his eyes that she couldn't quite capture without making him look angry. And it definitely wasn't anger she wanted to portray.

When May finished with her attempt, she studied the drawing. She had managed to capture his appearance overall. She took the piece out of her sketchbook and tacked it to the wall, then stepped back and folded her arms against her painting apron.

"What are you doing home?" her father asked from the doorway.

May turned and gave him a smile. "Bertha asked me to trade days off, and even though I just had Friday off, I didn't mind. But I thought you were going to be gone until late?"

"My meetings ended early. We managed to resolve all of our issues without too much trouble." He came into the room to join in her perusal of the sketch.

"I'm always amazed at how closely you can master a person's expression. You have managed to show Lee's serious nature."

"It only seems to work well when I know them personally. I doubt I could sketch out a stranger with as much luck." She cocked her head to one side, then the other. "Still, there's something about Lee's eyes that I can't quite figure out."

"I think you've drawn him faithfully." Her father stepped

closer to the sketch and leaned down. "You've definitely managed to portray the intensity of his nature, and much of that is in the eyes."

May appreciated her father's encouragement. "He reminds me of my samurai warrior. Or perhaps the warrior reminds me of Lee and his dogged nature to bring justice to the world." She stepped over to her painting. "I wish I knew more about the men who called themselves samurai."

Her father joined her at the easel. "I studied a bit about them, but of course not being one myself, I will never have a full understanding of their beliefs and determination.

"You've done a good job on the armor. I've been privileged to see a great many sets of armor. The Tokyo National Museum has taken a special interest in the history of the samurai. For which I personally am quite glad. They founded their museum in 1872, taking many of the pieces the samurai were forced to give up. They display them for all to see, and while I was working in Japan, I was sent to Tokyo on many occasions."

"What was it like there, Father?"

He turned toward her. "It's unlike anything I've ever experienced. Even Japantown here in Seattle loses something in the comparison. Japan is unique unto itself. The people, the culture, it's all a completely different thing. It's like a secret code to anyone who isn't Japanese. Intriguing and alluring, yet just out of reach."

"I want so much to experience it for myself one day." She couldn't disguise the longing in her voice. "I so wish Mama would have wanted to hold on to her heritage."

"It was hard for her to leave yet impossible for her to stay. If you'd known her pain, you would have understood. Please don't be too hard on her."

"Of course not," May replied with a sigh. "I do not wish

to be the cause of her enduring more pain. One day I will have enough money that I can go to Japan and visit our family. They may not welcome me, but they will have to deal with me." She winked. "And as you know, I can be just as fierce as my samurai warrior."

Her father laughed and put his arm around May's shoulders. "You would make a formidable samurai, my little May. But perhaps it would be better for you to put your energy into your friendship with Lee."

She glanced back at the sketch. What was it that she wanted from that friendship? Was it possible for them to have something deeper? Would society ever allow for that?

"Papa, what do you really think of Lee?"

Her father seemed to consider the question. "I think he's a good man. He was an honorable youth with integrity and courage, and I see nothing in the man he's become that would suggest otherwise."

"I think . . . maybe . . ." She let the words fade into silence.

"You're in love with him?"

She gave a nod. "I've always loved him as a friend. He was so good to look after me and keep me from harm."

"I know, but I suspect it's something more than that now."

"I don't know what it is exactly. I am trying to figure that out. I think I might be in love with him, but I've never known love for a man. That's why I asked Mama how she knew for certain she was in love with you."

Her father laughed. "And what did she say?"

"You overheard part of it, but the thing that touched me deeply was she said you made her feel safe and that you didn't force her to be something she wasn't. Lee's that way with me. He always makes me feel safe, and he's never asked me to be someone other than who I am."

Father squeezed her shoulders. "It won't be easy for you. His parents will never approve, even though I believe Lee is in love with you as well. I would not, however, advise you to make Lee pick between his family and you. That would be a very hard decision for a young man."

May leaned her head against Father's chest. "Why must they hate me so much? I never did anything to them. I was always respectful and kind. Why do they judge me because I'm part Japanese?"

"They judge in their ignorance, May. They haven't even tried to understand their anger and resentment toward the Japanese or anyone else."

"I've never understood such heartlessness. Poor Mama hides herself away in the house day after day, year after year. She only goes with you to those few places where she knows she won't be judged based on her bloodline."

"We've been blessed to have a few friends and a church body who don't care about such things, but May, the world is cruel, and those people who aren't are few and far between. There is very little understanding for those who break the rules and marry outside of their color."

"But I'm as much white as I am Japanese," she said, pulling away from his embrace. "How am I supposed to get by when neither side accepts me? They punish me for something I had no control over."

"My poor May. Life has been very harsh with you. I've hated watching it—knowing there was nothing I could do to alter the attitude that followed you."

May glanced again to her painting. The reds and golds were in sharp contrast to the blacks and grays. Each part of the armor seemed to come alive, and the variety of color only served to make it all the more beautiful. Why couldn't it be that way with people? She looked again and caught sight of the kanjis she'd put on the chest plate.

May drew her father's attention to the tiny symbols. "This means 'courage' or 'bravery.' I thought perhaps it had been included on the armor to give the warrior encouragement."

"A reminder, perhaps, that steadied his heart for the battle to come."

"Do you suppose God could give me courage to steady my heart?" she asked.

He took her into his arms and hugged her tightly. "My little May, God is ever with you to strengthen and defend you. He will give you courage for the battle. Just be true to Him. The truth, as the Bible says, will set you free."

Lee sat across from Glynnis at the elegantly appointed table his mother had arranged for what she hoped would be the announcement of the young couple's wedding. She had put out her finest table setting, the Meissen porcelain—a collection that originated in the late 1700s and had once belonged to her great-great grandmother. Added to this were the Baccarat crystal stemware and the Tiffany chrysanthemum silverware with the family's monogram on each piece. If anything could be said of Regina Munro, she could set a table fit for a king.

It was actually an artistic delight to sit at his mother's table. She had used her finest silver candelabras, despite the house being electrified, and had arranged white hothouse narcissus and tulips with pink roses in silver epergnes despite fall florals being in vogue. The narcissus, tulips, and roses were suggestive of something bridal. No doubt this was done intentionally.

Lee had agreed to the dinner after his father's visit demanding they set a date and make a formal announcement. Glynnis would be twenty-one on the following day and had put into place her plans for elopement. She and Lee had managed to keep both sets of parents in the dark, and though Lee despised deceptions, he had felt compelled to help Glynnis in her endeavor simply for the sake of love.

"You two have put this off for long enough," Lee's father said as they lingered over dessert and coffee. "I would like to announce your engagement tomorrow. Perhaps we could even post the planned date for the wedding."

Glynnis cast a shy smile in Lee's direction. Her parents exchanged a glance, then looked to Lee in anticipation of his approval.

"Glynnis and I haven't had a chance to discuss it. Perhaps you would excuse us to have a little time to ourselves." Lee looked at each of the parents with a raised brow. He hoped his questioning expression would encourage all present to release them without further commitment.

"I suppose it's only fair that they have time to talk about the date of their wedding," Mrs. Faraday said, smiling. "It is a very important date."

"There is a calendar for 1910 in my desk. It was a gift," Lee's father said as if explanation was necessary. "Why don't you go to my study and consider your wedding date there?"

Lee got to his feet so as not to give anyone else a chance to speak. "Glynnis, shall we?" He came around and helped her from her chair.

"Please come to a conclusion as quickly as possible," his

father encouraged. "We don't want to keep the Faradays all evening."

A glance at the Faradays' hopeful expressions nearly caused Lee to stop midstep. He couldn't help feeling guilty for this farce. Still, neither he nor Glynnis had actually lied. Neither had made a declaration of love nor suggested that they were marriage bound. That had been entirely dreamed up by their parents. Plans made by two old men to better their business affairs with no regard for their children. Lee and Glynnis had allowed for the coupling at dinners and parties, but they had been careful to make no pledges or promises.

They reached the study and went inside. Glynnis couldn't help but stifle a giggle.

"You would think they would have figured all of this out by now." She swept past Lee to look out the window on the dark night. "I believe it's still raining."

"Are you packed and ready?"

She turned back to him. "I am. I have most of what I'll take with me at my friend Minnie's house. My maid has slipped things out and taken them to her over the last few weeks. Mama has noticed a couple of my dresses missing, but I told her that the maid was tending them for me, which wasn't a lie."

Lee smiled. "I hope you know what you're doing."

"I do." She took a seat by the fireplace.

Lee joined her there but paused long enough to add another log to the waning fire. Once it was in place, the fire immediately brightened as it began to burn. He sat down beside Glynnis and eased back. "This has been exhausting."

"I know, but now it has come to an end. I'm so grateful to you, Lee."

He studied her for a moment. Her blond curls were masterfully arranged atop her head with ribbons and pearls woven in to add beauty. Not that she needed them. Glynnis Faraday was quite lovely. Lee might have fallen in love with her had their parents not made it such a forced issue.

"I'm glad I could help. Your friendship has been important to me, and I just want you to be happy."

"I know I will be." She turned to better look at him. "But what about you?"

"I think I'll be happy . . . eventually. It's going to be difficult to bring my parents around. First, they will have to deal with their disappointment of our marriage not taking place. Then they'll have to battle their prejudices as I explain I've fallen in love with May Parker."

"So you really love her?"

"I do." A spark seemed to set his heart ablaze. "She's wonderful. She's brilliant and kind and everything I've wanted all of my life. I still can't help wondering why I never saw it until now."

"Sometimes we're blind to the things that are right in front of us. Look at our parents. They've made up their minds that things will be a certain way, and they have no room for further argument."

"It's true. It didn't matter how many times I explained to my father that I wasn't in love with you, he would always just pat me on the back and tell me love would come in time."

"What a terrible thing to say. Love should already be there before you pledge your life to someone. I can say without any doubt or hesitation that my love for David supersedes any other love in my life. Even that which I hold for my parents."

"But aren't you afraid that they will disown you and have nothing further to do with you? You only have one mother and father. When I think of how my love for May will divide my family, I hesitate. Not because she isn't worth it . . . she is. But because I don't want to go against the Bible and dishonor my parents by taking a stand against them."

"But they're wrong. Their pride and judgmental attitude is not what God encourages us to have. The Bible clearly says God does not look upon outward appearance, but at the heart. You have told me over and over that May loves God and that her heart belongs to Him."

"That's true."

"I cannot imagine it being wrong for you two to love each other and marry."

Lee nodded. "Even legally there are no laws banning interracial marriages. Washington is one of only a handful of states that allows for it."

"Leave it to you to know the law." Glynnis smiled and reached out to take Lee's hand. "Trust God to guide and direct you, Lee. For once, listen to your heart."

"And what do we tell them?" He motioned his head toward the door.

"I have the perfect solution. We'll promise to make everything clear tomorrow."

He chuckled and squeezed her fingers. "I'll leave it to you to make that announcement."

15

The day was half-done when Lee received an urgent summons from his father. He knew full well it would be about Glynnis. She had planned to leave with David that morning after a quick marriage ceremony. Lee had offered to be a witness for them, but David had already worked out all of the details, knowing that Glynnis would have a hard enough time just slipping away.

They would marry and catch the first train east on their way to Chicago. David had been accepted by his former teacher and conductor Frederick Stock to play in the Chicago Symphony Orchestra. He would play with the orchestra and teach violin, while Glynnis would use an inheritance left her by her grandparents to help them get established in their new life.

Lee couldn't have been happier for her, but he clearly needed to hide the fact that he knew about the situation. His father would suffer greatly if Glynnis's father thought Mr. Munro had been keeping things from him. Appearing in his father's study, Lee was less than happy to find his oldest brother, Liam, also in residence.

"I suppose you've had word from Glynnis Faraday?" his father asked.

"Good afternoon, Father, Liam." Lee took a seat in a large and very comfortable leather chair. "And, yes, I've had a note from Glynnis."

"So you know that she's run off to elope with some musician."

"Yes." Lee glanced at his brother, who was watching him carefully. Liam's scrutiny was nothing unusual. All their lives Liam had been the one to ascertain if his younger brothers were speaking truthfully.

"You don't seem overly surprised or heartbroken," Liam declared. "My guess is that you knew about this."

"I knew that Glynnis didn't love me." Lee hoped that would be enough to satisfy his brother.

"And you made it clear to me on more than one occasion," his father interjected, "that you didn't love her. You no doubt drove her away."

"I do love her as a dear friend, but no, I do not love her as a husband should a wife." Lee continued to stare unemotionally at his father.

"So you aren't upset at her actions." It was more statement than question.

"No, I'm not. I believe one must be true to their heart."

"Bah! What nonsense," Liam exclaimed. "Your marriage was arranged. It was a well-thought-out plan by our father and hers. You should have made her happy, Leander."

"She wasn't unhappy with me." Lee crossed his legs and picked a piece of lint from his gray trousers.

"Did you know about this? Did you know that she was leaving this morning—eloping with that violin player?"

"Why would Glynnis have given me the details of her

elopement to another man?" There, he hadn't lied, merely turned the questions back on his father, but still he felt guilty. "My knowing would change nothing."

"This is pure nonsense. Faraday has gone after her, but of course she's ruined. She'll either have married and bedded that low life, or worse, Faraday will find them living in sin. Either way, her reputation is completely destroyed. I cannot have you marrying her now." Lee's father got up and paced the room. "This will ruin everything George and I had planned, and all because of the whim of a young girl. A silly, addlepated young woman who can't possibly know what real love is."

"Glynnis is hardly silly or addlepated. She's quite intelligent and no man's fool. You forget that she had additional education."

Father paused to slam his fist down on his desk. "Yes, and I blame that as well. Women have no need for education other than that of how to take care of a household and family."

All the while Liam watched Lee. Lee didn't acknowledge it, but he could feel his brother's gaze burning into him. Liam had long used such tactics to intimidate, although Lee found them more amusing than frightening. Hoping to irritate his brother, Lee leaned against the back of the chair and rubbed his temples.

His father stopped and looked at him hard. "I suppose you're bored with this entire matter?"

"Frankly, yes." Lee gave a stretch as if to exaggerate his point. "There is nothing I can or would do to alter what has happened." He got to his feet. "If that is all, I have a case that needs my attention."

Father shook his head and sank into his chair. "I might have known you wouldn't care. Go on with you, then. Go back to your criminals and ne'er-do-wells. We'll talk of this later when I have a better idea of what is to be done. George will send me word as soon as he can."

Lee opened his mouth to make a comment, then closed it again. There was no use in trying to persuade his father that nothing needed to be done. "Good day to you both."

He reached the foyer, and the butler handed him his hat and opened the door. Lee stepped outside and was about to breathe a sigh of relief when he heard Liam demand his hat as well. There was no sense in trying to ignore or outrun the man. When Liam wanted to speak to you, he would stop at nothing to make it happen.

Lee waited on the portico, hat still in hand. When Liam emerged, Lee fixed him with a questioning gaze. "Yes?"

"I mean to have a word with you," Liam replied.

Donning his hat, Lee walked down the steps and headed toward his carriage. "Might I drive you somewhere?"

"No, I have my own carriage and driver." He followed Lee a few steps along the walkway, then stopped. "I think you knew all about this. Perhaps you even helped Miss Faraday in the planning."

Lee turned to face his brother. "And what if I did? Not that it matters what you think, but as I said, Glynnis Faraday is no man's fool. She needed no help from me to arrange her life. She cared for someone else, as do I. We weren't meant to be together." He hadn't meant to confess his feelings for May, but now that they were out there, he wouldn't deny them if Liam pursued the matter.

"Father was counting on that merger."

"I thought it was a marriage we were speaking of—the love of a man and woman and happily ever after."

Liam all but growled. "You know what I mean. The business end of this marriage was important to our father. You could have at least been considerate of that."

Lee shrugged. "I never learned to mix business with matters of the heart. I am sorry that Father is disappointed, but if he and George Faraday wish to conduct business together, I see no reason they can't continue in that direction. Faraday has no other daughter or son to marry off. He might as well attend to his business dealings without the complication of the heart."

His brother eyed him carefully. It was almost as if he were sizing up game to be shot. Lee didn't care for the fact that he was the prey. He started for his carriage and waiting horse.

"You're in love with someone else." It was just a matter-of-fact statement, but it bore the weight of the world.

"I am." Lee didn't stop walking, and after a moment, he heard Liam following at a slow, methodical pace. His brother never hurried for anyone.

"Who is it? Perhaps our father can strike a better deal."

"May Parker." Lee waited for the words to register with his brother. Liam would remember the scrawny little Japanese girl and be appalled all in the same heartbeat.

Lee heard Liam stop following, and he turned to face him. He didn't say a word but met his brother's contempt head on with a stern, no-nonsense stare. "That's right. May Parker. We met up again at the expo. She works there at Fisher Photography."

After what seemed an eternity, Liam spoke. "You realize you will be disowned if you carry forward with any plan to marry her."

"I do." Lee smiled, which only served to further irritate his brother.

"You would cast aside your family for that . . . that . . ."

185

"Be careful the words you choose, brother. Whether you speak those that follow through broken teeth and torn lips will depend on your discretion."

Liam had never been one to involve himself in physical altercations. He might hire someone to stand in for him, but he wasn't at all capable of defending himself with any real success. He raised his chin slightly and narrowed his eyes.

"You are disgusting. She is of mixed race."

"And I find that quite appealing. She's beautiful, and not only that but she's a child of God. I find that far more important than any other issue."

"Her people don't believe in our God." Liam barely breathed the words.

"May and her family are Christians," Lee replied.

"They cannot be saved. They are alien to the concept, and while her white father may well know the truth, I believe his actions of taking a Japanese wife have voided any possible salvation he might have had."

"When did God appoint you as judge?" Lee fought back the urge to pummel his brother. "No! Do not bother to answer that. You are blinded by your prejudices and hard heart. God judges not on outward appearances, but that is all you know how to do." Lee climbed into his buggy.

God, help me in this, please. I need to stand firm, but I don't want to argue with someone who refuses to see.

And that was the simple matter of it. His brother was completely unable to see the truth. His contempt and judgmental attitude had robbed him of the ability to see the reality set before him. Lee released the brake and snapped the lines.

"Walk on."

Addie and May helped Esther into the Hansons' carriage and carefully tucked blankets around her. Addie had brought several pillows to cushion the ride home and to make sure that Esther would be as comfortable as possible.

"I know this isn't going to be very easy on you," Addie said, surveying her work, "but it's the best we can do."

"It will certainly be better than riding the trolley home," May offered.

Esther nodded and squirmed a little to adjust her position. "It will be perfect. Don't worry so much. Besides, I just had to get out of that place. I hate hospitals. So much despair and death. Two of the women in my ward died yesterday. I didn't want to be there one minute longer."

"I truly understand. I felt the same way," Addie assured her.

May climbed into the seat opposite Esther, and Addie did likewise with the help of her driver. Once everyone was ready, the driver put the carriage into motion and headed down Fifth Avenue.

"It's so kind of you to do this," Esther said, looking first to May and then Addie. "I don't deserve your kindness after all that went on in the past."

"As I've said before, the past is in the past," Addie replied. "You've been forgiven, and we'll speak of it no more."

Esther shook her head. "I've never known Christians like you. I mean, I've known people who said they were Christians, but they sure never forgave like you have."

Addie shrugged. "You know my past. It's not one to be proud of even though I had very little to do with the choices put upon me. However, I want to be forgiven that past and the choices I did have responsibility for. That encourages me to forgive and forget the wrongdoings others have done to me. I couldn't hold those things against you or even my dead brothers and feel completely free of the wrongs I've done."

"I want to be like that," Esther admitted. "But I'm not sure I know how."

"Just give it to God and then follow through. When angry feelings arise regarding the bad things people have done to you, give them again to God. Do it over and over until those things no longer haunt you. Forgiving offers us a release— a freedom—from those self-made prisons that come from holding on to anger and a desire for revenge. And, Esther, that freedom is so much better than anything revenge has to offer."

Esther nodded and looked out at the city. "I also need to let go of my worry. I honestly don't know how God is going to provide for our needs. My mother isn't able to make much money. They were dependent on what I could earn. Even with your generosity and pretending to owe me additional wages, it's going to be hard for us."

"But God knows what you need," May piped up. She had been deeply moved by Addie's words about forgiveness. She knew there were those whom she needed to forgive. "He knew I needed to hear what Addie had to say about forgiveness. He knows what we need even before we ask Him. I've learned this over the years."

"It's true," Addie agreed. "I used to be afraid to ask God for the things I needed. I wasn't convinced He cared. I didn't think He'd hear me."

"I'm afraid I don't know how to pray very well," Esther admitted.

"It's something we've all had to learn." Addie smiled. "Especially me. I didn't grow up in a Christian home, as you know. We didn't pray at all, not even over meals."

"We did, and prayer was still hard for me." May shrugged. "It doesn't seem it should be such a hard thing to just talk to God, but it can be."

"After all, it is *God*," Esther said, looking rather perplexed. "What if I say the wrong thing?"

"If we speak to Him from our heart, can we say the wrong thing?" Addie asked. "Even if we speak out of our anger at something that has happened, or out of disappointment or grief, is it wrong to take everything to God in prayer?"

Esther seemed to think about that for a time. Finally, she shook her head. "I honestly don't know. How can I?"

"By reading the Bible, we can know what other people did. We can see how Jesus prayed, how He taught His disciples to pray. We can always and should always go back to the Bible. There are many beautiful prayers there, especially in the Psalms when David was beside himself with grief or worry."

"Who was David?" Esther sounded so forlorn.

May reached over and squeezed her hand. "He was a king, but first he was a shepherd boy. It'll take time to learn all the things you'll want to know, but just take it a step at a time, Esther. Start in learning to pray. It's really not hard. You just talk to God as you would your earthly father. I know you've spoken of how much you love your father—how close you are."

"Were. Until he got sick. He seems so silent now."

"Perhaps he needs to learn to pray as well."

"I don't know if he even knows how to be right with God. I didn't know until you helped me, May. I thought I was a

Christian because I knew God existed and I wanted to be good. I had silly notions, I suppose."

"We have all had them," Addie said. "That's why the Bible is so important. God has given the Bible to us so that we might learn the truth. You can trust that the answers are there, and that God will guide you to them. You may be the one to change everything in your family."

Esther's eyes widened a bit. "Could God really use someone like me?"

Addie and May exchanged a smile. "Yes!" they said in unison.

Esther allowed a smile to edge her lips. "I'd really like that. Just thinking about God using me to do something gives me a sense of excitement."

"Oh, before I forget," May said, opening her reticule, "I want you to have this. I know you said your parents wouldn't take charity, but I thought of something you could say and not be lying about it." She handed Esther the one hundred dollars that she'd been paid by the Tamuras.

Esther's expression changed to shock. "I . . . I can't."

"You can," May insisted. "Addie and I talked about this. If your parents ask where you got the money—"

"They will," Esther interrupted.

May nodded. "Just tell them it came from folks at the expo."

Addie handed Esther an additional amount of money. "We're from the expo—you wouldn't have met us otherwise." She smiled. "They shouldn't question it, since the Seattle Electric Company paid your hospital bills. It won't seem strange that the expo officials would want to help as well, especially since you were employed there."

"I don't . . . I don't know what to say. This is a lot of

money." Esther didn't even look at the bills but clutched them close to her breast.

"It is," May agreed, "but it should see your family through for a time until you can get on your feet. Perhaps even longer."

"But you must take this time to rest and recuperate. Too often people don't allow themselves to fully heal, and then they take ill."

Esther let out a long breath. "I'm so deeply touched by your generosity. I don't know what to say except thank you. I'll never forget this."

"That's enough," Addie said, patting her knee. "More than enough."

16

May arrived home and found Lee's horse and buggy in the drive. She gave Gaspar a little attention before heading inside to see what had brought Lee for a visit. She heard her father and Lee talking in the large parlor before she had even set two feet in the door. They seemed to be having a laugh about something and sounded to be thoroughly enjoying each other's company. Wouldn't it be wonderful if she and Lee could somehow marry? Her mother and father would adore him as a son-in-law, even if his parents despised her. She frowned at that thought. Could she spend the rest of her life with in-laws who hated her so completely?

Mrs. Moore appeared and took the cloak May was already discarding. "As you can hear, your father and Mr. Munro are in the front parlor. Your mother is upstairs dressing for dinner."

Glancing down at her own attire, May thought she should probably change before bursting in on Father and Lee.

"Has Mr. Munro been asked to stay for dinner?" she asked.

The housekeeper nodded. "He has agreed to join the family."

"Good." May smiled. "I'm going upstairs to change my clothes. If anyone asks after me, tell them I'll be right down."

She hurried up the steps, thinking about what outfit she would choose. Lee saw her almost exclusively in her Camera Girl work clothes, and she wanted to wear something that might impress him. She knew it wasn't necessary, but there was still a little bit of the silly, romantic girl in her that desired to capture the attention of her beau.

Her wardrobe was full of beautiful clothes. Her mother and father had always seen to it that she lacked nothing. Spoiling their only child came easily, but May would have felt special even without these pretty gifts. She looked through the gowns and settled on one that was the same color as her eyes. She had received many compliments when she'd worn the green silk brocade—not that she'd had that many opportunities, but she knew Lee would enjoy it.

The light tapping on her bedroom door let May know that Willa had come to help. "Come in," she called as she worked to get out of her black skirt.

"Mrs. Moore said you would need me."

"Yes. Are you finished with Mama?" May asked, dropping the skirt to the floor.

"I am." Willa came to her and helped her step over the pile.

"I want to wear the green silk brocade, and I'll need help with my hair. I want to pin it with the matching ribbon."

"Very good, miss. And what of the pearl drop earrings and necklace?"

The set had been a gift to May on her twenty-first birthday. "I think that would be perfect. However, we need to hurry. The dinner bell will ring in ten minutes." Willa nodded and began pulling pins from May's hair.

Their determination won the day, and when the dinner

bell sounded, May was just reviewing her reflection in the mirror. It was exactly as she had hoped. The square neckline of the bodice lay nicely, and the puffed sleeves reached to her elbows, fanning out to cream-colored lace trim. The basque waist accentuated her tiny frame, and the skirt splayed to the floor in a fuller manner than most of the straight-lined gowns of the day. It was neither too fancy nor too drab, and the color accentuated her complexion and eyes in such a way that despite its rather girlish lines, May looked very much grown up.

Willa added one final pin to her hair and then nodded. "It's beautiful. You're beautiful, miss."

"Thank you, Willa. Let's hope Mr. Munro is impressed as well."

May headed downstairs and had just stepped into the hall when the pocket doors to the front parlor opened. Lee and her father were laughing about something, but both sobered when they caught sight of her. Lee had been speaking and fell silent while May's father came forward to give her a kiss on the cheek.

"Don't you look beautiful tonight," Father said, taking her hand. He twirled her around as he might have when she was a little girl. "Sometimes I cannot believe you're all grown up."

"Nor can I." Lee's added comment was barely audible.

"Thank you for your kind words. I thought I owed it to Lee to dress a little more carefully this evening. Lately he's only seen me in my uniform."

"You looked quite lovely in that as well. However, I will admit you are stunning, and it leaves me quite speechless."

"She is stunning," Mama said from the stairs.

All gazes turned toward the older woman. Father dropped

his hold on May and went to receive his wife down the last few steps. Mama had chosen to wear a plum-colored silk with black tulle overlay. It was one of her favorite gowns.

"And so are you, my dear," Father said.

"You are beautiful, Mama." May was very happy she'd taken time to dress for their dinner. Even the men looked fine in their dark suits and ties.

"That color suits you quite well, Mrs. Parker," Lee said, offering her a smile.

"Shall we go to dinner?" Father said, tucking Mama's arm around his as she reached the floor.

"Yes, of course." Mama smiled and glanced over her shoulder. "I'm sure Lee won't mind escorting May."

"Not at all." He took hold of May in a rather possessive fashion, with his left arm slipped around her waist and his right hand taking hold of her hand. It drew her snug against his side. "Shall we?"

May nodded, afraid that if she tried to speak, the words might not come out. Everything felt stuck in her throat. How was it a simple touch could render her unable to talk?

By the time they reached the dining room, Lee maneuvered his hold to be more proper. He paused beside her chair and reluctantly let go with a sigh. At least May heard a sigh. It could have been her own.

Lee pulled out the chair for her and assisted her into it, while Father did the same for Mama. May had never felt quite so grown-up or nervous. There was no real reason for feeling this way, except that she now knew she was in love with Lee and was hopeful that he was in love with her. Just knowing her own heart, however, changed everything.

Lee watched May with special interest all evening. It was as if he were seeing her anew. She was all grown up—a beautiful woman worthy of love and affection. He thought of his earlier reservations. Worries about his parents suddenly seemed unimportant. How could he cast aside love for May just because his parents wouldn't approve? What if they did disown him? Didn't the Bible say that a man should leave his father and mother and cleave unto his wife?

By the time dessert was served, Lee had convinced himself to ask for her hand. But in the back of his mind that niggling discomfort of dishonoring his parents returned to haunt him. How could this ever work? He frowned.

"Lee, is the blackberry soufflé not to your liking?" Mrs. Parker asked.

He straightened and shook his head. "It's quite delicious, especially with the fresh whipped cream. Thank you."

"You looked momentarily distraught."

He forced a smile. "Yes, well, there is a lot on my mind. Things are very busy at work."

"I'm sure as a police detective you are ever alert to all that's going on around you," May's father replied.

Lee dabbed his mouth with the napkin. "I am trained to be and do my best to be alert. I'm happy, however, that the expo is nearly done. There have been so many problems of late, and my team is trying hard to keep everything running smoothly. The accident with the runaway trolley only added to the complications. There are those who wish to sue the expo officials, though the accident was not at all their fault. The Seattle Electric Company has been good to pay medical bills for those who were injured, but of course there are those who are still unhappy. We've had people sending their lawyers to our offices at the administration building for information to aid their cases. It's most assuredly made my job more difficult."

"And then there's Mario Bianchi," May declared. She put aside her fork and leaned forward just a bit, as if to tell a secret. "Lee thinks the man is going to try to steal the Japanese samurai armor."

"Is this true?" Mrs. Parker asked.

"I'm afraid so." Lee reached for his coffee cup. "Bianchi is an old nemesis of mine. He forges art pieces and replaces them with the copies. This way he can steal the original and no one is the wiser. At least not for a while. Sadly, I'm sure there are some paintings he's replaced that have never been found out. He's that good."

"And this man wants to forge the armor? Wouldn't that be quite an extraordinary feat?" Mr. Parker asked.

"It would, but if anyone can do it, Bianchi can. He has connections to talented but devious artisans who live for such challenges."

"How terrible. How will you find him?" Mrs. Parker asked.

"I honestly don't know. We've spotted him a couple of times at the fair, but otherwise he always manages to get away. Still, thanks to May accidentally taking a picture of him, I've been able to let others know what he looks like. My men are keeping their eyes open for any sign of him."

May's mother fixed her with a concerned look. "You saw the man?"

"Yes, Mama. But there was never any risk to me. I was sketching the armor and taking photographs of it, and he just happened to be there. He was also there another time, but again there was no threat to me whatsoever. Too many people were around for him to do anything."

Lee didn't want to correct her and further worry her mother, but Bianchi would never let the number of people around cause him distress should he need to defend himself. That was, in truth, one of the things that concerned Lee. Bianchi's need to save himself would leave him little hesitation to endanger the lives of others.

"Well, I think it might be nice for Lee and May to have a little time to themselves, don't you, Kame?" May's father said, getting to his feet. "They might prefer to talk about something other than work."

"I agree." Mrs. Parker smiled and allowed Mr. Parker to help her to her feet. "Lee, it was delightful to have you with us. I hope you'll come by more often."

Lee got to his feet. "I plan to, Mrs. Parker." He waited until they were gone from the room to turn his attention back to May. "Where would you like to go?"

"Come to my studio. I want to show you the samurai. I've made great strides with it."

Lee helped her from her chair and took hold of her arm. "I have something I'd like to discuss, as your father guessed."

She glanced up to look into his eyes. "I have something to say to you as well."

They passed through the large parlor into May's studio. She led him to the painting and stood back. "First things first. What do you think?"

Lee studied her work and nodded. "It's amazing the way you've brought it to life. What are these marks on the side of the breastplate?"

"They are the kanji for 'courage' or 'bravery.' I love that someone thought to paint them on the armor. I like to think it reminded them to be strong."

"That's quite amazing how you've captured such tiny

detail." He moved to the other side and considered the painting again. "The canvas isn't as big as you originally planned. Why did you decide to make it smaller?"

She shrugged. "I was impatient to start, and getting the larger canvas would take time. I did have Father order one, however. I still intend to make the larger one."

"Would you paint it for me?" She looked at him, and he lost himself in her emerald eyes. "For us," he whispered.

Her gaze never left his. "What are you saying?"

He took hold of her hands. "I'm in love with you, May. I want to marry you."

"I want that too. I've fallen in love with you and can't imagine my life without you."

Lee pulled her close, relishing the way she wrapped her arms around him and placed her head on his chest. He rested his chin on her head and sighed. "I don't know how we can ever make this work, but I know I will never love another as I love you." May said nothing, so Lee continued. "My parents will have nothing to do with us. You know, don't you?"

"I do," she said without moving away.

Lee never wanted to let her go. "I know your parents will approve."

"Yes," May replied. "They already love you as a son. They would be more than happy to welcome you as a son-in-law."

He raised his gaze to the ceiling. *Oh, God, why couldn't it be the same with my father and mother?* Why did they have to have so much hate in their hearts for people who were different?

"I can't help but feel like this is impossible. I don't want to dishonor them—to lose them forever, but neither can I lose you."

"You aren't going to lose me, Lee." She pulled away and

looked him in the eye. "You were the one who taught me that we serve a God of impossibilities." She gave him a crooked smile. "It would seem to me that this situation is quite impossible, so we should probably give it to Him and see what He can do with it."

"I know you're right. I know that if this is right, and I feel it must be, God can work through all the obstacles. Still, I must admit I have some fear regarding the price."

May nodded and reached for his hands. She pressed a kiss on each one. "We should probably pray—don't you think? Pray together and ask for wisdom. God gives it to all people liberally, you know."

This made Lee smile. "Without upbraiding."

Again, May nodded. "He'll show us the way."

17

Days later, May couldn't stop thinking about Lee and his declaration of love as she worked on the photographs at the Fishers' shop. She had agreed to come twice a week to the Fishers' new shop downtown when the expo closed. She would sit in the store window there and touch up photographs just as she was doing at the expo. Meanwhile, Lee would go back to working downtown as well. She couldn't help but wonder what the future would hold for them. All night long she had been restless in her sleep, and when she awoke, she would pray. There were no easy answers for their situation, but she felt confident that God could provide exactly what they needed.

The over-the-door bell rang, and a fashionably dressed gentleman entered the store. May glanced up, surprised to find Lee's older brother Liam. She only vaguely remembered him, but he bore enough resemblance to Lee that it was either him or the middle brother, Newell. There was a hard glint to his expression, just as Lee often had, but in Liam's case the look seemed cruel.

He frowned. "May Parker, I presume."

May stopped her work. "I am."

He moved closer. "Do you know who I am?"

"I believe I do. You must be Lee's eldest brother, Liam. You look too much like him not to be related. Although I suppose you could be Newell."

"I am Liam Munro." He sounded rather irritated, and May could only suppose he had come to argue with her about her feelings for Lee.

May put her brush aside and wiped her hands. "How can I help you?"

"You can leave my brother alone. Whatever feelings you have for him must be set aside. If you truly care about him, you will put an end to this notion of love and marriage."

"And exactly how would that prove that I care for him?"

Liam studied her a moment. "If Lee continues with this desire to marry you, the family will disown him. He will be forever disinherited and left to his own doings."

"Does your family care so little for him that they would cast him aside for following his heart?"

"I assure you that the family cares very much for him. Enough that we do not wish to see him embarrassed and shunned from the society of his peers for marrying a Japanese woman."

"What petty friends Lee must have if they would put him out of their company for marrying the woman he loves."

Liam all but growled. "It isn't petty. It is the way our society functions. There are rules, and those rules must be abided by in order to . . . keep order. Interracial marriage is not an acceptable concept. It creates far more problems for everyone."

"In what way?" She crossed her arms against her painting smock and stared at Liam without blinking.

"In every way. You know yourself as the child of an interracial marriage that the years were arduous and painful. You were made fun of and cast aside for being neither white nor Japanese. Would you wish that for your own children?"

May said nothing. She had considered this many times as she allowed her feelings for Lee to grow. Their children would only be one-fourth Japanese. It was possible they would bear no sign of their heritage or that their heritage would blend into a striking beauty rather than a mark of disdain. She knew what Liam was talking about—knew that she had paid a price for her parents' love. Still, she wouldn't deny them that love, even with the pain it had caused her.

"Mr. Munro, I don't believe you care what I think," May began. "However, I care deeply for Lee and am praying for him in this matter and every other that concerns him. Perhaps you would be wise to do the same and commit this matter to prayer rather than berate me."

"I have taken it to prayer and sought the Bible for guidance, which is more than I can say for my brother. The Bible makes it clear that interracial marriage is unacceptable to God."

"I do not believe that is true, Mr. Munro. I, too, have sought the Scriptures. As a Christian, it is my duty to consider every matter in light of the Word of God. I believe praying over a matter is not only important but absolutely necessary. I have also sought the counsel of our minister, who has many years of education and experience in the pulpit. He assures me the Bible does not speak against interracial marriage, and in fact, he pointed out many situations where God ordained marriages between people of different countries and peoples."

"He tells His children not to marry outside of their people in Deuteronomy."

"He told His children not to marry the people of other countries because they served other gods," May countered. "If you bother to read the context of those Scriptures, you will see that. Just as the verse about being unequally yoked is about believers partnering with nonbelievers. It has nothing to do with the color of their skin. You must remember that the Bible clearly states in First Samuel, chapter sixteen, 'For the Lord seeth not as man seeth; for man looketh on the outward appearance, but the Lord looketh on the heart.' I believe this should clarify the matter completely."

"The Bible also says that God intends for each person to stay with their own kind."

May gave him a patient smile. "If you are referencing the Scriptures in Genesis where God is creating animals, I hardly see how that is an indictment against people of different cultures marrying. Whenever God has addressed this issue, it has had to do with matters of faith. He knew how hard it would be for a person of Jewish faith to marry a worshipper of Baal and have any peace in their household. Fortunately, Lee and I both worship the God of the Bible."

Liam looked at her for a long moment as if trying to decide whether he might challenge her declaration. Instead, he turned back to the matter of their family.

"Our father and mother will never accept you as Lee's wife. You will forever set yourself against them and put Lee in an impossible position."

"I'm well aware of their feelings on the matter, and it grieves me. I am praying for them. However, any separation would be on their part and not mine. I only desire unity."

Liam pounded his fist against her small art table. The action sent brushes and paints flying and brought Addie Hanson from the back room.

"What in the world is going on here? I do hope that you intend to pay for the damages, sir."

Liam looked at the mess and reached into his coat pocket. He pulled out some money and tossed it on the counter in front of Addie. "This should be sufficient."

"Now, if you don't mind," Addie said, looking quite stern, "I must ask you to leave."

Liam looked as if he might say something in protest, but instead, he glared at May. "You have the ability to keep tragedy from befalling a good family. Perhaps you might reflect on that."

He turned and stormed from the small shop, leaving May quite shaken. She turned to Addie, who held out the money. "This is rightfully yours. You've always supplied your paints and brushes."

May shook her head. "I don't want his money."

"I heard everything that was said. I'm so sorry you had to endure that," Addie said, opening the cash register. "I'll put the money aside in here and let Mr. Fisher know what happened."

"It's no different than what I had to grow up with. I never had close friends because their parents were worried about mixing our cultures. They always took issue with me because I was part Japanese."

"People took issue with me because my father and brothers were criminals. Because of that, they were certain that I was just as worthless." Addie offered May a smile. "People will always find a reason to belittle others or find fault, especially when they're insecure in themselves. It's easy to point out that someone has a different faith or a different skin color. Simple enough to make fun of someone for being too fat or too thin, too tall or too short. It's much harder to look past the differences to the heart, as God does, but we are called to do just that."

"That's why I don't want to be angry with Liam. He has his reasons for how he thinks and believes. I feel sorry for him. He was taught to hate, and he will likely teach his children to carry on the tradition. It's heartbreaking."

"It is. I suppose all we can do is pray for their eyes to be opened," Addie replied. "And teach our own children to love as God intended."

May sighed and began picking up her paints and brushes. "I will never teach my children to look down on someone else because of their differences."

"Nor will I." Addie came around the counter and knelt to help May pick up her supplies. "I'll get something to clean up the floor." She straightened and glanced at the door. "You don't suppose he'll come back, do you? I'll be leaving in a few minutes to go be with Pearl so that Mr. Fisher can come and develop photographs."

May shook her head. "He won't be back. He made his point."

Addie touched May's shoulder. "Don't let him steal your joy. You and Lee have something wonderful. Give this trouble to the Lord and trust that He can make things right."

May wanted to believe exactly that, yet there was doubt in her heart. *But what if He doesn't?*

Mario Bianchi surveyed the work being done. The armor was coming together in good order. The average person would never guess that the piece arranged before him wasn't decades old. The men he hired were very skilled. They also knew that if they spoke about the forged armor, they'd go to jail. Bianchi was no fool, however, and wasn't about to take a chance. He was paying them enough to guarantee they'd keep their mouths shut. Plus, they knew his reputation for resolving problems and that if they didn't keep quiet, they'd end up dead.

There was something so very satisfying about that. Nothing more needed to be said or threatened. Keeping quiet might result in another opportunity to earn a large sum of money. Speaking meant certain death. What could be easier to understand?

"Boss, you wanted to see the spaulders when they were finished," a grubby-looking man said from across the room. "They're done."

Bianchi went to where the man sat. The spaulders were long pieces that fit at the shoulder and came to a point on the upper arm just above the elbow. They constituted six thick leather rows, which had been bound together and lacquered quite heavily. The workman had used his artistic capabilities to make the piece look weathered and aged. Bianchi wasn't entirely sure how the man had managed to make it look so good, but the spaulders were perfect.

"Good job, Haru. Is it ready to be assembled?"

"Yes, Boss."

Bianchi nodded. "Then let us get it done. The days are passing much too fast."

He left the man and made his way to another table, where final construction of the helmet was taking place. The gilded family crest lay beside several photographs of the real pieces. Bianchi picked up one of the photos and held it closer beside the forged piece. The match was excellent. He nodded his approval and replaced the picture on the table.

Everything was coming together. He smiled. In another week, they would change out the real armor with this beautiful forgery and settle up with Hillsboro before heading off for San Francisco, where Bianchi had another customer waiting to discuss a particular painting they desired to purchase.

Once in his makeshift office, Bianchi sat at his desk. Lee Munro was still doing his best to make Bianchi's life miserable, but it was of little matter. Let him. Munro went by the book and had little imagination. If he had, he might have made things much more difficult for Bianchi, but Munro's devotion to observing the letter of the law had served Bianchi well. They both knew exactly where they stood with each other and what the other was capable of. It had been total chance that they'd found each other again in Seattle, but soon Bianchi would be gone, and Munro would be left to figure out what had happened. With any luck, no one would understand it all until months from now. And that suited him just fine.

Of course, Munro had made things much harder. There were half a dozen plainclothes police officers posted around the armor exhibit, making it impossible for Bianchi to go there and further study the armor. He didn't like the fact that he couldn't study particular parts of the armor. It was, after all, attention to detail that would give him the edge when making the copy.

Munro also had given a copy of Bianchi's image to every ticket taker at the front entrance. It was only a drawing—but a very good drawing. At least that's what his man told him. He had gone to the expo one Saturday to see his brother, who was working there, and spotted the drawing posted at the front gates.

Bianchi had laughed when told about it, but it was a nuisance. Munro was good at creating problems and hadn't failed to impress this time around.

"Soon it will no longer matter. You can't best me, Munro. You never could." A thought came to mind. "And just to prove it, I believe I'll come to the exposition one more time."

"He's sure growing." Addie held baby Joseph and admired his long eyelashes. He was a beautiful baby and quite adored.

"One week old yesterday. I'm completely in awe of how fast he changes," Pearl said from where she sat nearby. "Even Otis thought his legs looked longer today."

"He's perfect in every way." Addie reluctantly handed him over to his mother for a feeding.

Pearl had little trouble getting him to latch on. He had taken to breastfeeding quickly and seemed quite content to do his part. The entire thing fascinated Addie, who had not grown up around babies. She wondered if she would come to motherhood as naturally as Pearl.

"How is Esther?" Pearl asked, once she had Joseph settled.

"She's doing quite well. May and I took her home from the hospital. They live quite poorly. The building is hardly better than living on the street. The outside is brick, but the interiors are quite inadequate. It reminded me of living in the Yukon, but I think when we lived in our tent, it was almost better. There are vermin running around the place, and trash is everywhere. Esther said they do what they can to clean up, but other tenants seem not to care at all."

"How sad. What a terrible place to have to live when recovering from injury."

"Yes, it's little wonder her father is so sick. Still, Esther said it was better than the hospital, where there are constant reminders of death." Addie paused and shook her head. "I'm not so certain. They don't even have electricity."

"Poor girl. I am sorry for her."

Addie tugged on her sleeve to straighten it. "Of course, she's worried about getting work. I told her the city is growing so fast, I doubt seriously that she'll have any trouble."

"And her father? Is he worse?"

"That's less clear. He seemed to be about the same when I saw him last, but Esther says he's much weaker. She doesn't believe he will last until Christmas, although she says that's his desire." Addie went to the large basket of laundry and began to sort out what needed to be ironed. She'd already set up the ironing board and heated the irons so that she could make herself useful to Pearl.

"You don't have to do that, you know."

"But I want to." Addie picked up one of Otis's shirts and spread it out on the ironing board. "I can talk and iron at the same time."

"You're so good to look after me."

"You did the same for me. I'm more than a little bit thankful for you and Otis and all the years you watched over me. I love that I can help in some way."

Pearl gazed down at her son. "I might have had Joseph in the middle of the exposition had it not been for your sweet husband carrying me to the hospital. Poor Otis certainly couldn't have managed that. You've both been so good to us with stopping by to check on us and bringing us dinners and such."

"It's our way of supporting you, as Christians are supposed to do for one another. You'll soon enough be back on your feet and have to do it for yourself. I recommend getting a housekeeper. At least part-time. You could have someone come in and clean and do laundry. Maybe even cook."

"They'll never cook as well as you, Addie. Goodness, but we miss your meals."

"And now I rarely cook at all. We have a woman to do that for us. I'm telling you, Pearl, it's not easy getting used to having help."

"Yet you're suggesting it for me."

Addie laughed. "I didn't say it was bad. Just that it's taking me time to get used to it."

Pearl stroked the baby's head. "I could never understand women wanting a nanny to watch over and care for their children. I longed to have my own baby to love. I don't want another woman raising Joseph."

"Nor would I."

Pearl glanced up. "Are you and Isaac hoping to have children soon?"

Addie ran the iron over the front of the wrinkled shirt. "We've discussed it, and whenever God chooses is fine for us. We're just happy to be together."

"You're such a perfect couple. I can't imagine you with anyone else, Addie."

"I can't either." She flipped the shirt to the back and smoothed it out before changing irons. "I can't imagine being happier, Pearl. My life is so good. When I think back on the past and all that I've gone through, I'm just so grateful for the way God has redeemed the lost time."

"God is definitely good. He always knows what we need before we ask."

"I'm praying He'll work out things for poor May. She was accosted by the man who will be her brother-in-law if she marries Lee Munro."

"Accosted?"

"Well, at least verbally, although he did make a mess when he smacked her table and sent paint and brushes flying."

"Goodness, what was that all about?"

"The Munros do not approve of Lee marrying May because she's half Japanese. They are very prejudiced. May told me that they moved away from their neighborhood when Lee was fifteen because they couldn't stand that people of other races were living around them. In particular, May's mother."

"This city is full of people like that. So many have forgotten that they, too, were once strangers in this land."

"Mr. Munro was quite adamant with May that the Bible speaks against interracial marriage, but May held her ground, quoting Scripture and defining the context of his. She's a brilliant young woman, and I can't imagine why anyone wouldn't want her in their family."

"We should pray for her, Addie. When you come here, we should pray for all of the girls. It won't be long, and they'll all go their separate ways for the most part. Bertha will come and work for us full-time, and May will be here a couple of days a week, but I think it would be so good to keep them all in prayer."

Addie picked up another iron. "That's a wonderful idea, Pearl. I would like that very much, and there is no time like the present."

Pearl shifted her son. "I agree. Let's pray."

18

Lee was anxious to meet up with May and take her to lunch. For days, he'd been battling one problem after another. He had multiple thefts of goods, an evening robbery at one of the restaurants, and several altercations to contend with. Two of which had sent men to the hospital. He hadn't been able to even leave the expo until well into the evening.

It seemed that as the exposition wound down, crime was heating up. Maybe the criminals sensed a lack of concern and regard by the owners of the shops and exhibits. He'd noticed that himself. People seemed anxious for things to just be done. So many of the foreigners with exhibits were ready to return home to their own culture and way of life. Lee couldn't fault them for that.

He approached the photography shop window and found May bent over her work. For a few moments, he just watched her. She seemed quite keen on giving the photograph's sky a wash in blue. Her hand delicately guided the brush to touch only those places where the paint was needed. May's focus was so intent that she didn't even notice that someone was watching her, or if she did, she didn't acknowledge it.

After a few minutes, Lee made his way inside, and even when the bell rang, May continued to work. One of the other Camera Girls approached him.

"Can I help you?"

"I'm just here to take May to lunch," he replied.

At this, May looked up and smiled. "Lee!"

He loved the way she said his name. It was a cross between a celebratory expression and a pledge of adoration. He had no doubt whatsoever that her love for him was real.

He offered a brief smile. "I felt bad for being gone the last couple of days. Have you time for lunch?"

"I do. I was just finishing up. Let me wash my brush and put away my paint." She gave the postcard a wave in the air before pinning it up. "This will need to dry before I can move forward on it."

He watched her deftly handle the cleanup of her station. May had always been meticulous with most any task given to her, but today she seemed especially particular. Once she had everything sorted and cared for, she stood and began unbuttoning her smock.

"Where would you like to dine?" she asked.

"I don't care. I just want to be with you." He had tossed and turned all night thinking of her and how wrong it felt not to have seen her that day. Now they were together, and all was right with the world. At least for the moment.

She seemed thoughtful as she hung up her smock. "Why don't we walk over to the Nikko Café? Even though they only have American food, I love the Japanese designs for the interior. I'll pretend we have gone to Japan."

"To a restaurant where they serve meatloaf and potatoes," he replied, grinning.

"Exactly." She laughed and took up her small purse. "Mary,

if Addie arrives before I get back, would you tell her I'll have the postcards for the Harlington family done by two?"

The girl behind the counter nodded. "I'll see to it."

May took up a patterned black-and-red jacket. Lee helped her into it, then stood back to admire her. "You are quite lovely."

"I found this jacket a few days ago tucked away in my closet. I thought it was perfect for the Camera Girl attire."

"It really is, but I think it has more to do with the woman wearing it than the cut of the piece." He opened the door and allowed May to pass through before following her out into the cloudy day.

"It's chilly out here. It wasn't all that warm in the shop, but thankfully we have a little stove, and Otis keeps it going in order to keep all of his chemicals at the proper temperature."

"I'll keep you warm," Lee said in a low tone as he put his arm around her. He wasn't generally given to public displays, but having not seen May for two days brought out the courting suitor in him. Having her in his arms made his heart beat a little faster.

May giggled and moved a little closer. "I am not opposed to that idea."

They walked to the café, where they found a crowd had already gathered. Inside, Lee quickly found them a small round table with two chairs. It was one of only two tables left. He seated May, then took the other chair for himself. Within moments the attentive waitress was at their side suggesting the special—ham steaks with potatoes and green beans.

They declined and instead ordered pot roast with potatoes and carrots, warm bread and butter, and two cups of coffee.

Once the waitress left them, Lee leaned forward and took hold of May's hand.

"I've missed you. I'm sorry we've been so busy. Every day I wanted to come by and see you, then something new would develop, and I'd find myself buried in paperwork and argumentative people."

"I missed you, too, but thank you for sending me a note of explanation. Otherwise, I might have worried." She bit her lower lip and looked down. Lee knew this was a sign that she had something she needed to tell him but was uncomfortable with the topic.

"What's going on? What is it that you need to say?" he asked.

May smiled. "Is it that obvious?"

"I'm a detective." He shrugged and gave her a reassuring smile. "I am detecting discomfort on your part."

She toyed with the edge of her coat. "Liam came to see me a few days ago."

Lee stiffened. "I can guess what he was about, but tell me anyway."

"He told me I needed to let you go, or the family would disinherit you."

"Straight and to the point. Good old Liam. I suppose he argued his points against interracial marriage."

"He did." May met his gaze. "I argued back the context and truth of God's Word." She smiled. "You know me."

"I do, and I love you." Lee gave a heavy sigh. His family seemed determined to ruin his happiness. "I won't let them tear us apart. I've been thinking long and hard on this."

"And what are you going to do?" May asked.

Just then, the waitress returned with their coffee. "The food will be right up," she told them as she left.

Lee took a taste of the strong brew more to delay his reply

than to sate any thirst. He replaced the cup on the saucer. May watched him the whole time.

He was determined to resolve this. "I intend to go to my parents and ask them why they hate Asian people so much. For truly they seem far more prejudiced against them than anyone else. I know that something happened before I was born, but no one will talk about it. It involved Liam somehow, but even he won't speak of it. I don't know if it's just too painful or if they are embarrassed by it, but the topic is never allowed. I intend to find out what happened and why it has made them so bitter."

"Do you suppose knowing will help our cause?" She lifted the cup to her lips and took a sip.

"I honestly don't know. I can't help but believe talking about what happened might loosen the hold it has on them. But then again, what do I know about it? Nothing. Nothing except that it caused great anger and a solid resolve against Chinese and Japanese people."

The waitress arrived with their food, and Lee offered a quick prayer. Looking up, he found May's head still bowed. She murmured an amen and glanced up.

She lifted her fork. "We'd best get to it before some calamity befalls us and forces you to leave."

As if speaking the words could conjure the situation, Lee noticed a man walking across the dining room. He was headed for the exit.

"Bianchi," Lee muttered and jumped to his feet. His chair fell over with a loud bang, and the room went momentarily silent as everyone gawked to see what had happened.

Bianchi's gaze met Lee's. The man had the audacity to smile before he bolted for the door. Lee lost little time in following him.

They raced across the exposition grounds. When they were back on Pay Streak Avenue, Lee nearly lost sight of the shorter man. Luckily Bianchi cut a path for one of the theater buildings, revealing himself clearly. Lee followed.

Inside, the place was dark. Lee stumbled into the auditorium, where the sound of footsteps echoed off the empty walls. His eyes adjusted quickly—in time to see Bianchi leap onto the stage. Lee raced down the aisle and took the steps two at a time to cross the stage as Bianchi disappeared behind the curtain.

Lee wrestled with the velvet draping and finally managed to step into the darkness backstage. Once again, he had to wait a pace to let his eyes adjust.

"You can't escape me forever, Bianchi," Lee called out.

"I seem to have done a good job of it so far," the man replied from what sounded like stage right.

Lee turned and headed in that direction. "I'm on to you and your interest in the Japanese armor. I figure Hillsboro has hired you."

"You figure that, eh?" This time the sound came more from the center of the stage. "I should remind you that your guesses are seldom right."

Halting his steps, Lee turned around and listened. Scuffling sounds came from behind yet another curtain. A door opening and closing? Lee tried to move as silently as possible toward the noise. When he drew near to where the sounds had seemed to originate, there was no sign of Bianchi.

"Why don't you come out and face me like a man?"

Nothing. No sound. No reply. Somehow Bianchi had managed to give Lee the slip once again. Lee looked around as best he could in the dark. He didn't even have a match to try to see where Bianchi might have gone.

His foot hit something, and Lee knelt to the ground to feel for whatever it was. His hand touched a metal ring. He gave it a pull, and the same scuffling sound proved this was where Bianchi had made his exit. The trapdoor led somewhere beneath the stage and likely to another location where Bianchi could leave unnoticed. Lee didn't bother to follow. It was of little use. The man was an expert at disappearing, and Lee had no idea what lay below.

Making his way back to the restaurant, Lee tried to figure out a way that he could catch Bianchi without risking a lot of other people's lives. Bianchi knew Lee was concerned about that. There had been many a time when Lee could have fired shots at Bianchi, but there were too many people around him. People who might have been hurt—or worse.

However, Lee did have one advantage. Bianchi needed to be at the expo. He obviously wanted to be close to the armor for the sake of getting the copy as near to correct as possible. Bianchi might even be studying the layout in order to figure a way to exchange the forged piece with the original. Surely he wasn't stupid enough to think Lee and his men wouldn't be on the guard for just such a move?

Lee found May just as he'd left her. She smiled up at him as he reclaimed his seat. "Did you catch him?"

"No. The man has an uncanny ability to disappear."

She picked up a piece of buttered bread. "Still, everyone makes mistakes. I'm sure he will and that you'll be there to catch him when he does."

Lee nodded, but he couldn't hide his disappointment. "The man has vexed me for years. After our encounter in Washington, DC, I've done what I can to keep up to date on his activities, but it isn't easy. I had to rely on reading stories in newspapers from New York and other places that have large art museums. By the time I got wind of things and wrote to the various police departments, it was old news. I don't have much hope when it comes to putting him behind bars."

"Seek the Lord, Lee. He has all the answers you need. Even regarding your family's hatred of Japanese people." She smiled and held up the bread. "This is really good. You should try it. Not a hint of sawdust."

He surprised her by leaning forward to take a bite of the piece in her hand. She was right. It was delicious. She was also right that he needed to commit the problems to God and seek His wisdom in capturing Bianchi and talking to his family.

Lee arranged to show up at his parents' house around suppertime. They generally sat down to eat around seven or eight in the evening, but tonight it was edging toward eight thirty when the bell finally rang and his parents came downstairs.

He was certain the butler had announced his presence—at least to his father—but no one had bothered to come down or send word. Lee tried his best not to be offended. His father was still quite angry regarding Glynnis, no doubt. Lee had received a wire from her. She and David had reached Chicago and were comfortably settled. It made him glad that at least someone had achieved their dreams of a happily ever after.

Making his way into the dining room, Lee hoped his planned questions wouldn't cause too much upset. He hadn't been invited to dine, and he didn't want to further stir their ire. On the other hand, he needed to understand their bitterness, and putting them in a situation where they would have to endure him or miss out on their dinner seemed one way in which he could manage the situation. It was rude of him, but at the moment, he simply didn't care.

Neither his mother nor father seemed surprised to see him, and the dining table was laid for three. This confirmed that the butler had announced his presence and that his parents had asked for another place to be set.

"Good evening, Leander," his mother said, coming to where he stood. She raised her cheek to him, and Lee gave her a kiss.

"Good evening, Mother."

"Lee, to what do we owe this . . . surprise?" his father asked, taking his place at the head of the table.

Lee assisted his mother into the seat at his father's right, then claimed the one on his left. "I thought it might be good to come and discuss a few things."

The kitchen maid immediately brought the soup. It looked to be some sort of creamy chowder. A good choice for a chilly day.

"Would you like me to offer grace?" Lee asked.

His father nodded, and Lee bowed his head. "Father, we thank You for the food we are about to eat, and for Your faithfulness to us. Help us, Father to be able to talk to one another without anger and bitterness. In Jesus's name, Amen."

He glanced up to find his father watching him with an odd expression. "What are you suggesting?"

"Sir?" Lee knew what he was getting at but wanted a moment to think through his response.

"You pray for the ability to talk without anger or bitterness. Why should you pray for such a thing? This family has always managed to communicate in a reasonable manner."

"At times. But only when the topic was to everyone's liking," Lee answered. He sampled the chowder and smiled. "The soup is very good."

His father refused to give way. "I don't like it being supposed that there would be less than civil discussion at my dinner table. What is it you have in mind to talk about?"

Lee decided to just come forward with his plans. "I want to marry May Parker. I'm in love with her. I have been since I was a boy."

His mother gasped. "She's Japanese."

"Yes, she is—half. She's also half white. She's an American, born and raised in this country the same as you, Father, and me. She's a Christian who gave her heart to Jesus years and years ago. She's also an accomplished artist. May is many things and all of them good."

"You will not disgrace this family by marrying a woman of Japanese blood," his father replied in a calm, even voice. "The matter is not open for further discussion."

"I hate to be contrary, but I will not allow you to dismiss me quite that easily."

His father's eyes narrowed. "It is my table and my house. You will abide by my rules."

"Very well." Lee put down his spoon. "Then perhaps another topic would interest you more. I want to know why you hate the Japanese and Chinese so much. I know something happened before I was born—something that no one will speak of. I want to know what it was that caused such hatred."

Lee's mother looked worried. She dabbed the napkin to her lips. "Perhaps you should explain to him, my dear. It has been a great many years."

"It's none of his concern," his father fairly growled.

"I believe it is," Lee said. "It has tainted this family, followed us down through time. Everyone knows of the Munro family's bitter hatred of those with Asian origins. I want to know why. I think given the fact that I've had to live under this shadow, I should be allowed to know its cause."

Lee leaned forward in his chair and fixed his father with a stare he might have given when interrogating a criminal. He knew he could be intimidating and hoped his father was at least a little unnerved by Lee taking this stand.

For several long minutes, no one said a word. Lee could hear the faithful ticking of the grandfather clock and the occasional sound of clatter coming from the kitchen, but otherwise there was silence. Finally, his mother spoke up.

"Please, Artimus, just tell him what happened."

Lee could see that his father wasn't at all happy with Mother's request. He sat staring into space for the longest time, but finally he spoke.

"Your brother Liam was thirteen and worked that summer at the cannery. I had put him in charge of a group of young men who were new to the company. They were young . . . Japanese, a few Chinese as well." His father's voice remained monotone. "They were given the simplest of jobs, washing the fish. Liam oversaw this process and even at thirteen was a quality leader. But of course, the Japanese were an unruly bunch. The young men resented taking instruction from someone even younger than themselves. There was trouble almost immediately, even though I made it clear anyone causing problems would face immediate dismissal." He paused, looking uncomfortable. "Is it really all that important that you know every detail?"

Lee was surprised by his father's question. "If it pertains to why you hate the Japanese and Chinese, then, yes, I'd like to know the details."

Lee's father looked at his wife. She nodded, and he gave a grunt of dissatisfaction. "Very well. Liam took issue with how the cleaning was being handled. He pointed out problems and made the men redo several batches of fish. Of course, this caused problems farther down the line. When the cleaning job was still unsatisfactory, Liam warned that he would fire the men. They rose up against him and became aggressive. Liam was not concerned with their threats and dismissed them. One of the men hit Liam. This caused others to join in. They beat him to within an inch of his life, Lee. Beat him. The son of their employer!

"Some of the other workers came to the rescue and stopped them, but Liam was already near death. The police were summoned, and the workers involved were arrested, while Liam was taken to the hospital. We thought we would lose him."

Mother sniffed back tears and nodded. "He was just a boy, and they had been so cruel."

Lee had never heard Liam utter even a word of this story. "Why wasn't I told about this before now?"

"Why should you be? It was a black moment in our family's history. Once I was assured that Liam would survive, I went back to the cannery and fired every last Japanese man I could find. The Chinese immigration was already being limited by the Exclusion Act of 1882, and I was determined there would be no more Asians in my employ. I hired Mexicans and blacks, Indians, even, but no more Chinese or Japanese. Can you imagine how we felt later when we learned that a white man and his Japanese wife had taken up residence next door to us? It was added insult to our injury."

"You can hardly blame all Asians for the actions of a few men. You had others in the factory who stopped the fight

226

and saved Liam's life. Shouldn't they have been rewarded instead of punished by losing their jobs?"

"You don't understand, and I never expect you to," his father said, picking up his spoon. He sampled the soup and slammed down the spoon. "This is cold!" The maid came immediately to remove it.

"I have tried to understand, but the Parkers were in no way responsible for what happened. May and her family were only ever good to you and Mother. They are kind people who refrain from prejudice and judgment, even when being judged so harshly. I intend to marry May, and I don't want her to suffer because of something that happened nearly thirty years ago. The wrongs of one person, or even several, should not condemn an entire race."

"I will never allow a son of mine to marry a Japanese woman," his father said, his voice low and even. "If you marry her, you will no longer be my son."

Lee looked at his mother, then returned his gaze to Father. "And there is nothing I can do or say to change your mind?"

"Nothing."

Lee folded his napkin and placed it on the table. "Then I suppose this is good-bye."

His mother broke down in tears, sobbing softly into her napkin. Lee hated breaking her heart further, but it was her own prejudices and holding on to the past that were responsible.

"I find it difficult to imagine that a parent could reject their child because they didn't see things their way. It seems petty and unfeeling." Lee got to his feet. "Just know that I hold no malice or ill will toward either of you. I will always love you." He frowned at the thought that they would no longer be a part of his life. Still, he couldn't choose them over May.

"I will continue to pray for you as well. My heart's desire is that God would help you to see the truth of this matter."

Neither of his parents said a word as he walked from the room. Lee hoped the shock of the moment would bring about repentance, but he doubted it. Only God could change their bitterness into kindness . . . their hate into love.

19

"Mr. Hillsboro, I'm so glad you could come," Mario Bianchi declared as he let the tall, lean man into the warehouse.

"I was intrigued to be sure. You said the piece is nearly done. You're ahead of schedule."

"I am, yes." Bianchi smiled with great satisfaction. "My men and I have worked night and day to ensure the creation of this armor. We have managed to finish early. Well, we're nearly finished. We have touch-ups to do. It should be ready tomorrow, right on your original schedule."

"I want to see it."

Bianchi motioned toward another door. "That's why you are here. Come this way."

He headed through a room filled with old pieces of machinery. The place was filthy and smelled foul. Disrupted by human beings, rats skittered about in a frantic swirl, startling Hillsboro. Bianchi ignored it. He had found the rats and odors tended to discourage those who might want to snoop around.

"This small warehouse has proven useful to me in every way." He opened the door and walked into another room of machinery. This room was a little more organized, but not by much.

"What is this place?" Hillsboro asked, taking out his handkerchief and dabbing his nose. Apparently, the smell was too much for him.

Bianchi might have laughed, but the situation was far too important. "It is a repair shop, as you've probably already guessed. A friend of mine offered to rent it out to me since he was closing up the business."

"A repair shop for what?"

"For whatever needed repair," Bianchi answered in a sarcastic fashion. He turned and gave Hillsboro shrug. "Everything from furnaces to wagon frames. If it needed fixing, they gave it a shot. But now my friend is moving away and no longer needs the warehouse. I made arrangements to rent it for our particular needs."

He led Hillsboro through the room and around a large winch. Behind that was another door. Inside this room, Bianchi made his way to a row of shelving for machinery parts awaiting attention. Near the far end, he reached up and gave the shelf a nudge. The case didn't move easily, but Bianchi finally managed to slide it enough that the wall behind it was accessible.

"What are you doing?" Hillsboro demanded.

"You'll soon see." Bianchi reached over to one of the shelves and took up a pry bar. He wedged it into a spot where two wooden boards came together. It looked as if it were nothing more than part of the wall, but the effort soon uncovered an opening. Bianchi reached into the darkness and pushed open a door no more than four feet tall.

"Follow me," Bianchi said as he put the pry bar back on the shelf. He entered through the small door, bending nearly double to fit through. He knew it would be even more difficult for Hillsboro but only smiled. He rather enjoyed dispersing discomfort on those who irritated him.

Bianchi signaled to one of several men who awaited them on the other side. "Go guard the entrance."

The small Japanese man nodded and hurried past Hillsboro, who straightened to his full height.

"What in the world is all of this about?" Hillsboro demanded to know. He looked around. "Are these men living here?"

Bianchi gestured toward the cots, table, and chairs. "Of course they are. This job required working around the clock. There's a small bathroom off the back of the room and running water, along with a vented stove. Although they are allowed to cook only at night, when no one will catch sight of the smoke. I have worked hard to secure this place. This room doesn't even have windows. We work with the help of lamps and reflectors. But we've managed to get the job done. As you can see, the armor is nearly complete."

Hillsboro crossed the room to get a closeup look at the red-black-and-gold samurai armor. "It's beautiful."

"I agree," Bianchi said. "One of my best efforts. The men I've hired are all very good at what they do. They know not only the necessary craft but also how to get their hands on antiquated pieces of leather, silk, and metals. And they know how to keep their mouths shut."

Hillsboro leaned closer to the armor. "I can hardly wait until I possess the real piece." He reached out to touch one of the lacquered pieces.

"Don't!" Bianchi moved forward to stop him. "Some of the pieces are still drying."

Hillsboro looked surprised at Bianchi's declaration. He

stepped back and dabbed the cloth to his nose once more. "I forgot myself for a moment. The piece mesmerizes me."

"It's a good thing you don't have to work on it then," Bianchi said.

"When will it be ready to move?"

"Tomorrow. Evening." Bianchi crossed his arms. "I'll have it exchanged for the real one as we planned. We'll crate the original, taking every effort to protect it for shipping. I'll have it in storage at the train station, where you can acquire it for your trip back to New York."

Hillsboro glanced around the room. "How will you ever get it out of here?"

Bianchi laughed. "I have another door boarded up behind the tables over there. When the time comes, we'll easily get the crate out and off to the expo. I have everything calculated and planned. Have no fear."

"That's absolutely perfect." Hillsboro rubbed his hands together. "We'll be able to see the response of the expo attendees and the Japanese government. If they accept your piece as the real armor, then we will have little trouble proceeding." He let out a laugh. "The intrigue and planning are almost as rewarding as knowing I'll have the armor in my collection."

"I expect the balance of the money to be in my account by morning. I will check with the bank, and if all is as it should be, then we'll exchange the piece after midnight. That will allow it to be on display for the fifteenth and sixteenth. Although, I'd much rather wait until the armor is packed for shipping back to Japan. You may find the intrigue rewarding, but I do not."

"Isn't it more of a thrill to see them all fooled? I intend to visit the replica and hear the talk being bandied about.

There's something deeply satisfying in pulling the wool over the eyes of so many. Thoroughly exciting, wouldn't you say?"

"There is a satisfaction, I will agree." Bianchi knew the location of each of his forged paintings, and there was a sort of thrill in seeing them on the walls of grand museums, fooling the world. But with Munro hovering, Bianchi was more of a mind to err toward caution where the art piece was concerned.

"We will display it, and the world will stroll by, oohing and ahhing at your creation, while the ancient piece is safely packed away, awaiting my attention. It's all so very gratifying."

"For me, the payment will be the most gratifying for the moment."

"I'll see to it that the money is put into your account today, Mario. You will have your money and satisfaction." Hillsboro laughed and put the handkerchief under his nose.

Bianchi nodded. "It's always a pleasure doing business with you, Mr. Hillsboro. Let us leave this place and coordinate our final exchange."

May sat quietly sketching in the large parlor while her father shared various articles from the paper with her and her mother. It was one of her favorite ways to pass the evening. Usually, once Father finished with the stories he thought would most interest his ladies, he would pull out the Bible and begin reading from there.

"I think it will be interesting to see what is left behind," Father said as he concluded an article about the end of the exposition. The article spoke of how an immediate teardown would begin to rid the university campus of the temporary buildings, while great care would be made to keep the beautiful landscaping and the few permanent buildings that had been a part of the original contract agreement.

"I think the plans for the university and the overall growth of the city will see that area flourishing," Father said, folding the paper and setting it aside. He reached for his Bible. "Shall we move right ahead with where we left off last night?"

"Oh, please do," Mama said. She had been working on a piece of embroidery and paused to adjust the hoop.

May studied the two of them for a moment. They were quite content with their situations. This was their favorite time of the evening, just as it was May's. She turned to a new page and began to sketch her mother.

"I believe we were about to start Psalm one hundred twelve."

"Yes, that's right," Mama said, smiling.

A knock sounded at the front door, and May straightened in her chair. Had Lee decided to make a surprise appearance? She glanced at the clock. It seemed too late for him to come calling. In fact, it was quite late for any visitors.

Mrs. Moore knocked lightly, then opened the pocket doors. "Mr. and Mrs. Munro have asked to speak to you."

"Show them in," Father said, getting to his feet.

May and Mama did the same, putting aside their personal work. May knew this most likely wouldn't be a pleasant matter and breathed a silent prayer for God to take charge of the moment.

"Mr. Munro, Mrs. Munro," Father said, stepping forward. "How nice to see you again. Won't you be seated?"

The twosome exchanged a look, then moved to take a seat on the settee. May cast a sidelong glance at her mother and gave a slight raise of her shoulders at her mother's quizzical look.

"You have a very lovely parlor, Mrs. Parker," Lee's mother spoke up. "I expected to find Japanese décor, however."

"Thank you for your kind words. I find these American furnishings to be quite refreshing."

"Yes, but you're Japanese. I would have expected you to . . . well, I don't know. Promote, I suppose. Yes, I would expect you to promote your own culture."

May bit her lip to keep from blurting out a comment. She was determined not to shame her parents by arguing with the Munros.

"My culture has caused me a great deal of pain and regret," May's mother said, never looking away from the couple. "As you probably can guess, people can be quite cruel."

Silence rained down on the room as Mrs. Munro looked to her husband and said nothing more.

"To what do we owe the pleasure?" Father asked as the family took their chairs.

"This isn't a pleasurable situation, I assure you," Mr. Munro began. "We have come to ask that your daughter release her claim on our son Lee."

"Ask or demand?" Father questioned.

Mr. Munro's face reddened. "I have no desire to quibble over words. The matter is quite serious, and after speaking to our son, we felt it important to put this matter to rest."

"I see. And what matter are we talking about?" Father asked.

May folded her hands and tried her best not to speak out, but she was angry. Angry that they would come at such a late hour with their demands. Angry that they would ignore the pain they had caused her mother. And angry that they would bring their hate into this home of love.

"The matter of Lee and May getting married. We won't have it." Mr. Munro glared at May. "We cannot talk sense to our son, so we have come to encourage your daughter to be reasonable about this."

Father leaned back in his chair. "Well, I've never known May to be anything but reasonable. She gives careful thought to all of her decisions, giving them to prayer and seeking God's counsel. Have you done that yet?"

"Mr. Parker, this is a grave matter that cannot be allowed to continue. If our son marries your daughter, it will be an end to his relationship with us. We will cast him from the family, and while he isn't a first son, he is entitled to a sizable inheritance that he will not receive should he defy us in this."

"So the price of your son following his heart will be your alienation." Father spoke matter-of-factly and pressed his fingertips together. "That is a steep price indeed."

"We tried to make him see reason, but he will not. His brother has tried to talk to him. Liam even tried to speak with your daughter, and all to no avail. I want you to insist that May put an end to this once and for all."

"And why would I do that?" Father asked. "I happen to care for your son. He is a wonderful young man, and I would be proud to have him marry our daughter. He would be quite welcome in this family, and while I don't suppose we can ever leave him the grand inheritance that you might, I can assure you he will be blessed in love."

"Bah! Love is immaterial. Lee is on the precipice of losing all social standing, family connections, and the respect of his peers."

"And why would his peers lose respect for him?" Father pressed.

"Because of his choice of bride. A Japanese wife would never be welcomed by his friends."

"Then perhaps he needs new friends," Father suggested. He shifted his weight and crossed his arms. "It occurs to me that you should be proud of a young man who doesn't simply follow the dictates of a crowd. Lee is no man's fool. We have shared many conversations of late, and he has given a great deal of thought to his future."

"You may not approve of our social circle, Mr. Parker, but it is the society we have chosen and cherish. There are rules to every society, as you well know. I'm very certain you suffered rejection and other opinions from your own peers when it was learned that you took a wife who was not of your race."

"The human race was all that interested me," May's father said with a smile. "That and love. True love. My wife's love for me is epic, and mine for her will never end." He glanced at May's mother, and his smile broadened. "She is the light of my life and the most precious of all the blessings God has given me, along with May."

His words softened May's anger. How fortunate she was to have such love and protection. Her parents had always been there for her with great love and support. She thought of the horrors Addie Hanson had endured. From what little she knew of the woman's past, May knew she hadn't had a loving family. How blessed May was to have never known that kind of pain and betrayal. Mama and Father had always defended and encouraged. Their affection for her was strong and safe. Just like God's.

"I didn't want to do this, but I will do whatever it takes," Mr. Munro said, reaching into his coat pocket. He produced his wallet. "I will pay you, Miss Parker. Pay you whatever you want. If I haven't the sum with me, I will have it delivered first thing in the morning."

May's mouth dropped open before she could stop it. How dare this man try to buy her off. "I'm sorry, Mr. Munro, but my love for Lee isn't something you can pay me to give up. I'm quite insulted to think you would stoop to such low levels."

"I see nothing low about buying what you want. Name your price, Miss Parker."

"There is no price you can put on love." May glanced at her mother, who smiled and nodded. May felt strengthened by her mother's approval. "Do you honestly want to deny your son happiness—true love?"

Mrs. Munro looked away. Mr. Munro, however, was not to be put off. "Feelings. Emotions. They aren't the reality of life. Jeremiah chapter seventeen, verse nine states that 'the heart is deceitful above all things, and desperately wicked: who can know it?' Not only that, but the Bible makes it clear that children should obey their parents—that they should honor them."

"Ephesians six, I believe," May replied. "To be followed by verse four, stating, 'And, ye fathers, provoke not your children to wrath: but bring them up in the nurture and admonition of the Lord.' It would seem to me that this is a definite provoking. If Lee knew you were here, there would be a great deal of wrath, I assure you."

"May, we will not have a war of Scriptures," her father said, giving her a smile with his admonishment. He looked at Mr. Munro. "We are well aware of the Bible's teachings, and because of that, we know of no reason our two children should not be joined together."

"But there are Scriptures that stand against marrying other than your own kind. For example—"

May's father held up his hand. "As I said, we are not going to have a battle here tonight where we throw Bible verses out of context and look only at surface meanings. The Bible is the Word of God and should be admired and taken with the greatest of respect. I find so many people look only for verses that they can hurl at each other like spiritual rocks in slings."

"There is nothing wrong with quoting the Bible," Mr. Munro spat back. "It is the source of our faith."

"I agree, and as such we will maintain the deepest respect for it." May's father stood. "I would encourage you to reflect on the Word and your heart. We will do the same."

"I do not need to reflect on anything." Mr. Munro got to his feet. "I'm an elder at my church. I know my Bible. I assure you that God will not sanction a marriage between my son and your daughter."

May's father gave a slow nod. "Why don't we let God speak for Himself? I encourage you to go home and pray about this matter. Pray and read the Bible in full context of those verses you are so sure condemn. God is faithful and will reveal His will and ways if we but ask."

Mr. Munro opened his mouth, then closed it again. He assisted Mrs. Munro to her feet. They moved to the open doorway, and only upon reaching the foyer did Mr. Munro bother to stop and look back.

"I know the will of God, and it is not for my son to marry your daughter."

Mrs. Moore appeared with the man's hat and Mrs. Munro's cloak. He snatched both from the housekeeper and waited for her to open the front door while he put the cloak around his wife's shoulders. With one final piercing gaze directed at May, he turned and led his wife from the house.

May gave a shiver. How could she marry Lee with such

unabashed hatred from his parents? How could she force him to choose between her and them? She loved him. There was no denying her feelings, but in the back of her mind, she was also tormented by knowing she would be forced to explain to their children that she was the reason they could never see their father's parents.

"That was most unpleasant," Father said, reaching to help May's mother up from her chair. "I'm sorry that you two had to endure such a thing."

It was then that May saw tears streaming down her mother's face. Father pulled Mama close and held her as she cried.

May shook her head and jumped up from her chair. "I can't bear this."

20

May strolled through the Japan building late in the day. The exposition would close tomorrow and take all of these wonderful exhibits away. How she would miss them and Mr. Akira. Of course, she could visit him at his son's restaurant in Japantown, but she would miss the silk displays and the photographs of Tokyo and Mount Fuji. She hoped, even prayed, that she might be able to visit it all one day.

She stood once again in front of the samurai armor and smiled. It was such an amazing piece. She remembered her father said there were many exhibits of armor at the museum in Tokyo. Perhaps she and Lee could one day visit there together.

Thoughts of Lee caused a frown. She was quite concerned about her future with him. The Munros' late-night visit still haunted her. She hadn't told Lee about it. She had prayed about whether to say anything to him. Perhaps Father should be the one to talk to him and explain what had transpired.

It was so hard to imagine what God's will was in all of this. May had prayed almost continually through that first night, unable to sleep because of the blatant hatred in Mr. Munro's tone. Still, she wasn't at all sure what God wanted her to do. Did honoring one's parents mean following their demands? Surely when the demands went against God's Word, it wasn't necessary to obey them. Couldn't a person honor their father and mother simply by not speaking out against them or revealing their shame?

She had spoken briefly to her father about the matter over breakfast. He had been encouraging. He didn't think it was wrong for Lee and May to marry. He said he would always love Lee as a son whether they wed or not. May rather liked that, not that she was about to give up on becoming Lee's wife, but the fact that her father loved Lee meant a great deal.

The Japanese armor drew other viewers as May stood in silent contemplation. Perhaps those visitors would believe she was considering the artistry of the armor. Or maybe the code of the samurai. She smiled at the thought that they might note she was Japanese and wonder if the armor played some role in her life.

Thoughts of Japan once again came to mind. May knew there were family members still there somewhere—cousins whom she might be able to visit. They might only speak Japanese, though. Perhaps her mother could accompany May to Japan. Maybe they could all go. The expense would be quite high, and if Lee's family were truly to disinherit him, there would be no wealth to spare on something as extravagant as a trip to Japan. She could talk her father into paying for the trip instead of a lavish wedding. Not that she had ever had in mind to pursue an elaborate ceremony.

Again, she frowned. It was just so hard to believe that Lee's parents would not come to terms with the situation and give their blessing. Lee was their third child, true, but he was still their own flesh and blood. Couldn't the Munros find it in their hearts to let love triumph?

"It's such an interesting artifact," one of two men studying the samurai armor declared.

"I agree. Such a magnificent example. Just look at the detailed work on the breastplate."

May glanced to where the symbols for courage were drawn, wondering if the two men knew what they meant. She blinked. They were missing. She then studied the armor overall, giving extra concentration to specific areas. This wasn't the original armor. Just as Lee had feared, Bianchi had replaced the authentic Japanese armor with a very good copy.

She momentarily considered the people in the room to see if anyone else had noticed the forged piece. The two men were deep in conversation about the age of the armor and the history surrounding the times. They seemed to know quite a bit about Japan and its culture, but they hadn't noticed the armor was a fake. No one seemed the wiser about it.

May knew it was important to find Lee as soon as possible. She hurried from the room, passing Mr. Akira without a word. No doubt he would wonder at her rudeness. She would explain it to him later.

Making her way to the administration building, May wondered when Bianchi had managed to exchange the armors. The security was tight on the exposition grounds. Lee and the expo officials had seen to that. It wouldn't have been an easy feat at all. He would have had to bring the forged armor onto the grounds and to the Japan building unnoticed, then remove the glass case, switch the armor, and sneak off the grounds again, taking the original armor with him—all without arousing suspicion from the guards.

"May, are you heading back to the photography shop?" Mary asked, coming from the opposite direction.

"No. Something has happened, and I must find Lee. It's official police business."

Mary's eyes widened. "What's happened?"

"I can't talk about it just yet, but I'll return to the shop when I can. I'm sorry." May picked up her pace and all but ran the rest of the way to the administration building. She raced up the stairs and made her way inside. Fortunately for her, Lee was just coming down the interior stairs. He was studying a paper in his hands but looked up when she called his name.

"Lee, come quick. We have a big problem." She reached for his arm.

"What's wrong?"

May looked around at the various people coming and going. "Let me tell you outside. We must get back to the Japan building."

"Is it Bianchi?"

She nodded and led him outside and down the stairs. "But not in person. Lee, he's changed out the samurai armor. At least I think it must have been him."

"How do you know?" Lee paused at the bottom of the stairs.

"The kanji for courage are missing on the breastplate. The piece has to be a forgery."

"They were quite small as I recall."

She nodded. "Yes, but they're not there now, so the armor must have been exchanged for this copy."

Lee pulled her along and made haste to reach the Japan building. May had trouble keeping up with his long-legged strides, but once they were standing in front of the armor case, she took the time to regain her breath. She pointed to the dou.

"See, they're not there."

"How could he have done this?" Lee glanced around the room. "I had guards posted everywhere. I was especially attentive to this area."

"I don't know. I wondered the same myself. It would have been quite the task. He did an amazing job on the forgery, however, so I suppose the exchange was just one more point of consideration."

Lee studied the armor. "He does incredible work. The man is very talented. Pity it isn't something he uses for good."

"We need to tell the Japanese officials," May said. She knew that wasn't a job Lee was going to like.

He released a heavy breath. "I'll go now. Stay here and keep an eye out for Bianchi. He might show up to see how the armor is being received."

May nodded and watched him walk away. There was a hint of defeat in the way he carried himself. Others wouldn't have noticed it, but May knew him too well. He blamed himself. And if he was unable to retrieve the original armor, he would continue to blame himself until he could right the situation. He took his job very seriously.

As she waited, May noticed a variety of people, but none of them were Bianchi. She wondered what she would do if she saw him. It would probably be impossible to hide her recognition of the man. She couldn't maintain a stern-yet-stoic expression like Lee could. Her feelings were never easy to hide. Mama once said she wore her heart on her sleeve and her feelings in her expression.

It wasn't but a few moments before Lee returned with one of the Japanese officials. May wondered if it was the same man who had asked Lee to check her out when she was spending so much time with the armor. She stepped aside as they approached.

"As you can see, the kanji is missing from the breastplate," Lee pointed out.

The older man leaned closer to the display case. "It is. This is not our armor."

"No," Lee replied. "It's exactly as I feared, and I believe Mr. Hillsboro has probably had something to do with it. He probably hired Mr. Bianchi to make a copy of the original armor."

"The armor was a copy to begin with." The man straightened. "We did not believe the original would be strong enough to endure such a long trip to America. We worried the voyage might be overly rough due to storms." He looked at May and then to Lee. "But we want our copy back. This forgery is not nearly as good as the original. We used actual pieces of old, incomplete armors to create the one we displayed. It was altered and made over with some difficulty, and we intend to keep it. I hope you will seek out this Mr. Bianchi and reclaim our property."

"I intend to try," Lee said. "In the meanwhile, what would you like me to do to help you here?"

"Nothing," the man replied. "The forged piece is good enough to display for the day. We'll pack it up tonight after the building closes."

May could see that the entire matter was greatly troubling to the official. She wanted to offer some sort of comfort, but nothing came to mind. How could she hope to assure him that Bianchi would be caught when he had proven himself a master of escape?

"Come on," Lee said to May. "I've got to get back to

the administration building and let them know what's happened."

May followed him from the building, knowing there was nothing she could say to offer him any comfort either. She prayed instead, asking God to give Lee success in recovering the copy the Japanese had made and catching the men responsible for the entire situation. As she prayed, something came to mind.

"Lee, do you remember the Tamuras, who hired me to paint the picture of the armor?"

"Of course." He was probably ten steps ahead of her and stopped so she could catch up. "I'm sorry. I need to move quickly on this."

"I understand. The Tamuras said the armor had been in their family. Given that it's a compilation of pieces, it can't possibly have been a part of their family lineage. They must have been in on this."

"Good point. I'll send someone to find them. Now I'd better hurry."

She nodded. "Go. I'll see you later." He turned and sprinted off through the crowd without another word.

May watched until he had completely disappeared into the sea of people. She loved him so much. She had no doubt that the men he was seeking would be dangerous—perhaps even deadly.

God, please keep him safe.

She made her way back to the camera shop and noted that it was nearly time to close. When she came inside, May found most of the Camera Girls were already bringing back their cameras for the day. It was their last day—at least for their routine procedures. Addie Hanson was there as well, and Otis Fisher stood to the far side of the counter.

"As you know, this was our last day to take photographs. Tomorrow we will focus on camera sales and last-minute purchases of previously taken photographs," Addie explained. "Tonight, Mr. Fisher will finish with the undeveloped film, and the photographs will be available at the counter. Most of you will be free to roam around the expo one last time. I will be here to handle the sales, and Bertha will help with anything else.

"I just want to commend each of you girls for the wonderful job you did this summer. I want to let you know that Esther is doing quite well. I saw her yesterday, and she is clearly on the mend." She smiled, appearing quite pleased with everything. "Oh, and don't miss out on coming in at the same time tomorrow before you go strolling about. Mr. Fisher has a surprise for each one of you, and you won't want to miss out on the fun."

The girls began to whisper to each other, and even May couldn't imagine what was planned. Perhaps Mrs. Fisher would come to show off the baby, though that hardly seemed like the personal kind of surprise Addie suggested.

Addie picked up some of the souvenir business cards they handed out to customers. "I want each of you to have one of these for your memory books, and because it has the Fishers' new address. They live upstairs over the shop." She gave each girl a card.

May took one and gave Addie a nod. She had so very much enjoyed getting to know the young woman.

"Pearl and I have discussed our desire to stay in touch and to pray for one another. In keeping with this, Pearl has suggested we have a regular time of prayer at her house. We know, of course, that you will have jobs to keep up with and other responsibilities, but we will meet at Pearl and Otis's upstairs home on Saturday mornings at nine. If you can come, please do. If you can't come every week, that's still all right. Come when you can. And if nothing else, stop by the shop and just let us know how you're doing and how we can pray for you."

"This is a wonderful idea." Mary turned to Bertha. "I was feeling envious of you because you would be working for the Fishers full-time, but this will allow me to go on being a part of the family."

"I'm quite excited," May said. "Prayer is such an intimate and wonderful thing. To share it with my friends here would be a true blessing."

"Exactly," Addie said, finishing with the card dispersal. "Pearl and I know the power of prayer. Many of you do as well. We want to tap into that power and see all of us made better for the time we spend praying for one another."

"But I don't go to the same church that you go to," one of the newer girls said, looking rather skeptical.

"You serve the same God, Anna. We Christians are the church. We are the body, each one working at the things God has given us to do. Each of us supporting the other parts. If you serve the God of the Bible, with Jesus as your Savior, we are one body. Never forget that."

May smiled and nodded. Some of the other girls did likewise. It warmed May's heart to see her Christian sisters in agreement. She had made more than acquaintances while working here. She had made friends—friends in Christ who would pray for her and share the burdens she carried. The truest blessing of Christian fellowship.

21

May was still thinking about the closure of the expo the next day and had just finished packing her paints when a boy arrived at the shop with a message for her. She opened the note and read it.

Need your help. Meet me at the front gate right away.

Lee

The fact that he was asking for her help sent a momentary wave of pride through May. How wonderful that he trusted her to be able to lend him the aid he needed.

"Lee needs my help with something," she told Addie. "I'll be here tomorrow. At least I plan to be." The situation with the missing armor gave her some concern that perhaps Lee would need her to continue helping him tomorrow.

"What's going on?" Addie asked.

Thankfully the rest of the girls were busy on the other side of the room talking to Mr. Fisher. May lowered her voice. "Someone stole the Japanese samurai armor on display in the Japan building and left a forgery."

"How in the world did they do that?"

May shrugged. "Lee's trying to figure all of that out right now. I think he may want my help in finding that older Japanese couple I made the painting for. They must have had something to do with it."

"How awful. Well, I'll let Mr. Fisher know you've gone. Please be careful." Addie's expression betrayed her concern.

"I will be. Don't worry. Lee has it all in hand." She gestured to her things on the table. "I'll take those home tomorrow." She took up her cloak and pulled it on.

"I'll be praying for you both," Addie said, touching May's shoulder. "That couple may be older, but they could still be dangerous. Don't go into the situation without caution."

"Lee is a very cautious man. I'm sure he will have everything well thought-out."

Addie nodded and dropped her hold. "I'll pray just the same."

May headed out of the shop. It made her uneasy that Addie was so upset. She had to concede that Addie knew more about threatening situations and had reason to be afraid for May. Still, May knew Lee to be very protective—especially of her.

It wasn't very far from the shop to the front gate. May searched through the throng of people. Lee wasn't anywhere to be found. She made her way toward the gates and found a place out of the main flow where she could stand and watch the people coming and going. Hopefully she'd be easy to spot.

It had been an amazing exposition, and May would miss coming here to work. It had been so interesting to meet new people and interact with them while they watched her paint. She hadn't experienced a lot of negativity related to her Japanese heritage, and that had come as a pleasant surprise. Maybe since people knew the Japanese had a hand in the exhibitions and activities, they had looked beyond her appearance or even expected it.

So why couldn't people look beyond it all the time? Why couldn't Lee's parents accept her for who she was? She wanted to be their friend—wanted to love them as she loved Lee. How could they hate her without even knowing who she was?

"Don't move." The voice came from behind just as May felt something hard ram against her back.

"That hurt," she protested, trying to turn.

The man shoved the hard piece against her again. "I told you not to move."

May wasn't about to tolerate whatever this man had in mind. "I'm waiting for someone, so you'd do well to move on."

"You're waiting for me," the man replied. "Although you think you're waiting for Lee Munro."

A sickening feeling started in May's stomach. "Mr. Bianchi?"

"The one and only," he answered, sounding rather amused by her deduction. "I sent you the note to meet here at the gate. I'm glad to see you're very prompt and obedient."

"What do you want?" May tried to think of what she could do to escape the situation. People were everywhere. What could Bianchi want from her?

"I want you to listen very carefully my instructions. There are a great many people here, as you probably have already observed. A lot of them are children. I have a gun on you, but I won't hesitate to shoot as many as possible if you refuse to follow my orders. I'll aim at the children first."

"What are your orders?" she asked as a group of young boys crossed in front of her. She grimaced at the thought of Bianchi shooting them.

"I want you to board that approaching trolley with me. Step out and walk toward it."

May didn't hesitate to move. She wanted to do whatever it took to keep Bianchi from hurting innocent people.

"When we're on the trolley, try to find a place near the back," he commanded.

May walked slowly to the trolley stop. The conveyance halted, and about twenty people disembarked. May waited for the last of them to exit, then boarded with dozens of other people. She took a seat at the back of the trolley and wasn't surprised when Mr. Bianchi sat down beside her.

"Good. Now that we're here, I will explain my plans for you. If you cooperate completely, nothing bad will happen to you. However, if you refuse to obey, you will find yourself in dire straits, and so will Lee."

May turned to face the man. He had disguised his appearance. Black hair was now gray and longer, and he a beard and mustache. Theater pieces, no doubt. His eyes were a brownish-black, narrowly set, giving him a beady-eyed look that no makeup or wigs could alter. His nose was hawkish, and his lips were thin. As an artist she noted every detail, memorizing it as if she would be asked to paint him later.

"You stare so intently. I can see the ire in your bright green eyes. What a color for a woman such as you. I would love to paint you."

She had forgotten he was also an artist. "No, thank you. What do you expect of me?"

He smiled, but there was no joy in his expression. It was

more a look of tolerance mixed with intrigue. "We need you for insurance in case Munro figures things out."

"He already knows," May blurted. She immediately regretted her words.

Bianchi raised a brow. "And how is that?"

She knew there was no sense trying to keep it to herself. Perhaps if she told Bianchi everything he would drop his plans and flee.

"You failed to put the kanji on the breastplate. The original had the kanji symbols for courage. They are missing on your forgery."

"Ah, the trouble of counting on others to make a piece right. I couldn't keep studying the armor in person because Munro made it so difficult for me to be seen. Good thing I have friends in the theater, eh?"

"We've already told the Japanese officials that the armor has been replaced with a copy."

"Pity, but that makes you even more important. We need you to ensure that Munro won't follow us and interfere with our plans."

He glanced at the people on the trolley. Most were far enough away that they couldn't hear the conversation, but May wondered what would happen to them if they could. She didn't want to see anyone hurt.

"And what are those plans?"

Bianchi said nothing for a moment. Finally, he turned toward her. "We plan to succeed at what we started. Hillsboro will have his armor, and we will leave Seattle free men. You will be our guarantee."

"Why me?"

"Because you're Munro's woman. I've watched the two of you closely. It's evident that he cares for you, and because he does, I know I have leverage in using you against him. He won't dare to challenge me if he knows your life hangs in the balance."

May knew he was right. Lee would give his life for her. She had no doubt about that at all. The same was true of her for him. It was the reason she remained quietly at Bianchi's side and didn't even attempt to make a scene.

"So your plan is to take me on your trip out of town. When will enough be enough?"

Bianchi frowned. "What do you mean?"

"When will you set me free? I can hardly accompany you the rest of my life."

The trolley crossed a rough patch of track and jostled her against Bianchi. May reached out to steady herself, noting Bianchi had removed his hand from his pocket to steady himself too. She guessed that he had a gun in that pocket, which was what he had stuck into her back. She wondered if there might be a chance to get it away from him when the trolley stopped.

"Well?" she asked. "What is the plan for letting me go?"

"If Munro does nothing to follow us or create problems, there's no reason you can't be set free as soon as we reach another major city. Of course, heading east won't present a large number of cities until the train reaches the middle of the country. That will most likely take several days."

"You can't mean to keep me for several days," May replied, shaking her head. "Think of the problems that itself will create."

Bianchi shrugged. "I'm certain you will find ways to accommodate us in this endeavor. Personally, I have a client awaiting me elsewhere, and leaving with Hillsboro wasn't exactly my first choice either. However, the man has plenty of money, and I'm certain once he realizes that you'll make the difference between a peaceful exit from Seattle and trouble, he'll be happy to pay for your needs."

May looked out the window. How in the world could she convince this man that taking her was a terrible idea? If Lee caught wind of what was happening, he'd never allow Bianchi and Hillsboro to leave the city with her. But first he'd have to find out.

Lee made his way to the Sorrento Hotel and up the stairs to Tobias Hillsboro's room. He knocked on the door and waited for someone to answer. The officer who'd been assigned to watch the room appeared.

"What's going on, sir?"

Lee recognized him as Officer Harry Jacobs. "I'm trying to find Hillsboro. Is he in his room?"

"As far as I know he's never left."

Lee knocked again and finally the valet opened the door. Lee pushed past him. "Hillsboro, we need to talk."

"Mr. Hillsboro is no longer in residence," the valet told him.

Lee stopped and gave the man a stern look. "Where is he?"

The older man put his nose in the air. "I have no idea."

Rather than argue with the man, Lee made his way back to the front desk and asked for the manager.

He showed his credentials. "I'm Detective Munro with the Seattle Police Department. I am looking for Tobias Hillsboro. He is a guest of this hotel."

"Not any longer, I'm afraid," the man replied.

"When did he leave?"

"I'm not sure. His man came down to tell us they'd be checking out immediately, but evidently Mr. Hillsboro left days ago."

"Do you know where he was headed?" Lee glanced around the lobby, making sure Hillsboro wasn't biding his time there.

"The valet didn't tell me," the manager answered. "However, he had the doorman hail a cab. You might want to ask him."

Lee nodded. "Thank you. I will."

He strode across the lobby and out the door, where the doorman was helping an older woman into an automobile. Once the man stepped back, Lee approached him.

"Excuse me. I'm looking for Tobias Hillsboro. Have you had any interaction with him?"

The man looked around the area as if to make sure it was safe to speak. "And who are you?"

Lee pulled out his badge and showed the man. "I am a detective. I need to find Mr. Hillsboro."

This seemed to satisfy the man, who noticeably relaxed and gave a nod. "I haven't seen him for days, but his valet was here earlier and ordered a cab." He glanced at his pocket watch. "Wanted it to take him to the train station in half an hour. That was ten minutes ago. I don't know where he plans to go after."

Lee figured the valet would catch up with Hillsboro at the station, and then Hillsboro would likely head home to New York City with his treasure.

"Thank you." Lee turned to Officer Jacobs, who'd followed him like a faithful dog. "Jacobs, go back and trail the valet to the train station. I'll go and scout out Hillsboro. We should find our way together once the two men meet." The younger man nodded and headed toward the hotel.

Lee raced back to his horse and carriage. He wasn't at all familiar with the train schedules, so he didn't know if he was too late. He prayed he wasn't. He wanted more than anything to retrieve the armor for the Japanese officials. Well, almost more than anything. Most of all he wanted to find Bianchi. There was no way of knowing if he'd be with Hillsboro, but there was a chance. A chance Lee definitely had to take.

He should have had Jacobs call the station. Lee spotted one of the cast-iron police call boxes and pulled Gaspar over to the side. He started to climb down, then thought against it. The Gangrel Box System would only allow him to send a telegraphed signal to the station. It would signal the police to send help to the box's location. That wasn't what Lee needed. He glanced around again. He needed a telephone.

He put Gaspar in motion once more and drove the horse to a rapid clip. He wove in and out of traffic and finally came to a stop in front of Kellogg's Drug Store. He knew the owner and had used his phone on many occasions. It would save the time of explaining to anyone else.

Inside the drug store, people seemed intent on making their purchases, and Lee found it almost impossible to push his way to the back of the store.

"Excuse me. Police business," he announced and waited for the crowd to part. Once the people gave him a little space in which to maneuver, he found the pharmacist and motioned toward where he knew the phone to be.

"I need to make a call."

The man recognized Lee and nodded. "Sure thing, Detective."

Lee waited impatiently while the operator seemed to take forever in reaching the station. "This is Detective Munro. I need officers sent to the King Street train station. We need to stop Tobias Hillsboro and, if possible, Mario Bianchi. Have the officers meet me at the ticket office." He took only another moment to explain the urgency, then hung up and made a mad dash for his buggy.

He silently prayed, desperate to be successful in this matter. Only God could bring a successful conclusion. Hillsboro might not even be at the depot, but surely he wouldn't travel without his valet. The man was far too particular about appearances. Still, the valet had been at the Sorrento without him. Perhaps Hillsboro had more than one valet working for him. Lee urged the horse on.

Help me, Lord. Help me to capture these men and put an end to Bianchi's games.

22

I t was getting dark by the time Lee reached the King Street Station. He pulled his carriage up to the front entry, and when a baggageman approached, he explained the situation and handed the man a dollar.

"If you'll watch over my horse and buggy, there will be another dollar in it for you."

The man nodded. "I'll be needin' to move him over a ways, but I'll see to it that nobody messes with him."

"Thank you." Lee hurried into the grand structure, relieved to know Gaspar would be looked after.

Inside, the coffered ceilings stretched high above to display intricate artistic details in the trims and moldings. Seattle was quite proud of this station and with great reason. It was quite the feast for the eyes. People visiting here would find every amenity possible for their comfort. Waiting here for a train was said to be a very enjoyable occasion.

Lee made his way to the ticket office, and instead of waiting in line, he flashed his badge and went directly to the window.

"I need to know if you've seen a man named Tobias Hillsboro," Lee told the man behind the counter. "He's tall and lean, sandy blond hair that he parts on the side, clean shaven. He's about six feet tall and wears expensive clothes."

"No, sir, I haven't seen any man fitting that description," the ticket master told Lee.

Lee glanced around the depot. There were probably a hundred people milling about. It would be no easy matter to locate Hillsboro among them.

"If the man has money," the ticket master continued, "he may have a private car. There's a separate waiting area for those customers. It's beyond the ladies' waiting room."

It was at least something to check. Lee started to go, then turned back to the man. "Thank you. If a group of policemen show up, send them in the same direction."

"I'll do just that, sir."

Lee made his way as instructed. He opened the door to the private waiting area and glanced around. There wasn't anyone to be found with exception of a uniformed man who was cleaning up.

"I'm Detective Munro," Lee announced as he came to where the man was wiping out an ashtray.

"Yes, sir, how can I help you?"

"I'm looking for a man named Tobias Hillsboro." Lee rattled off the description once again.

"No, sir, I ain't seen him. I've been here all day, and nobody like that came around."

Lee sighed. "What's the procedure here? A man who has a private car would come here to wait and then what?"

"He'd let us know where he was bound, and iffen he hadn't let the private car agent know when he was comin', then we'd notify the office. They'd let him know when and on what train he could be arranged. Sometimes it don't work well iffen they don't call ahead or send notice. A man might have to wait a day or so to get his car hitched."

Lee nodded. He doubted seriously that Hillsboro would neglect calling ahead. The man seemed quite meticulous in his arrangements.

"If they call and make arrangements, would they come here to wait to board their car?"

"No, sir, not necessarily. They could have gone to the agent hisself and been escorted to the private car directly."

"Where can I go to speak to the agent?"

"In the main terminal, go down the hall past the magazine-and-newspaper stand. You'll come to a row of offices. It's the third one down on the left side."

"Thank you." Lee started to go. "Oh, if a group of police officers shows up, have them wait here for me."

"I'll do jes that, sir." The man gave Lee a reassuring nod.

Lee made his way back across the station, spotting six police officers coming through the front entry. He made his way to the men.

"I'm Detective Munro. Are you the men who were sent to assist me?"

One of the men stepped forward. "We are. I'm Sergeant Stevens."

"We are looking for Tobias Hillsboro." Lee gave the man's description. "It's likely he has a private car, so I'm on my way to see the agent who handles that. We're also looking for Mario Bianchi." He gave them a description of Bianchi and then a warning. "Both of these men are dangerous, and I think we must assume they are armed."

"We have seen the photograph of Bianchi," Sergeant Stevens replied.

"I'll meet you back here in a few minutes. Hopefully the

private-car agent can tell me where Hillsboro is. Oh, and Officer Jacobs should arrive before long. He's watching Hillsboro's valet. We're hoping if all else fails, the man will lead us to Hillsboro. Don't interfere with Jacobs."

"Yes, sir. We'll spread out and see if we can find Hillsboro and Bianchi and await further instructions."

Lee took off across the depot to where he'd been directed. He found the agent's office and stepped inside without knocking. A man at least twice Lee's age sat behind a wooden desk, stacks of papers surrounding him. He looked up.

"May I help you?"

Lee noted a wooden placard with a name. "Mr. Foster?" The man nodded. "I'm Detective Munro of the Seattle Police Department. I'm searching for a man who may or may not have a private train car."

"What is his name?" Foster asked.

"Tobias Hillsboro."

The older man nodded again. "Yes, he has been here. He arranged with me yesterday to have his car readied and secured to the evening eastbound train."

"Has the train yet departed?"

"No. I believe the time of departure is seven o'clock, but let me check to be sure." The man pulled out a stack of papers from his drawer. He looked over the first page and then the second. "Ah yes, here it is. The eastbound train will pull in at six thirty-five and depart at seven." Foster glanced up. "It's six fifteen. That should give you time to reach Mr. Hillsboro's car before they head out."

"How do I find it?"

The man gave Lee instructions. "The car is very near the depot platform. I'm just now closing up for the day," he told Lee. "If you want to wait, I can take you there myself."

"That's all right. Your instructions were quite clear. I should be able to find it."

Lee exited the man's office and found Sergeant Stevens. He relayed the information. "Gather your men and come to where Hillsboro's private car is situated. We'll search it for the armor and arrest him if it's on board. Hopefully Bianchi is there as well. We can definitely take him into custody. He has multiple warrants out for his arrest."

Lee lost no more time and made his way outside, following Mr. Foster's instructions to the siding track where Hillsboro's car waited.

The train car was nothing special from the outside. It looked rather standard, painted a navy blue with shaded windows set down the length of the car. Somehow Lee had expected more flourish from Hillsboro.

Light shown from the window edges in the fading evening light. The shades were heavy enough that if there was movement inside the car, it wasn't reflected. Still, Lee watched for any sign of the light being altered at the edges. If Hillsboro was inside, then he was seated and not moving at the moment.

Lee proceeded to the steps of the car and made his way up without pause. He didn't bother to knock but opened the door to the private car and stepped inside, hoping he would have the advantage of surprise.

Hillsboro sat in an overstuffed chair reading the newspaper. He lowered the paper. "Detective Munro."

"Hillsboro, I've come to reclaim the Japanese armor you stole from the exposition."

The man looked at him blankly. "I have no idea what you're talking about. I've stolen nothing. I did offer to purchase the armor but was refused an opportunity to do so. But of course, you know all of this."

"I know that you hired Mario Bianchi to make a very good forgery of the armor. I know too that the armor was switched out."

"And how is it that you came to this conclusion?"

"The copy isn't true to the original. Bianchi is quite good at what he does, but he missed a very important marker. The Japanese kanji for the word *courage*. It's missing on the replica."

"How interesting." Hillsboro folded the paper. "Well, you are free to look around, but I assure you, I do not have any Japanese armor on board."

"No, I don't suppose you would have it here," Lee said. His eyes narrowed as he considered where Hillsboro might have the armor waiting. "It's a pity, you know. The armor you have is . . . well, it's also a copy. The Japanese officials told me when I reported the theft."

Hillsboro's expression remained fixed, but Lee noted a fire that seemed to come to his eyes. "Why would they have a copy of the armor instead of the original piece?"

"They feared the original was too fragile to travel the distance to America. They arranged for a copy to be made using parts from other incomplete sets of armor. Then, like Bianchi, they remade what they needed to. The armor you have is virtually worthless, although the Japanese would like it back."

"Ha, they are lying. The piece is original, and they are trying to save face. The Japanese worry about things like that, you know."

"What I know is that the piece is a copy used for the exposition in order to save wear on the original. They do worry a great deal about the pieces of work that play such an important part in their culture and past."

Lee heard someone coming aboard behind him and presumed it would be Sergeant Stevens and his men. Lee smiled. "You'd do well to just come clean and tell me where the armor is. You might even be able to wheedle your way out of any charges by pleading ignorance, but we will have that armor returned to the Japanese officials."

He heard a gasp and turned to find May standing there with a poorly disguised Bianchi behind her. The two men's gazes met, and Bianchi had the audacity to smile.

"Leander Munro. As I live and breathe."

"Hopefully not for long," Lee said. He gave May a once over to ascertain if she was hurt. "Why is she here?"

"Because, as I told Miss Parker, you care for her, and therefore she is important to us. She will ensure our safety and welfare."

"In what way?"

"By going with us when we leave Seattle. You won't dare to follow us or wire ahead for others to take us in hand so long as she is with us."

Lee looked back at Hillsboro. "Right now, you don't have to face much in the way of charges, but if you take May with you and leave Seattle, I'll see you fully charged for kidnapping."

"Oh, come now, Mr. Munro. You can hardly charge me with such deeds. You saw for yourself that Mr. Bianchi arrived with the woman in tow. I had nothing to do with her being here. I'm just as surprised as you are."

Lee turned back to Bianchi, who was pushing May past Lee and making his way to where Hillsboro sat. Lee could see that May was afraid, but there was nothing he could do to ease her worries at this point.

"By the way, Mr. Bianchi," Hillsboro added, "Mr. Munro

tells me that the armor taken from the Japanese display was not an original at all. It was a copy created from odd parts available. They feared the original too fragile to make the trip."

Bianchi's face reddened as he looked to Lee. "He's lying."

"I'm not," Lee replied. "You can ask Miss Parker if you truly doubt me. She will tell you. When we spotted the mistake, that you made I might add, of omitting the kanji that was on the original, we went immediately to the officials. They told us that the piece they displayed was a copy."

"Yet they want the 'copy' back," Hillsboro added. "No doubt they are lying about the authenticity to save face. If a copy was stolen, it wouldn't bring nearly as much shame as losing an original piece of their history."

"That would be my guess," Bianchi replied. He peeled off his fake mustache and beard. "Itchy things." He tossed them aside, then reached up and took off the gray wig.

"Think what you like, but I'm telling you the piece you now own isn't worth anywhere near the money you must have paid Bianchi." Lee shrugged. "I'm still amazed that someone of Bianchi's talent could have forgotten that kanji. Your skills must be slipping."

Bianchi's face reddened. It was easy to see that Lee's comments were getting to the man.

"He's telling the truth," May affirmed. "The Japanese official said it's a copy."

Lee sensed the entire matter was getting under Hillsboro's skin as well. "You should also know that before coming, I arranged for more police officers to join me here at the train station. I have plenty of help, so even if the armor isn't here on board your private car, we will find it."

"You'll do nothing of the sort," Bianchi said, dropping

the wig to pull May to his side. "I have your woman. By leaving now and forgetting about the armor, you can keep her from harm. Pursue this matter or continue to threaten us, and I will kill her."

Lee felt his stomach churn at the thought of Bianchi having May in his control. He couldn't let them take her. "It would be the biggest mistake you ever made to try to force her to go with you." His voice was void of emotion.

Hillsboro moved, and Lee caught sight of a gun he pulled from his pocket. "It would be wise for you to go now, Mr. Munro. They will soon be attaching my car to the train, and then we will be off."

Lee could see the fear in May's eyes. He didn't want to leave her but wasn't sure what he could do at the moment. Then, as if to make up Lee's mind for him, Bianchi reached inside his coat with his free hand. He pulled out a large knife and put it to May's throat as he jerked her farther away from Lee. She went pale, and her eyes searched Lee's for answers.

"Don't hurt her. She's innocent of anything between us."

"True, but unfortunately she must be a part of this," Bianchi said. "Leave us now and collect your men, or I will cut her just to show you what I'm capable of."

Lee raised his hands. "I'm leaving. Don't hurt her. If she's harmed in any way, Bianchi, I will hunt you down. I will never stop pursuing you. I will make it my lifelong task to see you dead."

Hillsboro got to his feet and pointed the gun at Lee. "Go now. I assure you Bianchi won't harm your sweetheart— unless of course you do anything to interfere with our departure."

The door was only a few steps away, but Lee couldn't make his feet move. He couldn't leave May in the hands of these monsters. Yet what else could he do? He considered the gun he carried. He was certain he could never retrieve it before Bianchi or Hillsboro did them harm.

"I'm sorry, May. I don't have much of a choice."

She nodded. "I love you, Lee. I'll be all right."

"I love you too. I'll see to it that these two pay for what they're doing. I won't let them get away with this. I'll come for you."

"You do, and she'll be dead before you reach her," Bianchi declared. "That is my solemn promise to you, Munro. Please do not think me to be joking. I will do what I must. I cherish my freedom too much to allow you to take me to prison."

Lee moved backward toward the door. "You're both going to regret this."

May watched Lee leave and felt her hopes go with him. She prayed for strength and bravery. Prayed that Lee would be safe no matter her own outcome. Thoughts of Lee getting hurt or killed were just too much to bear.

"Could I please sit? I feel faint."

Bianchi moved her to another of the overstuffed chairs. He released her. May sank onto the cushioned seat.

"A copy is what I've paid good money to have in my collection?" Hillsboro asked.

Bianchi turned and faced him. "No. I believe, like you, that the Japanese officials only said that to save face. With their pride of culture and history, they would never allow a copy to be displayed. I know enough about those people to know that much."

Hillsboro's expression relaxed a bit. "Well, good. I figured it was just a ploy of Munro's, but I certainly don't want to get stuck with a worthless copy."

"But it is a copy," May interjected. "Just a copy."

"Shut up!" Bianchi commanded. "It isn't. I would have known."

"Because of your great knowledge of Japanese samurai armor?" May asked a little more snidely than she'd intended. "Yet you forgot the kanji."

"You had better be quiet." Bianchi stepped closer, waving the knife. "I won't hesitate to punish you. You will suffer if you fail to cooperate."

May shivered but kept her gaze fixed on Bianchi. She could well understand Lee's desire to capture this man and see him brought to justice. He was evil. Pure and simple evil. And she was his captive.

23

Lee caught up with Sergeant Stevens and the other officers. He found them talking to several railroad officials.

"This is the train that Hillsboro's car is to be hooked up to," Stevens explained. "My men are going on board to search through the baggage cars. They'll give a thorough search for anything out of the ordinary."

"Bianchi is in Hillsboro's private car over there." Lee motioned to the siding. "He has May Parker as a hostage. She's my fiancée, and he's threatening to kill her if we pursue or try to overtake them."

"I'm sorry, Detective Munro," Stevens said. "How do we contend with this?"

Lee shook his head. "I'm not sure. I think you should definitely have your men search the train, but other than that, I haven't quite come up with a plan."

"We were just about to hook Hillsboro's car to the main train," one of the railroad men said. "Should we not do that?"

"If you don't, Hillsboro is going to know something is amiss. He might try to take additional hostages if he doesn't get his way. The car is near the platform, and I certainly don't want anyone else hurt."

The oldest looking of the railroad men spoke up. "What if we hook him up to another train and pull him farther out in the trainyard? Away from the people. We can put him in a place more isolated."

Lee nodded. "We could make him believe he is being hooked up and the train is preparing to leave."

"Maybe once we get them separated," the man offered, "I could go aboard and tell him there's a mechanical problem. Maybe something wrong with the brakes or something else, and that there will be a delay. That will at least buy you time."

"Is there another eastbound out tonight?"

"We could lie and say there is," the man replied. "Or we can just tell him that the eastbound will be delayed due to the mechanical issues and that we'll have him on his way as soon as possible. In the darkness, he'll never know what's really happening."

Lee could see the potential, and a plan started forming in his mind. If they could get Hillsboro's car away from the public area and ensure the safety of the citizens, then they might have better options. May would still be in danger. There was nothing that he could do right now to change that. However, if they could convince Hillsboro that he'd soon be on his way, perhaps that would ease the tension, and they'd let their guard down.

Stevens instructed his men, then turned to Lee. "It's doubtful that Hillsboro is shipping the armor in his own name. What size crate do you suppose we're looking for?"

Another railroad official joined the men. "I have the manifest of additional freight. Since he has a private car, it's doubtful he has any small baggage on board the main train, so I don't think we need to search through the suitcases and such."

"No," Lee replied. "The armor stands about five feet tall, maybe five-five. They wouldn't break it down. It's too valuable as a whole. It would have to be crated in a wooden box, probably in straw to cushion and protect it. It would be the size of a casket, I'd guess. Probably a little wider."

Stevens turned to his men. "Do you have that? You're looking for a large crate or wooden box that could fit a coffin."

"They may have even used a coffin," Lee said, thinking that might be a clever way to disguise the piece and protect it. "Do you have any caskets being shipped east?"

The railroad man looked over the list. "Two. A Mrs. Platte and a Mr. Newman."

"I'm afraid we should probably start there," Lee said, not relishing the idea of disturbing the dead. Even if one of the caskets did contain the armor, the other would not.

"I'll take you to that car first," the man told the assigned officers.

Lee waited until they were on their way before addressing the other men. "We'll need to plan this carefully. First, Stevens, you need to find Officer Jacobs and take Hillsboro's valet into custody. Then we need to secure this area so that none of the innocent passengers get into the wrong location. After that, here's what I have in mind."

"I can't believe he caught up to us so quickly," Hillsboro said, trying to look out into the darkness without making himself a target in the window.

"Munro is a smart one, to be sure. He relentlessly chased me in DC. I wasn't free until he thought I'd been killed. It bought me a great deal of time. I accomplished several projects without him on my back." Bianchi looked to May. "It's a pity you two had to make this difficult for us."

"It's a pity you had to be a forger, Mr. Bianchi." May shook her head. "I can only imagine what you might have accomplished if you'd used your talents and money for good."

Bianchi laughed. "I did use it for good. My good. I've become a very wealthy man over the years and intend to go on being one. Leander Munro can play detective all he likes, but he's bound by the laws of this land, and I am not. I have the advantage."

"I suppose you might see it that way, but it really isn't so. You are very limited by what you can and can't do. After all, no one really knows of your accomplishments." May gave him a sad smile. "As an artist, I know I enjoy people knowing that I was the one to create a painting or drawing. You will never have that pleasure because when you do a good job, no one is the wiser. You will be a forgotten man once you're dead."

Bianchi gave her a hard look. "Don't think to play that game with me. Fame has never been important to me. I love knowing that I've pulled the wool over everyone's eyes. I love walking into an art museum and standing before a famous painting that thousands have come to see thinking it's a van Dyck or Reynolds. I've listened to their praise and known great satisfaction."

"But they're praising van Dyck's or Reynolds's ability and creativity. Not yours. Yours was just a copy of the original."

"A very good copy!" Bianchi shouted.

May shrugged. "But only a copy."

"Stop letting her goad you, Bianchi," Hillsboro said, grinning at May. "She's quite good at it, and you won't be thinking clearly much longer if you allow her to get under your skin."

Bianchi glanced at the man and then back to May. He gave a shrug and took a seat opposite her.

The gathering of chairs had been positioned so that four people might sit and face each other for conversation. May wanted no further conversation, however. She made a quick study of the room and wanted only to figure a way out of her situation.

Noises outside caught both men's attention, and Bianchi popped up out of his chair to join Hillsboro near the window. "What's going on?"

A knock sounded on the door, and Hillsboro nodded. "Go answer it. I'll have you covered."

Bianchi did as instructed and opened the door to find one of the railroad men. "Yes?"

"We're about to hook you up to the eastbound," the man declared. "You might want to take your seats. The coupling can be quite a jolt. As soon as we're finished, the train will be heading out, and you'll be on your way."

"Thank you," Hillsboro said, moving away from the window. "By the way, I was expecting my valet to join me. Has anyone seen him?"

"I couldn't say, sir, but I will check on it."

May noted Hillsboro's hand remained in his pocket the entire time. No doubt he was ready and willing to pull his revolver if the situation warranted it. She felt confident that should she bolt for the door, Hillsboro or Bianchi wouldn't hesitate to shoot her in the back.

"Very well." Hillsboro gave a shrug. "If he misses the train, I'll simply hire another."

She watched the railroad man leave and felt a sinking despair. They were about to pull out of Seattle. She would have no chance to tell her parents what had happened. She might never see them again. The thought brought tears to her eyes. They would be so worried if they knew what was happening.

"No use crying, Miss Parker," Hillsboro said, handing her a handkerchief. "If you and Mr. Munro cooperate, no harm will come to you."

She refused the handkerchief and turned her back to him. Hillsboro said nothing, but Bianchi couldn't seem to refrain.

"I think she should cry. Cry and be afraid. She knows the situation is dire because that suitor of hers is dangerously careless when it comes to the lives of other people. He won't care so long as he gets his man."

"Then why have her here at all?" Hillsboro asked. "Honestly, Bianchi, make up your mind. Either he cares and will keep his distance because of his concerns, or he won't. If the latter is true, then I'd just as soon put Miss Parker from my car. She's a liability for the both of us."

"No, he'll play by the rules. I didn't mean to suggest he wouldn't." Bianchi looked rather worried. May wondered if she could somehow use that against him.

The train car lurched, and May gripped the arm of the chair. It was the first time she'd really noticed the lovely blue-and-white patterned Chintz that had been used for the upholstery. The fabric featured Renaissance men and women in various garden settings, as well as the gardens themselves with lovely blue trees and arched stone bridges. In another setting, May would have liked it very much. Now, however, the pattern was forever ruined for her.

There was a grinding sound of wheels and metal coming

together, then the train moved forward. May felt as if she might be ill. Was Lee really going to let them take her away from Seattle? Surely, he would figure out a way to stop them.

The train picked up a little speed, but not much. May supposed they had to go slowly through the city. She glanced toward the windows. All but one had the shades pulled. She'd have no chance to see where they were going.

They hadn't gone very far when the train slowed, and then the movement halted altogether.

"What's going on now?" Bianchi questioned and moved to the window. He carefully maneuvered to see outside. "It's pitch black out there. I can't see anything."

After about five minutes, a knock sounded once again at the door. May wasn't surprised when Bianchi made a mad dash. Hillsboro got up slowly and made his way to the door as well.

The same railyard worker appeared and stepped inside, moving to the right, where Mr. Hillsboro was approaching. "I'm sorry for the delay, Mr. Hillsboro, but we've got a problem with a locked brake. Shouldn't take very long to fix."

May noted that Bianchi had drawn his knife and held it behind his back. The man was positively paranoid about his situation. She stood and eased over to where the men were talking. With a little bit of luck, she might be able to throw Bianchi off-balance and make a run for it. But what if Hillsboro shot the railyard worker? She didn't want that.

She was halfway to the men when, to her surprise, Lee came through the door. Bianchi saw him and raised his knife to attack. May didn't take time to think but lunged at Bianchi as he thrust the knife, knocking him sideways. She lost her own footing as well but rolled away from the man just in case he thought to swing the knife her direction.

There was a scuffling sound, and a man declared Hillsboro to be under arrest. May got to her feet as the other man came around Lee and helped him manage Bianchi. Lee glanced her way and then came to her once Bianchi was in handcuffs.

"Are you all right? Why did you do something so foolish?"

"He had a knife. He was going to kill you. Oh, Lee, are you truly all right?" She started checking him over and found a cut on the shoulder of his coat. "Are you hurt?"

Lee pulled the coat away from his shoulder. "I'm fine. It didn't go all the way through. You must have thrown him back before he could plunge it in."

She threw herself into his arms. "I was so afraid he'd kill you."

He hugged her close. "I'm just fine. You saved my life." He pulled back and searched her face. "Marry me, May. Please marry me."

"Of course I will, but only after we talk once more to your parents."

"Why?"

She smiled. "To tell them that I don't wish to dishonor them, but that I love you and plan to marry you because I believe it's God's will. And that I will be praying that one day they will be able to let go of the past and love me and any children we have."

He touched her cheek. "And we'll let them know you risked your life to save mine. Maybe that will help to persuade them."

"Even if it doesn't, I know we are meant to be together. I feel so certain that it is God's will for my life that I can contemplate nothing else. I know together we will serve Him and honor Him."

"Yes," Lee agreed, leaning to kiss her. "I know this as well."

May heard a man clear his throat. "Uh, Detective . . . we've got the men in custody. Will you be accompanying us to the station?" the other officer asked.

Lee pulled away and shook his head. "No, Stevens, I must see that Miss Parker gets home safely. I'll be down to the station shortly after that."

May watched as two officers led Bianchi and Hillsboro off the train.

"Did you find the armor?" Lee asked Stevens.

The man nodded. "Yes, in the large coffin marked for Mrs. Platte."

"Good work. You and your men did an excellent job. I'll put in a good word for all of you."

The man straightened and gave Lee a nod. "Thank you, sir." He turned and went to assist with the captives.

"By the way, Hillsboro," Lee called out. "The armor you have really is a copy. I didn't lie about that. But I'm sure your place in New York holds many pieces that are real. I intend to wire the New York police so that they can do an inventory while you're busy here in Seattle. Maybe I can send your valet there with a Pinkerton man, and he can give them a tour."

Hillsboro scowled but said nothing as his escort pulled him along.

Lee pulled May back into his arms. "Now, where were we?"

24

The previous night had held more than enough excitement for May. Unfortunately, she couldn't just rest up and ponder the matter for long. She was due at the photography shop for their final day. Mama hadn't wanted her to go after having gone through so much, but May assured her she was fine and felt more than obligated to make an appearance on the last day of the fair.

Lee arrived to take her by carriage as he had most days since they had found each other again. May's father insisted on speaking to Lee before they left. He had only gotten to talk to Lee for a few minutes the night before.

"I want to thank you again, Lee. May told us all the details of what happened. I still feel ill when I think of what might have happened."

"God was good to us, to be sure." Lee smiled at May. "I told my folks about how you saved my life and how they should be proud to welcome you into the family, May. They said very little, but I think it impressed them that you would risk your own life for mine."

"I hope they can see it as proof that my love for you is real. I've been praying God would change their hearts." She looped her arm through his. "But we really must go, Father. I'm sure you can talk Lee into coming for dinner tonight or tomorrow to share all the details of what's happening to Mr. Bianchi and Mr. Hillsboro."

"What about it, Lee?" her father asked. "Can you join us tonight?"

He grinned. "I would love to."

"Wonderful. Then I'll just have to wait until later to sing your praises." Father glanced at May. "And you be careful. Don't accept any more notes unless you're certain they're from Lee."

"I won't. We've already decided that when he sends notes to me, he'll sign them with the kanji for 'courage.'" She looked up and gave Lee a smile. "And I'll sign with the same."

"Good. I don't want anyone else to threaten your life." Father leaned down and gave her a kiss on the forehead. "Take good care of her, Lee."

"I promise I will."

Lee helped May into the carriage and gave a wave to Father. May settled into the leather upholstery, smoothing the red-and-black coat she'd chosen to wear again.

"I really like the cut of that coat. It complements your figure quite nicely," Lee said as he put the horse in motion.

"Uh, thank you." May felt a momentary sense of shyness at the thought of Lee studying her figure. She glanced down at her black skirt. It was the last time she would wear her Camera Girl uniform. Up until this job, she had rarely worn black.

"Are you excited to be done with the exposition?" Lee asked.

"To a degree. I'll miss the girls and Mr. Akira. And of course the Japanese displays. However, Mama has agreed to work with me on my Japanese language studies. I'm quite excited. I want more than anything to get good at speaking Japanese so that one day we can visit Japan."

"I think going to Japan would make a lovely wedding trip, don't you?"

She looked at Lee and smiled. "I do. I've been praying about it. Lee, I know if your parents disown you as they've threatened, you won't get your inheritance. I want you to know that the money doesn't matter to me at all. In fact, I can help earn money, too, by touching up pictures for Mr. Fisher. I've already told him I'll do it part-time to promote his new shop. But a trip to Japan will cost a great deal. I don't want you to think that we have to take this trip right away. We can save up and wait. I'm a very patient person, as you know."

"I do, and I appreciate your patience. However, I have managed to put aside a nice savings from monies gifted me in the past and from my salary as a policeman. Until recently, I didn't have much in the way of expenses. I lived at home, and my parents still insisted, despite not liking my job, on paying for everything. I think we can use that money for the trip and still have some left over."

"We haven't even talked about when we want to marry." She hoped he wanted to wed as soon as possible. She certainly did. She might well be a patient person, but she was in love with Leander Munro and wanted to claim him as soon as possible.

"Well?" he asked, looking at her with his brows slightly raised.

"Well, what?"

"When do you want to marry me?"

"As soon as possible, but . . . I still want to speak to your parents." She frowned. "I really would love for them to accept your choice of me."

"I know, I'd like that, too, and I'm praying God will change their hearts. But it will probably take time."

May nodded. "I suppose so." She sighed. "Back to being patient."

"That doesn't mean we can't set the date. Then in a few weeks, we can go talk to them, but no matter what they say, I want to marry you as soon as I can."

She felt the same way. "I'd like that very much, Lee. What if we set the date for just after the first of the year? That way Mama and I will have time to make arrangements."

"That's just a few months away. I think I can wait that long." He glanced at her and grinned. "I feel like giving out a yell."

"I do too. I can't believe we are finally together again. When you went away, I thought I'd lost a part of myself. In truth . . . I did. You will always be such an important part of who I am."

Lee said nothing, but he wore a very satisfied expression. Finally, after a couple of blocks passed, he looked at her with that same intent manner he got when considering a case. "Do you suppose your mother would teach me Japanese as well?"

May laughed. "I'm certain she would. After all, she likes you very much."

"It doesn't seem possible that this is the last day of the exposition," Addie told the gathered Camera Girls. "I have to admit that I shall miss all of you."

"We'll miss you as well, Addie," Mary said, shaking her

head. "I don't think my new job as a nanny will be anywhere near as much fun."

"Oh, but you've not yet had much time with my husband's nieces. Mina and Lena can be quite adventurous, and I believe you may find yourself overwhelmed at times."

May held up an envelope. "I've had a brief letter from Eleanor. She mailed it when they reached Seward."

"Well, please read it to us," Addie instructed.

Just then, the door opened, and Pearl Fisher came into the shop. Behind her was her husband, Otis, pushing a baby pram.

"Oh, the baby!" Bertha gave an uncharacteristic squeal. She hurried over to see the infant. "He's so handsome."

The girls gathered around the baby carriage and oohed and ahhed at the newest Fisher.

"Is he a good baby?" one of the girls asked.

"He is," Pearl replied. "He's very good and is already sleeping quite well. He sleeps for four and sometimes five hours at a time. I don't feel that's too awful a schedule at all."

"May was just about to read us a letter from Eleanor," Addie told the couple.

"Oh, please continue. I'd love to hear how she's doing." Pearl glanced at her husband. Otis nodded his approval.

The girls moved back to let the Fishers come farther into the mostly disassembled shop. May took the letter out and began to read.

"'Dear May and anyone else who might want to hear from me.'" May looked up and smiled. "I believe that covers everyone here."

She looked back at the letter and continued. "'Alaska is most impressive. The mountains are quite large and plentiful. The land seems to stretch out for miles and miles, as does the water. I've never seen so much water in my life.

"'The weather has been cold and rainy, delaying our help-ers who are coming from the village to lead us back to the camp. I don't really mind, however. We've been living in tents, and it's all a grand adventure. I've been able to take a few very nice pictures despite the rain but haven't been able to develop the film just yet, so I cannot send you any photographs. But I will, as this place is much too beautiful to refrain.'"

May looked up once again. "She has a few personal lines for me, but ends by saying that you may all write to her if you wish. I have the address for you to use if you'd like to have it."

"I would," a voice spoke up from behind Mr. Fisher. Es-ther peeked around the man and smiled. "Surprise."

"Oh, Esther!" Addie declared. May moved to join her as she made her way to Esther's side. "It's much too early for you to be up and around," Addie said. "Come and sit down." She grabbed one of only two chairs still left in the tiny shop.

Esther sat down and looked up at Addie. "You have your husband to thank. He wanted to surprise everyone, so he came and got me in the carriage. I didn't have far at all to walk because he got special permission to drive in through the delivery gates and bring me here."

"Where is he now?" Addie asked.

"He wanted to keep an eye on the horse. The crowd was upsetting the poor animal."

"I don't doubt it. They sometimes upset me as well," Pearl announced. "Especially with Joseph. I'm quite protective of him."

The girls laughed and once again began fussing over the baby while May and Addie fussed over Esther.

"How are you feeling?" May asked, putting away her let-ter. "I've felt bad that I haven't been able to come visit."

"Don't. You and Addie have already been so kind, especially in helping me get a job."

May was surprised by this news. "What are you going to be doing?"

"I'm going to work at one of the dress shops downtown. The owner goes to church with Addie."

Addie shrugged. "She mentioned she would need to hire someone for the Christmas season and possibly longer if they worked out. I knew Esther couldn't return to work just yet but told my friend about her need of a job."

"I met the woman, and we talked about what I would be able to do and how soon I could start, and she hired me." She leaned in and lowered her voice. "The pay is quite good, and I'll be able to help my parents again."

"That is good news, Esther. I have good news too. Although I have no ring to show for it, I'm engaged to be married."

"That police detective?" Esther asked.

May nodded. "Leander Munro is his name. We've known each other since we were children. His parents don't approve of me because I'm part Japanese, but I'm hoping that will change as I prove myself to them."

"Well, we will just add that matter to our prayer time," Pearl said, coming to join them. "I find that there is nothing that can't be managed with prayer."

"I agree," May said, feeling quite satisfied. "I agree with all my heart."

"Ladies," Mr. Fisher called for their attention. "I have a special gift for each of you. Besides your final paycheck with bonuses included, Mrs. Fisher and I want to gift you with your very own camera."

He disappeared into the back room for a moment and

returned with a large Kodak box. He set it on the floor in front of them and opened the top. Inside were boxes of Brownie cameras. He handed them out to each of the Camera Girls, and when he got to May, his eyebrows arched ever so slightly.

"I hear you are getting married. Perhaps someone will take photographs for you with this camera."

"I'd be happy to do that," Mary volunteered. "If I'm invited to the wedding."

May laughed. "You are all invited to the wedding. It will be small, most likely, but you are my dearest friends . . . besides Lee, of course."

"Of course," Addie said, putting her arm around May. "I know I'll be there."

"I should hope so," May replied. "I was hoping you'd be my matron of honor."

Addie hugged her close. "I should be proud to do so."

Nearly three weeks later, Lee escorted May into the music room where his parents often enjoyed spending their evenings before dinner. To Lee and May's surprise, they had sent written invitations for the young couple to join them.

As a gift, they had brought one of May's paintings—a floral arrangement done in hues of deep crimson, ivory, and pale pinks. Lee had arranged to have it framed and knew if his parents would look past the fact that a half Japanese woman was the artist, they would very much enjoy the piece.

They were announced and entered the room to find Lee's parents looking quite welcoming. His father rose to his feet.

"Father, Mother." Lee gave each a nod. "Thank you for

inviting us to come tonight." He held up the oil painting. "May wanted to bring a gift. She made this for you."

This brought Lee's mother to her feet, coming to see what the gift might be. Lee pulled away the cloth they had used to wrap it in.

"It's . . . it's beautiful," Mother said, reaching out to touch the frame. "May . . . painted this?"

"I did."

"She's quite talented, Mother." Father stepped forward to better see it, while Lee continued. "In fact, the university is going to buy one of her landscapes of the area."

"That is quite impressive." His father's tone was guarded. "Congratulations."

"Thank you. It wouldn't have happened except that Mr. Hanson, one of the professors there, had purchased one of my paintings for his house, and when the president of the university saw it, he insisted on knowing about the artist."

Lee couldn't help but be proud of May and her talents. She had so long kept things hidden away in her home without anyone knowing anything about her ability. Now word would get out, and she might very well become a celebrated artist. If Bianchi escaped the jail cell he was now in, perhaps he would attempt to forge one of May's paintings. The thought caused him to shake his head.

"I'll put this on the mantel, and you can arrange for it later," Lee said. He settled the painting to one side, then went back to May. "We were quite surprised to get your invitation."

"Yes, I imagine you were," Father replied. He motioned for them to take a seat. "I cannot say that this is an easy meeting for us."

"I am aware of that." Lee took a seat beside May. "However,

I'm grateful for the time and that you would set aside your discomfort. May and I have wanted to talk to you about . . . well, everything."

"Before you say anything more," his father said, holding up his hand, "I must say something first." He glanced at Lee's mother and then to Lee and May. "We are most grateful to May for saving your life. When we heard the details of what happened, it made us realize . . . well, we were troubled at the thought that we might have lost you, Lee."

"You nearly did." Lee gave May a tender look. "May was very brave, albeit foolish, to rush a man with a knife. Still, I must say I'm quite grateful for her actions."

"As are we. I suppose I must also admit that we have been unfair to May."

"You have been." He wasn't about to tell his father that their attitudes had been without pain.

"We spoke to the minister," Mother chimed in. "We were quite moved by something he had said one Sunday. It shamed me, I must admit. He shared a story from the local news of a man who'd been beaten and left for dead. It turned out, we knew the man quite well. Mr. Cranston. You know him, Lee."

"I do." He turned to May. "He used to live next door to us."

"I see." May looked back at Lee's mother. "Please go on."

The woman nodded. "Apparently a group of young men— white men—attacked and robbed him. Several people walked by the man, not willing to get involved. They thought he was drunk or even dead and wanted no part in the situation. After several people ignored him, an older Japanese man came forward and helped Mr. Cranston. He picked him up and carried him to the closest doctor, who then called for an ambulance."

"The Good Samaritan retold," Lee commented.

"Yes," Mother continued. "The pastor spoke of how shameful it was that people passed by and refused to even ask poor Mr. Cranston what had happened. They judged him falsely—that he was a reprobate. The pastor said even if he had been, he was a human being, and only this poor Japanese man had bothered to show him love. I was quite moved."

"As was I," Lee's father said. "I have walked the same route as Cranston many a time. It could have been me."

"It could have been," Lee murmured.

"Lee." Mother rose and went to him. He got to his feet. "We spoke with Reverend Cornwall about you and May. He assured us that the Bible says nothing about it being a sin for you to marry—just as you told us before." She looked at May. "But it will take us time to get used to the idea and to fully change our hearts. We know it's wrong to hold a grudge against an entire people for the actions of a few."

Lee patted his mother's hand. "It's enough that you are willing to attempt a change of heart. I know God will help you both in this matter, just as He can help us all to be better neighbors to those around us."

"It will be hard for the two of you," Father interjected, standing. "You must realize that. Even if we change, our friends probably won't."

"But as you change, they will take note. You are a strong leader of your own social circle. You are also a very persuasive man, Father." Lee met May's gaze and smiled. "Once you come to realize how wonderful May is, how kind and generous and giving, I believe you will find ways to convince others as well."

"It's hard to break with tradition and our own training,"

Mother said, leaving Lee to go to May. May, too, got to her feet. "May, you must understand that we have been taught to believe the things we do, and that it was further instilled in us by examples of people around us. It is wrong thinking—I can see that now. But I can't say that I will be able to easily change. You children must be patient with me."

Lee gave a bit of a chuckle. "May is the most patient of all people, and the most loving. And as for me, well, I'm neither, but I, too, am trying to change."

"If we put off the wedding until spring," May began, "do you think you might be willing to attend? We'd very much like your blessing, but I can understand if January is too soon for you."

"Nonsense," Lee's father declared. "We will be there. Not only that but we will work to convince Liam and Newell to come as well. We have two months in which to get the job done."

"God's performed bigger miracles in much less time," Lee said. He went to his father and surprised everyone by embracing him. "Thank you for this. You have made me happier than I have words for."

As Lee let him go, Father met his gaze. "I confess, I still feel a great deal of anger toward those who harmed Liam."

"I can understand that, but you must forgive them so that you'll be forgiven as well. That doesn't mean you approve what happened. It merely means you've given it over to God to manage. The freedom of giving it to God will amaze you."

"I will try, son. I will try."

Later that evening as Lee drove May back to her parents' house, he couldn't help speaking about the turn of events.

"I never anticipated that."

"I did," May said, adjusting her lap blanket. "I've been

asking for just such a change at the prayer meetings with Mrs. Fisher and the girls I used to work with. Addie and I especially have given it a great deal of prayer."

"I admire your faith, May. I know God can do anything, but somehow, I wasn't sure it applied to my parents and their prejudices. I'm sorry to say that my faith was weak in that area."

"Let this strengthen it, then. I know God is going to make us into a wonderful family. I know one day your mother and father are going to completely cherish us and their grand-children."

Lee nodded and urged the horse to go a little faster. "Let's go tell your folks. I'm sure they've been praying as well."

Epilogue

In January, May and Lee were married in a small but beautiful ceremony. They settled down to live in a fashionable house given to them by Lee's parents as a wedding gift. Lee had surprised May with the news of the house the night before the wedding ceremony, and she had been delighted to find it partially furnished with the promise of a big shopping trip to buy more. But most of all, May had been excited about the trip they would take to Japan.

And now that the time had arrived and May stood at the rail of the westward-bound ship, she could hardly contain herself.

"This is so exciting, Lee. I can't believe we're finally on our way."

"Well, we will be soon. They still have to raise the gangplank and anchor."

May turned to him and met his steely, blue-eyed gaze. "This means the world to me. It means the world that you would also encourage Father and Mama to come along. I know Mama would never be brave enough to venture back to Japan on her own."

"Well, our ability to speak Japanese leaves much to be

desired. We needed someone who could do it well, and your folks are both proficient." He reached out and touched her cheek. "But I'm very glad to be making this trip with them, and especially with you. I have a feeling this will be a blessing to all of us."

"I do too. The letter Mama received from her cousin made it sound as if everyone was excited to see Mama again. I pray that's the case and that no one treats her poorly. She has such a tender heart."

Lee stroked her cheek. "So do you."

May put her hand over his. "I couldn't be happier."

"You may feel otherwise after four weeks of travel—and that's if things go well."

May knew the voyage wouldn't be easy. Her mother and father had both shared their stories of the long days at sea and the storms they had encountered. Everyone was hopeful that their sailing would go easily and without storms, but May knew that anything was possible.

"It's going to be strange being away from America for so long," she said, turning to gaze back on the docks. The men were pulling up the gangplank now, and she wanted to watch as the ship moved into the sound.

"Five months is a long time, but it hardly makes sense to go all the way to Japan and not take our time, especially when your relatives are offering to take care of us. Your father told me about the museum in Tokyo, and I must say I'm looking forward to visiting there as well."

"As am I. Father said there are beautiful cherry trees in Tokyo, and we should get there in time to see them in bloom. Won't that be wonderful?"

"So long as I'm with you, May, it will all be a glorious adventure." He turned her back to face him and pulled her close.

May hoped she could be forgiven a public display since they were on a ship getting ready to depart. She stretched up on tiptoe and put her arms around Lee's neck. "Knowing you has made me a better person . . . a happier person."

"I love you, my darling wife."

"I would tell you *daisuki*, which Mama says is the Japanese way to say 'I love you'—if there was one Japanese way. They don't speak it like we do, but they do love as we do. Mama says the Japanese way is more of action rather than words."

"I like the idea of action," Lee said, tightening his hold.

May smiled and pulled him down to meet her lips. "Then let me show you that I love you. Now and for the rest of my life."

If you enjoyed *Knowing You,*

read on
for an excerpt from

The
HEART'S
CHOICE

by Tracie Peterson and
Kimberley Woodhouse

Available now
wherever books are sold.

1

The downright icy air around him burned his lungs as he inhaled, but it couldn't take away the sense of euphoria that filled him. After all these years of hard work, he'd gained the position of a lifetime!

The head of the brand-new Carnegie Library.

He, Mark Andrews, was the head of the Carnegie Library!

Of course, his father probably wouldn't be excited. Or impressed. Angus Andrews wanted Mark to love ranching. Plain and simple. But being a librarian had been Mark's dream. He'd gone after it and obtained it. Not only was he the librarian, but he was in charge of the whole place.

In the darkness of the early morning, he stared up at the large Second Renaissance Revival–style building in front of him. The deep, bracketed eaves above the pilastered entry made the dome above stand out.

From the domed, octagonal entry to the gray sandstone from the Columbus quarries making up the base to the deep red of the brick exterior, the structure was beautiful.

"There's the cowboy."

Mark turned at the voice breaking the silence of the morning to hold out a hand to Judge Milton Ashbury. "Good morning, Judge."

No surprise that the man used his childhood nickname. Though he'd left the ranch, people around here would probably always call him Cowboy.

"Ready for the big ceremony? I know you haven't had much time to get settled."

True enough. Mark had arrived four days prior and had spent every waking hour with the books. "I'm looking forward to today, sir. Thank you."

A high-pitched *yip* diverted his attention downward.

"And who's this?" Mark crouched down to pet the white ball of fur.

The older man let out a long sigh. "Marvella's newest passion. His name is Sir Theophilus."

Mark raised his eyebrows, working hard to keep his amusement to himself.

It didn't work. A snicker escaped.

The little thing couldn't weigh more than a few pounds and seemed all fur. It bounced around on its tiny little paws, stabbing at the dirt and snow in the street, and then at the judge's pants.

Mark cleared his throat and gave his best effort to swipe the mirth off his face. "My apologies. It's a gallant name."

"Don't apologize. I think it's ridiculous as well, but you know my wife. Her group of church ladies named him. Apparently they are now working through the book of Luke, and it seemed apropos." The man's bushy white eyebrows, mustache, and beard all wiggled as he rolled his eyes. "And since my loving wife thinks I need more exercise, I've been declared the one to walk him in the mornings instead of 'pacing the halls,' as she puts it." With a shake of his head, he peered down at the little dog. "As long as no one thinks he belongs to me, I don't mind. I have a reputation to uphold, you know."

Mark chuckled. "Well, it *is* barely six a.m., sir. I think you're safe." He glanced around. "There aren't too many folks out at this time of day."

"Which is a godsend." The judge straightened his coat with the hand not holding the leash. "I wouldn't want to be seen with this little fluff ball too often."

And yet despite the man's gruff words, there was no denying the twinkle in Ashbury's eyes. If Mark wasn't mistaken, the good judge liked the little dog but wouldn't ever admit it. "He certainly is cute. How much will he grow?"

One bushy, wild eyebrow shot up. "This is it, young man. He's full grown, or so my wife informs me."

"Oh." Mark grinned. Maybe it was best to change the subject. "How are things with you? I know you were voted in as the district judge while I was in college. Are you enjoying the position?"

"Very much. All except for the travel. It's a large district to cover, and while most of the larger cases are transferred here to Kalispell, I still need to travel out to the other areas." He stuffed his left hand into his coat pocket. "At my age, it's beginning to be wearisome."

"I can imagine." Montana was a rugged land and not always easily accessible. "Can you request that all cases be brought here?"

"As our great state keeps growing and more districts are added, yes, eventually. Until then, I'm afraid I will have to travel, which is much easier when the snow is no longer on the ground." Another yip from Sir Theophilus made the judge check his pocket watch. "I better head back, Marvella will be waiting."

"Please give her my love, sir."

Judge Ashbury laid a hand on Mark's shoulder and stepped a few inches closer. "We're all proud of you. It's wonderful to have you back home doing what you love— what you were called to do. I know things have been difficult with your father over the years but remember that he loves you. Marvella and I have been praying for the Lord's will to be done. You're family to us, and we're glad you're home." The man's eyes filled with a sheen of tears. He dipped his chin and cleared his throat. "I'll be back for the dedication ceremony later."

"Thank you, sir." Mark struggled to clear his own throat. He blinked several times as he watched the man and his tiny dog walk back toward the Ashbury mansion.

The judge and his wife understood Mark like no one else. They'd been like a doting aunt and uncle, filling the aching hole left in his life when his mother died. Mark had been a mere five years old. The Ashburys had poured into Mark from the time his family arrived in Kalispell to now. They clearly saw the passion in Mark for intellectual pursuits. They'd encouraged him and cheered him on. The judge had even lent Mark book after book from his own prized collection.

Mark straightened. Had he ever let the couple know how much they meant to him? How much he appreciated their belief in him?

The judge's words just now conveyed a lot. Soon Mark would make a point of sharing with them everything that was on his heart and mind, but it would need to wait until the library was up and running.

And after he had a long heart-to-heart with his father. Which was long overdue.

When Mark went out east for college a decade ago, Dad hadn't liked it but let him go. Probably hoped that time away from the ranch would prove Mark wrong—that he would miss the ranch and everything related to it. Instead it solidified Mark's love of words and books, his desire to earn the directorship of a large library, and his passion to share the love of books with people who hadn't had the chance to know the precious gift of reading. What doors reading could open. The dreams it could spark.

And yet . . .

Deep down, Mark sensed he'd failed. Oh, not his dreams or the Ashburys' hopes for him. However . . .

Had he failed his father? Dad's expectations had been high. Still were. And he and his father had let deep rifts develop in their relationship.

He could only pray that coming home and spending time with his father would allow mending to take place.

Enough. He needed to focus on the matters at hand. In the moonlight, Mark glanced across Third Street and allowed the thrill of the coming day to take over. With swift strides, he crossed the road and walked up to the library's main entrance.

Andrew Carnegie, one of America's leading philanthropists, had given a generous donation of ten thousand dollars to the city for the library. The only provision was that the city had to provide the land and the funding to keep the library operating. So they purchased two lots here on the northeast corner of Third Street East and Second Avenue East.

Etched into the sandstone above the double doors was *CARNEGIE*, a testament to the wealthy man who didn't want to die rich. And in fact, Mark had heard that libraries were being built across the country thanks to Mr. Carnegie.

What an amazing thing to do.

Mark would be eternally grateful. Not just for the library, but for the opportunity of the job. He had high hopes and dreams for this place. For his home. To educate people. Help kids who, like Mark, wanted a life beyond ranching and farming. To have the opportunity for a college education.

Not that farming and ranching were bad. Not at all. But books and reading opened up doors to entire worlds beyond Kalispell.

It wasn't a bad town. No. In fact, he loved it here. That's one of the reasons he came back. But if he had the chance to impact the next generation, he wanted to take it. Especially with the age of machinery upon them. The world was changing at an alarming rate, and their best option was to keep up with it the best they could.

They weren't living in the nineteenth century anymore.

Standing at the foot of the stairs, Mark smiled again. The entry was angled to the northeast corner of the block with the dome rising high in the pre-dawn sky. The tall wood doors welcomed him.

As he took the nine cement steps up to the front, his smile grew. Today was the day.

The dedication.

He slipped his key into the door, unlocked it, and opened it to the eight-sided entryway. The smell of lemon oil—which he'd used to detail and polish all the wood in the building— filled his nose.

The new construction was full of rich wood trim. From the hand-carved banisters on the multi-angled staircase that led to the daylight basement, to every window and door in the place, the craftsmanship was of the highest quality.

As he closed the door, he took a long slow breath and let the true aroma of the library take over.

The unmistakable smell of books.

Lots of books.

More than four thousand tomes filled the shelves. He'd cataloged, placed, and *knew* each one of them.

Breathing deep of the scents he loved and the satisfaction of a job well done, he filled his lungs and let his chest puff out. Just a bit. This moment was worth it. No one was around to see him anyway.

In a few hours, they would open the doors and hold the dedication ceremony. And in a couple weeks, the library would be open to the public. There were still furnishings and decorations to bring in and many little projects to do. Thankfully, he wasn't in charge of all that. The women of the Ladies Library Association were handling that side of things.

He strode toward the front circulation desk, where he would make his place every day. He turned on the light, then made a circle under the dome of the entry. Each window and door in the place had a beautiful, butted head casing with a hand-carved rope pattern in it. They drew the eye upward to the dome and high ceilings—the visualization of knowledge and higher learning. The oak floors shone in the light. He could imagine hearing footsteps throughout the library of those eager to read and learn.

He made his way to his desk, shed his coat and hat, and hesitated.

Kate.

Would his sister come today? He'd sent a note out to the ranch, but he hadn't heard back. It had been quite a surprise to come home and find Kate married. To a fellow Mark had never heard of. The man wasn't even from Kalispell.

But Harvey Monroe must be a decent guy if Dad had agreed to the wedding.

Dad . . .

Mark let out a deep sigh. Things hadn't been great between them lately. If he was honest, things hadn't been all that good since Mark left for college. Especially since he hadn't come home to the ranch after his schooling. But he was back now. He could make amends. Spend time with his family. And hopefully prove to his father that what he did was important.

A knock on the front door drew his gaze. He checked his watch. Wasn't even seven yet. Who could that be?

Mark strode to the door and unlocked it, then opened it a few inches.

"Mr. Andrews." The gangly kid handed him an envelope through the space. "Your father asked me to bring this by."

Mark took the envelope. "Thank you."

But it was no use, the kid was already loping down the stairs.

With a tear to the envelope, Mark then pulled out a piece of his dad's ranch stationery.

> *Mark,*
>   *I am calling a family meeting this evening. It is imperative that you be in attendance. 6:00 p.m. sharp.*
>
>   *Dad*

Mark walked back to his desk and set the missive down. Just like Dad to demand an audience. So much for hoping that his family would come to the dedication today. He hadn't seen them since he returned—even though he'd sent several messages out to the ranch. Perhaps Kate would come. Clearly, he wouldn't see his father there.

Shaking his head against the negative thoughts, he refocused his attention on the excitement of the day.

He could deal with his father later.

RIVER VIEW RANCH—ANDREWS FAMILY RANCH—TEN MILES NORTH OF KALISPELL

"I've come to a decision."

Angus Andrews placed his hands on the arms of his favorite leather wingback chair and narrowed his eyes. Even though they were clear and full of fire—as always—they couldn't hide the fact that Dad was aging. A lot.

More than Mark could have imagined.

He sent a glance to his sister. When Kate had answered the door, she'd hugged him tight and introduced him to her husband, but Dad hadn't given him as much as a how-are-you before insisting they all sit for the family meeting.

The man hadn't changed a bit. Whatever he said was law.

Kate took her seat next to Harvey and sent Mark a sympathetic look.

"This is how things will go. Kate and Harvey will continue running the ranch like they have been. All the day-to-day, hands-on work. Mark will take over the books and the management side of things. With all his college education, he must have some good insight into how we can grow. Kate and Mark will be equals in this endeavor. This is your ranch now. I'm getting too old and haven't been feeling all that great. I need to hand everything over to you two." Dad thrummed his fingers on his knee.

Mark had been expecting this from his father in the years to come, but not so soon. He'd hoped for some time to settle in and have a chance to prove himself. How was he supposed to answer his father honestly and honor him at the same time? "I'm not sure I will have time for all that, Dad. My work at the library will keep me busy."

His father grimaced. He waved off Mark's words. "After a time, I'm sure you'll be back here permanently, otherwise you wouldn't have come home. Get the library going, and then come back where you belong."

The man never listened. Never. As much as Mark hated the temper he'd inherited from his Scottish father, he let it seep to the surface. "I came back home, yes, but my job is the director of the library." There. At least he didn't allow it to boil over.

"Your *job* is to do what your father says." Dad's right hand pointed out the window. "I built all this for you. Don't be ungrateful."

Mark did a silent count to ten. "Kate is more than capable of running the business end and the physical end now that she has Harvey. You have plenty of hired ranch hands. She lives for this place. You know that."

"This ranch is for *both* of you. Now stop arguing with me." Red infused his father's face.

Enough. The ordering had to stop. "Dad, I'm the director of the library." Was he wrong to—in essence—tell his father no? Was he dishonoring the only parent he had left?

"Don't be so contrary, young man." His father pushed to his feet and shoved a finger at him.

Mark stood as well but kept his tone low. Forceful, but

low. "You never listen. I thought after all these years things would be different." He stepped toward his sister and leaned down to give her a hug. "Come see me soon?"

"Of course." Unshed tears glistened in her eyes.

He turned his gaze to his new brother-in-law. "It was nice to meet you. I'm sorry for the circumstances, but perhaps we could chat at the library sometime?"

Harvey gave him a sympathetic smile. "Nice to meet you too. Next time I'm in town, I'll look you up."

Mark headed toward the door without another glance at his father. It was for the best.

"Don't you walk out on me, Cowboy!"

The words halted his feet. He couldn't—wouldn't—look back. His face toward the door, he kept his words calm. "I'm not walking out, Dad. I'm giving us both some space so I don't lose my temper and say things I will regret. My mind is made up. I never wanted to run the ranch. I appreciate all you put into this place, I do. But you know I don't love it like Kate does."

"Always choosing books over your family, aren't you?"

As silly as the words were, they still stung. Mark spun around. "I'm not choosing *anything* over you, Dad. I thought you would be happy and *proud*. I've worked hard for this. I've been given an incredible opportunity. And I'm back home where I can spend time with all of you." As his gaze spanned the room, from Dad's fury to Kate's anguish to Harvey's discomfort, his heart twinged.

Dad fisted his hands. "Proud? When you've wasted ten years gallivanting around doing whatever you pleased. I allowed it, but now it's time to come home and do your duty. I didn't raise a quitter."

No. He would not let the words that sprang to mind have

their entrance to his heart. Dad didn't mean it. The heat of the moment always brought out the worst in him and he said things for dramatic effect. How often had he and Kate joked about their father's bluster?

Kate held up a hand toward each of them. "I think we all need to sit back down. Perhaps have some dinner and cool our tempers."

Dad shook his head. "No. I'm not sitting down to dinner with him. Is that still your answer, Mark? You gonna tell me no again?"

Mark took a long breath and then exhaled. "I'm sorry, Dad. But my answer is no."

"*Fine!*" His father's roar echoed off the walls of the room. "Do whatever you want. Kate will inherit the ranch. From this day forward, you're disowned. You hear me?"

"I heard you. I'm guessing all of Kalispell heard you." As much as Mark tried to keep his voice under control, the words burst out of his mouth in equal volume to his father's. He stomped out of the room.

Why had he ever come home?

He couldn't sleep. He kept getting up to pace the room while the events of the evening replayed in his mind. Why couldn't Dad see Kate's passion for the ranch and be grateful? Especially now that she was married to a husband who seemed to love the ranch too.

Mark pulled back the drapes and gazed out into the darkness. There was so little sunlight these days. Winter had brought its long, dark nights. At least the dedication ceremony had gone well. The people of Kalispell seemed more than pleased to have the new library in place. A crowd had waited outside in the cold, they'd been so excited. Two schoolteachers from the local high school even made arrangements to bring their classes over to learn about the Dewey decimal system.

He let the curtains fall into place and went back to the bed. Sat on the edge. Mark prayed. For wisdom. For healing. He didn't want to hurt his dad or dishonor him, but he'd made a commitment to the town—and to God—regarding the library.

"Lord, I need wisdom to deal with this matter. I love my father, but I love my work at the library as well. Since Dad paid for me to go to college, I thought he understood my passion and the plans I had for the future. Plans I feel certain are ones that You have ordained for me. If I'm in the wrong, please help me to see that and be willing to acknowledge it. Please show me what to do."

Every last bit of anger he'd held onto from the evening dissipated. The whole ride home, he'd muttered under his breath about his father's outburst and how the older man was clearly in the wrong. What a waste of time and energy.

And what irony to accuse his father when he'd been equally wrong in his response.

"God, I'm ashamed of my behavior toward my dad, but he brings out the worst in me. Help me to bite my tongue when I need to. Which is probably a lot more than I think." He blew out his breath between his lips.

Why was his relationship with his father so full of conflict? Why couldn't they understand and accept each other? Was the only way to rectify that to give up everything he'd worked for—his hopes and dreams . . . ?

Mark's throat tightened. Could it be? He bowed his head, but his heart hurt as he prayed, "Is that what You want me to do, God?"

Tracie Peterson is the award-winning author of over one hundred novels, both historical and contemporary. She is often referred to as the "Queen of Historical Christian Fiction," and her avid research resonates in her stories, as seen in her bestselling HEIRS OF MONTANA and ALASKAN QUEST series. Tracie considers her writing a ministry for God to share the Gospel and biblical application. She and her family make their home in Montana. Visit her website at traciepeterson.com or on Facebook at facebook.com/TraciePetersonAuthor.

Sign Up for Tracie's Newsletter

Keep up to date with Tracie's latest news on book releases and events by signing up for her email list at the link below.

FOLLOW TRACIE ON SOCIAL MEDIA!

Tracie Peterson

@authortraciepeterson

TraciePeterson.com

More from Tracie Peterson

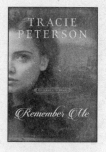

Haunted by heartbreak and betrayal, Addie Bryant escapes her terrible circumstances with the hope she can forever hide her past and with the belief she will never have the future she's always dreamed of. When she's reunited with her lost love, Addie must decide whether to run or to face her wounds to embrace her life, her future, and her hope in God.

Remember Me
PICTURES OF THE HEART #1

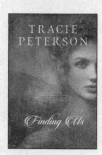

While taking photos at an exposition in Seattle, camera girl Eleanor Bennett meets a handsome stranger, Bill Reed, who recognizes the subjects in one of her portraits as a missing woman and her child. As they hunt for the truth, Eleanor and Bill will have to band together to face the danger that follows.

Finding Us
PICTURES OF THE HEART #2

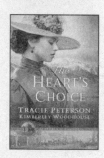

Rebecca McCutcheon is the first female court reporter in Montana. During a murder trial she's covering, she's convinced that the defendant is innocent, but no one except the handsome new Carnegie librarian, Mark Andrews, will listen to her. In a race against time, will they be able to find the evidence to free the man before it's too late?

The Heart's Choice
THE JEWELS OF KALISPELL #1